LOU AND THE WHALE OF A CRIME

The Squamish Mysteries

INGA KRUSE

Illustrated by
TREVOR WATSON

The Marketing Chair Press

Illustrations and cover by Trevor Watson

Paperback ISBN: 978-1-7773001-0-4

Ebook ISBN: 978-1-7773001-1-1

To my Lovies - Denzil, Erika and Rowan.
You hold my heart steady.

CONTENTS

CHAPTER ONE

There has always been excitement when a big moving truck rolled into this sleepy neighborhood in Squamish. People walking their dogs, a cyclist, and the guy sweeping his driveway all stared when the moving truck lumbered by.

The truck pulled into the driveway of a house with a "sold" sign in the yard. Before it even stopped, the side door of the van opened, and Lou leapt out. She swept her mess of red hair into a quick ponytail and surveyed the street. She waved at a lady walking her corgi and flashed an enormous smile as she shouted, "Hi neighbour, my name is Lou, and we are moving into that house." She pointed to the white two-story home.

The lady returned her wave, smiled and replied, "Welcome to Pine Street!"

Lou watched her walk off, her tiny dog sniffing at every shrub. As Lou assessed her new neighbourhood, she wondered what secrets these tidy homes might hold, and more importantly, how she could discover them.

Lou clumsily bent over to tie up her Doc Martens boots and strolled across the yard toward the house.

As she walked, she whistled to get the attention of a giant Great Dane who had slept through the big arrival and remained snoring in the van. When he realized he was being called, he unfolded his long legs and shook his massive head to wake up. Stepping out onto the sidewalk, he went to catch up with his girl.

Lou gave his ear an idle scratch as she looked at her new home. She fed the dog a cookie from her pocket and said, "Rocky, you missed all the cool mountains and ocean views on the way up here!"

Rocky, seemingly unconcerned, drooled a puddle of cookie crumbs as he noisily munched his treat.

She looked around and noticed the blooms on trees and the tulips in the garden. "April sure is pretty around here," she mused. Lou had been looking forward to getting here and starting to explore this new and interesting place on the west coast of Canada. On the last stretch up the highway from Vancouver, she was riveted to the window, gawking at the mountains that looked like they had simply grown straight out of the ocean. There were so many of them everywhere she looked, and most of them had snow on their tops. The jagged peaks seemed to go on forever; Lou had never seen anything quite so stunning.

As her eyes moved down to take in the water and its shore, she checked her map. "Howe Sound," she whispered to herself. Lou was fascinated by the many shades of green of the trees and shrubs that seemed to grow between the rocks and filled up the cracks in the mountains. She noticed the water was perfectly still and reflected the peaks like a mirror. Lou was wondering how the ocean could be so tranquil. She also knew about the killer whales that lived in these waters. She had been determined to see one on her first day, so her nose remained glued to the window the whole way from Vancouver.

Lou noticed her parents had left the van and were talking to the movers. They did not seem happy. Her mother was frowning and winding up for an argument as she pointed at the moving truck driver. Her father looked embarrassed and was trying to settle this drama down.

The mover struggled to get a word in. "Mrs. Dalrymple, I assure you we were careful with your furniture."

Mrs. Dalrymple was not convinced. "We were driving behind you and you stopped suddenly so many times, I can't imagine there aren't broken chairs and tables!" Lou could tell her mom was grouchy. It had been a long ride, and this move was a big deal for Lou and her family.

Mr. Dalrymple stepped in to try and calm his wife down, but his voice trailed off before he could get anything out that could help. He stopped trying to talk and resigned himself to waiting for the storm his wife was brewing to be over.

Mrs. Dalrymple finally finished chewing out the driver, who slouched off to unload the truck. She called across the yard, "Lou, please stop playing with the dog and come see the house."

Lou whispered to Rocky, "Mom's super stressed. We might want to keep out of her way."

Lou marched to the front door, leaving Rocky to sniff every blade of grass in the front yard. Mr. Dalrymple was fiddling with the lock and dropped his key chain. Lou kindly picked it up for him. Mervin Dalrymple was a kind but nervous man. He usually looked rumpled and wore clothes that were always a size too big. As he tried to manage the keys, his balding head was beaded with sweat which made his sparse few hairs flop over his forehead. His glasses slid down his nose and as he pushed them up; he dropped the keys again. Lou caught them and unlocked the door.

"Thank you, Bunny," he replied. "I am a little rattled and tired. It was such a long drive."

Lou opened the door as her mother came up the two steps to join them on the front porch. Now that everybody realized they had actually gotten there, the stress fell away. They all looked at each other with excited expressions because they were walking into their new house for the first time.

This peaceful moment of anticipation was suddenly interrupted by a distinct sound Lou and her parents knew well.

They spun around and saw Rocky bearing down on them at a full run up onto the front porch. He looked like a giant black and white bear careening towards them. He barreled past, knocking Mrs. Dalrymple's purse off her shoulder and stepping on Mr. Dalrymple's foot. He licked Lou's ear on the way in. By the time everyone got their balance again, Rocky was lying on the carpet inside waiting for them.

Mrs. Dalrymple turned on Lou, griping, "How many times have I told you to keep a leash on that dog?"

Lou wanted to mention that it wouldn't have mattered if she did have him on a leash, but then decided against it. Mom hadn't fully settled down yet.

Rocky sat up and tilted his head, knowing they were talking about him so maybe that meant he would be getting a cookie.

Mrs. Dalrymple huffed at Rocky but still scratched his ear and marched into the kitchen to make sure the cleaners did a suitable job. She was wearing her usual pencil skirt with stockings and high heels and her stylish car coat for travelling. She took off her jacket and pulled a silk scarf out of her purse. After smoothing her black stylish bob, she put the scarf over her head and tied it in a knot at the back of her neck. Lou knew her mother was now in her housework mode, and, somehow without getting so much as a smudge on her, she would clean and unpack. Lou knew that getting things put away would calm her mom's stress. She was happiest when she was busy organizing.

Lou and Rocky went upstairs to tour the bedrooms. Rocky led the way and disappeared into one of the rooms down the hall. Lou went to see where he was and found him sprawled on the floor, stretched as long as he could make himself. It reminded her of the last time they measured him with his paws up on her dad's shoulders. They were amazed to find he was two meters tall.

She leaned in the doorway with her arms crossed and asked, "Hey lazy dog, what are you doing?"

Lou's father appeared behind her and put his arm around her

shoulder as he scanned the scene. "It seems he has picked this room for you."

Lou snickered. "More likely he thinks this is his room."

Together, Lou and her dad stepped into the room and sat on the floor next to Rocky. He swung his giant head onto Lou's lap and thumped his tail.

A thoughtful look crossed Mr. Dalrymple's face. "You know Lou, I hope you are excited to start in a new school and make friends. I know now that you are fifteen, you will be more able to deal with this big change, but I hope you'll give yourself time. School starts next week after their spring break. Are you worried about anything?"

Lou chewed a ragged nail while she thought about the question. She couldn't decide where to start, so she blurted it all in one shot. "Dad, I hope people like me here. I have all this crazy red hair, I am taller than all the kids in my class and I have enormous feet. When we lived in Halifax, they teased me about all of it. That is what I am worried about."

Her dad sat on the floor next to her and held her tight. "I know you had a hard time. Those kids that bullied you were mean to lots of people. I always wondered what was wrong in their home lives that they take it out on other kids."

"I know, Dad. They didn't really hate my hair, but they wanted to find something to pick on me about."

Lou had cried when she left her hometown in Nova Scotia. She knew she would miss the wild coast of the Atlantic Ocean, her hikes with Rocky through familiar neighbourhoods, and her teachers. She didn't list her friends because she didn't really have the sort of friends she would miss.

As she remembered her maritime home, she looked up at her father and waited for him to answer. "Bunny," he reassured her, "you will be able to make a fresh start in a new school. You are an outstanding student, and we know your teachers will love you. They always do. And as for friends, I know you will have a bunch

5

of them in the first week!" His face shifted a bit. He sounded less confident about the "friends" part, but she was grateful he had tried.

Mrs. Dalrymple stuck her head in the doorway, which interrupted the impromptu heart-to-heart. "You picked a nice room, Lou. Mervin, can you please make sure the truck is being unloaded properly?" She disappeared before either Lou or her father could reply.

Mr. Dalrymple let out a grunt as he stood and stretched. "No rest for the wicked, I suppose," he called over his shoulder as he made his way out of the room. Lou smiled because Dad always said that when Mom assigned him a chore.

Rocky woke briefly and noticed people were moving. Not spying any treats, he put his head back down and returned to his snoring.

The family had already spent a good portion of the weekend unpacking when the doorbell rang. Mrs. Dalrymple fixed her hair in the mirror and answered the door. Lou heard her out on the porch chatting with two ladies. "They brought a plant for the garden," Lou thought. "She will like that for sure."

Lou tackled boxes the movers had piled in her room. Her dresser, bed, desk and night table had been placed exactly where she wanted, but she had to move her big cabinet. Not thinking to ask for help, she put her back against the side and pushed. Rocky got out of the way just in time. She frowned at him and muttered, "You could make yourself useful and help me move this."

Sensing she wasn't pleased, he plunked his bum on her bed and made a droopy face.

Once the cabinet was in the right place, she searched for a specific box.

"Ah, there it is!" She cut open the box marked *spy tools*. As she pulled out carefully wrapped items, she chatted with Rocky. "None of these got broken in the move."

Rocky looked interested as she unwrapped each item. She inspected and listed off each piece as she put it in the cabinet. "Periscope, cup cam, lock picking kit, bug book, teddy cam, pen firecracker, invisible ink, and batteries. It's all here, Rocky."

She hunted for another box and strained to lift it onto her desk. This one was labelled *spy parts and pieces*.

As she opened it and checked the contents, she noted, "I will need more supplies soon." She decided that this box should go under her desk because that was her workspace. She found her desk light and plugged it in. Standing back with a pleased grin, Lou said, "We are back in business, Rocky."

By Sunday afternoon, Lou was bored with unpacking her room and began dumping out boxes into drawers to get it done. It was unseasonably warm, so she was wearing shorts and a t-shirt. As she was concentrating on stuffing sweaters into her chest of drawers, a shock of cold, wet nose landed on the back of her thigh. She spun around, wiping her leg only to see Rocky plunk himself down.

"Well, dopey dog, you have my attention now. What do you want?"

Rocky stood up and went to the door, looking back and wagging his tail. Lou clued in that he was as ready to explore their new area as she was. "Okay, let's go see if Mom will let us out. Cross your legs; it will help our case."

Lou and Rocky loped into the kitchen where Mrs. Dalrymple was holding two large bowls in her hands. Her eyes flicked between the bowls and the cupboards, a deep line forming between her eyebrows. With a frustrated sigh, she turned around and put the bowls down on the counter. As she sat on a stool, she pulled the scarf off her head and huffed, "None of my enormous dishes fit into the cupboards. I have been trying to figure out where to put things for hours. And what is with this heat in April?"

Sensing a rant about to happen, Lou interrupted. "I finished my room. Can I take Rocky for a walk?" And as if on command, Rocky walked to the front door and nosed at the handle.

Mrs. Dalrymple surveyed the scene, deciding maybe it was better to get the two of them out from underfoot anyway. Nodding, she replied, "Okay, you can go out for the afternoon, but if I can find a pot and cutlery, dinner is at six."

Lou tied up her bright blue Doc Martens boots and she and Rocky were out and away before her mom could say anything more.

CHAPTER TWO

After the two explorers were out of sight of the house, Rocky sat down so Lou could unclip his leash. She gave him a solid back scratch, and he shook himself all the way to his tail. They were ready to go and see what there was to see.

As they meandered down the street, Lou realized they drew attention along the way. Everybody stared at this unlikely pair walking along the sidewalk. A giant dog off its leash walking with a gangly, frizzy-haired redhead in big boots was an unusual sight. Lou supposed people tended to notice when newcomers came to town.

It was the end of a spring break with a summer-like feel; there were people everywhere in their shorts enjoying the sun. Lou decided she would get herself and Rocky an ice cream. She found a small ice cream shop and Lou bought two cones. She spotted a park across the street with a picnic table in the shade. The table was near a cement path that wound through the park. People were walking, running and riding their bikes in the warm sun. "Busy spot," thought Lou.

Rocky settled on the grass to eat his ice cream cone in one bite while Lou sat at the table near him. As she ate her ice cream, Rocky put his head on her lap and watched the people and dogs go by. Lou patted Rocky's head and said, "We will have so many places to explore here, big dog, but today we can just watch the people go by."

Lou slowly finished her ice cream and watched a group of kids she assumed would be going to the same school as her. Some of them seemed friendly enough. She noticed they looked no different from the kids she left behind at her old school. There were the cool girls, the jocks, the emo kids and the nerds, same as always. She sighed and absently chewed her nail.

Her nails had grown back during the ride across Canada. Her mother was ever vigilant, saying, "Would you stop chewing up your nails please, you will ruin them and look like you have stubby hands!"

As Lou was contemplating what could make her long fingers look stubby, she was startled by a kid on a skateboard doing a close flyby. He was moving at high speed and noticed too late that he startled a girl and an enormous dog. He slowed a bit and turned around to wave sorry, then he pumped his foot and was racing away again.

Lou settled Rocky back into his nap and thought about the boy who had skated by them. Dressed in all black with his hoodie up, he had a streak of blue in his long black bangs. He looked like he would be a senior in her high school, which she found herself hoping for.

Once Rocky seemed ready to go again, Lou thought she should probably head home and help with supper. She got up and tapped Rocky on the head. "Let's go dude, I'm starving."

Lou was certain which street to turn onto until it she realized it was the wrong one. She tried another one she thought might be in the right direction and found it was still not the route. The more she walked, the more turned around she got. Getting home should have been easy with a giant cliff always in sight, but she was still lost.

Her parents hadn't had the chance to get her a new phone yet, so she would have to figure it out herself. She found herself trying to navigate by the sun but figured out that she needed to be more familiar with the streets to make that work.

Lou was getting frustrated, "How could I be so lost on my first weekend here? I usually have my phone or even my compass for just such a crisis," she thought to herself.

The pair started down a trail she thought might lead them to the dog park. According to the Squamish community website, there was a dog park right at the end of her street. If she could find that park, it might lead her home.

Wild shrubs lined the sandy trail. As they walked, Lou kicked pebbles down the path. Rocky lagged behind, sniffing bushes and lifting his leg to pee on every one of them. This was his trail now. He was claiming it.

Instead of a dog park, she found another smaller path that led down an incline to a tiny lake. When Rocky spotted water, he was ready to bolt and go for a swim. She put her hand on his snout to indicate stop. She had nothing to dry him with, and she knew her mother would flip out if Lou brought a big, soaking wet dog into their new house. Putting a hand on his solid forehead, she said, "You don't get to go for a swim today, but maybe we can come back another time."

She heard voices coming from the lake and thought maybe there were people down there who could give them directions. She and Rocky made their way down to a small beach just big enough to launch a canoe or a small rowboat. Standing on the beach, she tried to figure out where the voices were coming from. Rocky was listening too, and when she looked over at him, his hackles were up, and his head was down. She hushed him. "It's just people, Rocky. Chill out."

The voices got louder, and they sounded angry. Lou loved eavesdropping, so she grabbed Rocky by the collar and they both tucked into the tall grass. When she hunkered down, she could see through a gap in the grass. There she spotted two men in a small paddle boat. They were both in dirty overalls and hats that looked like they had been pulled out of a woodchipper. They had big beards, and when they took sloppy swigs of their beers, they left a trail of foam running down their chins.

"What are they doing?" Lou wondered. "And why do they sound so mad?"

It looked at first to Lou like they were fishing since they had rods on board, but as they bickered, she noticed they weren't using the rods or looked like they had been doing much fishing. Then she heard what they were saying.

The bigger man took his hat off and wiped his forehead with a dirty rag. He sneered at the smaller man, "Calvin, you got us into this mess, at least you can keep your mouth shut about it!"

Calvin looked offended and fired back. "I didn't get us into nuthin', Jake. It was your stupid idea! And besides, I ain't told nobody, I swear."

Jake was frowning as he fiddled with something on the bottom of the boat just out of Lou's view.

Lou forgot to close her mouth and a mosquito buzzed right into it. She spat it out quietly, careful not to miss any of their conversation. She was thinking hard about what was going on, irritated with herself for not having her binoculars in her backpack.

Was she actually seeing and hearing this? She thought to herself that they were for sure up to something. Lou was convinced.

Rocky had made himself a spot in the grass. He looked at her as if to say, "What are we doing here?" Lou whispered at him to stay so she could move a little closer to the lake. She knew she would have to sit perfectly still in the tall grass so she wouldn't be seen.

Lou watched as Jake picked up a small black fabric bag about the size of a grapefruit and made sure it was tied up. He handed it to Calvin, who sealed it with plastic and tied a brick to it. They tied two more bags and continued to argue about who was at fault.

Calvin was restless and fiddling with a fishhook. He kept glancing around until he caught his thumb on the hook and swore a blue streak. "Jake, this is the last time I am covering anything up for you. You come up with some harebrained plan and I am supposed to figure out how to make it work?"

Jake pointed his finger at Calvin and barked, "And figure out how not to get caught too! You are in for your share, so shut your trap."

Calvin grumbled, "I am sick of sitting out here hiding these things!"

Lou was riveted. They were up to something shady for sure, and she had a front-row seat. She knew she was up to the task of sleuthing out the mystery or even catching them red-handed. She had always been a suspicious person and she even kept a notebook of suspicious activities and people. Lou knew a lot about conspiracy theories and investigations, but she had never had one dropped in her lap like this.

She continued to watch and listen while it started to get dark. She needed to leave soon, but the men started paddling. Lou couldn't tell where they were headed, so she sat still.

Jake grabbed the first brick with the attached bag and carefully put it in the water. As he watched it sink, he looked around, trying to find something at the edge of the water. Lou ducked back so she wouldn't be seen.

Calvin pulled a notebook and pencil out of his overalls, licked his finger and flipped pages. Jake called out, "Calvin, this one is near the west beach about fifteen feet out, mark it down!"

Calvin made a note of it. They repeated this procedure two more times, seeming satisfied they had made enough notes to find them again. They paddled back to the little beach and pulled their boat out of the water.

Lou stayed out of sight. Even if the men had been paying

attention, she and Rocky were deep enough in the grass not to be detected. It dawned on Lou this was not her usual harmless scheme or conspiracy theory. This seemed like it could be much more serious. Lou still had no idea what they were up to, but for sure it was something nefarious and criminal. She was getting nervous about being discovered in their hiding spot. She hunkered down further and hoped Rocky would stay where she told him to. But she was getting hungry, and her stomach was almost growling loudly enough to alert the men in the boat.

Fortunately, as the men pulled the boat out of the water, they were still grumbling at each other. They kept it going as they left, carrying their boat up the path. Now that they had left, Lou started buzzing with the possibility of solving a mystery, or better yet, maybe catching real criminals.

Lou thought the coast was clear, but just in case it wasn't, she whispered, "Rocky, sneak!"

She moved stealthily out of the tall grass, staying low to the ground. Rocky followed behind, crawling on his belly, trying to be as inconspicuous as a massive dog could be. When they finally stood up, she saw that the men and their boat were gone. Lou made note of landmarks so she could find this place again.

Lou and Rocky made their way back up to the main road and tried to retrace their steps, looking for a route that would get them closer to their street. However, she wasn't truly concentrating too hard on the route because she was busy planning her investigation. How would she find these men? Would they come back to the lake? Should she set up a duck blind for surveillance?

As she was deciding which spy camera to use, Lou and Rocky found themselves arriving at a busier intersection. Lou had stopped to get her bearings when her father pulled up beside them. He lowered the passenger window and said, "Hop in, Bunny. You're late for dinner."

"Dad! Cool! How did you find us?" Lou opened the sliding door and Rocky hopped in, his weight tilting the van to the side. Lou settled into the passenger seat and buckled herself in.

Her father asked, "What have you two been up to for so long?"

Lou reluctantly admitted she got lost. "I got turned around and couldn't find my way back, so we just kept walking. We found a little lake and rested for a while, and now we're here." She didn't mention the criminal activity she saw. She was pretty sure her parents wouldn't allow her to use her spy gear or investigative skills to solve a real crime.

Mr. Dalrymple was driving slowly and checking street signs. Lou realized this place was new for her dad too, and he might also have trouble finding his way. Grabbing his phone, she asked, "What's our new address again? I'll put it into your phone and get us home."

After a lecture from her mother for missing dinner, Lou ate a reheated meal, went to her room and closed the door. She flopped onto her bed and pulled out her notebook and pen. She noticed it was looking a bit ragged from being in and out of her backpack all year. She mused she would probably need another one soon.

Lou started a fresh page and titled it *Lake Guys Criminal Activity*. She put a star next to it, indicating importance. Then she spent the rest of the evening jotting down notes and trying to figure out which spying technique would work best. She made a to-do list:

- Check a map and find out where the lake is
- Search up local names Calvin and Jake
- Use coffee cup spy cam or periscope???
- Make surveillance schedule at lake
- Drag lake?

When she finished her notes and made a detailed diagram of the lake and shore, she closed her notebook with a decisive snap. She was convinced it was a crime, and she would solve it.

Lou's door opened, Rocky sauntering in to settle down for the night. Her parents followed behind him. Mr. Dalrymple inspected the door handle to see how the dog opened it. Looking around at the nearby rooms, he discovered the house had the same handle on every door. Rocky was tall enough to put it between his teeth and crank the lever. Absorbing the implications of this, Lou's father muttered, "Well, I guess there will be no keeping him in a room he doesn't want to be in."

Lou piped up, "Or out of a room he wants to be in," causing the whole family to chuckle.

Mrs. Dalrymple followed her husband inside and leaned against Lou's dresser. She was wearing her favourite robe and fuzzy slippers. Her mother was at her most relaxed when she was ready for bed.

As she rubbed moisturizer on her hands, Lou's mother asked, "So Lou, how are you liking your new town so far?"

Lou thought about it for a second and answered, "It's nice for what I saw of it. I plan to go exploring a lot and will try not to get lost again."

Mr. Dalrymple chuckled softly. Her mother put her hand in her robe pocket and pulled out a distinctive white box. Lou leapt up and squealed, "A new phone! Thank you! AAAAAH! When did you get it?"

Mrs. Dalrymple handed it over. "While you were out exploring today, your Dad went to get it. It's connected and ready to go."

Lou hugged them both and immediately started unpacking it. She had a sudden thought. "Do we have Wi-Fi?"

Her dad smiled indulgently. "Yes, Lou, of course we do, I had it set up before we even got here. I'll go get you the password."

As her dad left the room, Lou turned to her mother and thanked her again.

Smiling at her daughter, Mrs. Dalrymple reassured her, "We wouldn't send you to high school with the broken phone you had. Besides, we want you to be able to communicate with us and with all the new friends you're going to make." She kissed Lou on the head and said a final goodnight before leaving the room.

Lou smiled, sniffing the air as her mother closed the door behind her. Her mother still smelled like lavender hand cream, the same as she did at their old house. This comforted Lou.

As she was getting ready for bed, someone slipped a piece of paper under the door, with what looked like the alphabet on it. Rocky got to it first, picking it up in his mouth and bringing it to Lou.

The drool-covered scrap of paper stuck to her hand. "Thanks, slobber monster," she said as she looked at the wet paper and saw what used to be the Wi-Fi password.

Rocky was pleased with himself and sat waiting for a treat. Shaking her head at him, Lou said, "I don't have anything for you. Besides, you've had plenty of cookies already today."

He seemed to understand and started spinning in slow circles until it felt just right to lie down. He melted onto the floor in a giant ball and exhaled deeply, making his lips flap loudly. Lou gave him a light pat on the head as she climbed over him and into bed. He was already snoring.

Lou brought the covers up to her chin and wiggled around to get comfortable. It dawned on her that tomorrow was going to be her first day at a new school. Her stomach lurched a little as she pulled the covers over her head to try to sleep.

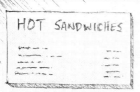

HOT SANDWICHES

CHEF'S SPECIAL

DESSERTS/ DRINKS

CHAPTER THREE

L ou's alarm clock went off at seven, but she was already awake. She hadn't slept well, having had nightmares about not being able to find her classes.

While she had lain awake at three in the morning, memories of being teased and bullied spun through her head. She couldn't shake her nervous stomach through most of the night. As she always did though, she had talked to Rocky about it. He didn't seem to mind being woken up in the night to listen to Lou's troubles. He had shifted his position on the floor to put his chin up on Lou's bed.

She had lain on her side, nose to nose with Rocky and said, "I don't know what I would do without you. You always listen and seem to be the only one who gets me. So, tell me, Rocky, what does a girl need to do to make friends in a new place?"

Lou had cried a few tears, then, when she realized that her only friend in the world was a dog. Rocky had rubbed his big floppy ear on her cheek; he had always wiped her tears like that. Eventually, she had dozed off again, and Rocky had stretched back out and resumed his snoring.

Despite the rough night, Lou felt a little more positive about everything. After showering, she was excited to put on the outfit she had bought for her first day. She thought to herself, "These are super cute if I do say so myself." She put on the polka dot navy tights, a black skater skirt, a black-and-white striped shirt, and a bright yellow raincoat. She hoped her style would fit in with the other kids. Her hair was another matter. She did her best to tame the frizz and comb it into a more orderly mess. Finally, she gave up and put it up in a ponytail.

Lou's mother was banging around and muttering to herself in the kitchen. She was dressed for work in a perfectly pressed white-collared shirt and a dark grey suit. Mrs. Dalrymple was tall and slim and always impeccably groomed, especially for work. When she carried her black leather briefcase and wore conservative heels, she looked every bit the responsible bank manager that she was.

Lou flopped down on a stool after grabbing a muffin from a tin on the counter.

Her mother turned around, amazed to see Lou sitting there. "Impressive kid, you're up and ready well before the first bell rings."

Lou nodded as she chewed, looking thoughtfully at her mother. "Mom, are you starting your new job today already?"

Absently throwing a granola bar into her purse, Mrs. Dalrymple replied, "I hadn't intended to work my first Monday here, but there is some sort of crisis that I need to jump in and deal with. I didn't even get details about what I am solving, but they wanted me to come in urgently."

She glanced around the kitchen, spotted what she was looking for, and tucked her phone in her pocket. "Bye, Lou. Have a wonderful day at school."

Lou waved weakly as she watched her mother march out the door. She lumbered over to the fridge, selected a yogurt, and sat back down. She set the yogurt in front of her, but didn't open it. She no longer felt like eating. Lou would have liked to spend a little more time with her mom before she had to go to school. All the worries from last night flooded back in her mind. Even in the morning light, she was more nervous and worried about the new school than she thought.

A minute later, Mr. Dalrymple wandered down the stairs in a robe he must have pulled out of a moving box and one slipper. "Oh, good morning, Lou! Hey, is your mother still here? I was going to ask her if she knew which box my other slipper is in?"

Lou came out of her thoughts and answered, "No, she left."

A few seconds later, Rocky lumbered down the stairs carrying a slipper in his mouth.

"Thanks, Rocky," Mr. Dalrymple said as he let him out in the backyard. "I'll take you for a walk later, boy."

Mr. Dalrymple fussed around the kitchen as he tried to figure out his wife's system and where things were located. He looked for coffee and spoons but only found towels. After he finally located what he needed, he leaned over the island to look Lou in the eye. "How are you feeling about your first day?"

Lou met his eyes and complained, "Dad, I am a little nervous. Actually, a lot nervous. What if I get teased or bullied again? I don't know why we had to move for Mom's job, and I won't even know one person!"

Her dad reassured her, "You'll figure it out and be as popular with your teachers as you always have been."

Lou winced a little. "Dad, I don't want to be popular with just the teachers. I want friends my own age who like me for who I am."

Lou's father reached out and thumbed her cheek. "Bunny, people will like you for who you are, all you have to do is show them."

Lou's dad was always her cheerleader, but he didn't get what high school was like for her. She didn't tell him about the mean girls who dumped blue powder on her hair to make it a better colour. She couldn't tell him. It would have made them both cry. Her mom understood the mean girl stuff better.

As Lou thought about all her worries, Rocky nosed the back-door handle and let himself in. He sat by Lou, putting his paw on her lap.

Lou smiled and said, "Rocky, how did you figure out our new door handles?" She scruffed his ear as she got up, went to her room to get her backpack. She stopped at her mirror and did one last check. Seeing that she looked okay she rushed down the stairs.

As she put on her boots in the front hall, her father said, "Maybe I should drive you today, so we are both sure we know the route."

Rocky heard the word "drive" and was out the door like a shot. Laughing, Lou replied, "Thanks Dad, that would be great, and Rocky wants to come too, apparently."

When they got in the van, Lou wondered how her mother had gotten to work. She guessed maybe a taxi. Until her mom's car arrives on a moving truck, she will probably have to take taxis a lot. Before she could ask her dad about it, he said, "Well, here we are Lou. Boy it is close by, just a six minute drive. This is your new school."

Lou recognized it from the website when she was researching her new home. A combination of middle and high school was an unfamiliar experience for her. It only had four hundred students, which felt small, but hopefully it would feel welcoming to her.

They pulled up to the front doors of the modern school building, and Lou took off her seatbelt. Her dad twisted in his seat. "Do you want me to walk you in?"

Lou looked horrified. "Daaad," she whined, "I don't want people to think I need my dad to walk me to class!"

He had assumed as much but had said it anyway to make her feel supported. He knew this was a big day for her. "Okay, Bunny, I just thought I would give you the option. Do you want me to pick you up after school?"

She shook her head and said a quick goodbye to her dad,

giving Rocky a pat as she got out of the van. She watched Rocky not-so-gracefully fold himself into the passenger seat as her dad drove out of the parking lot. Sighing, she took a deep breath, looked at her shiny blue boots and said, "Okay boots, do your magic." With that, she stepped into the school's entryway.

She was early and reported to the main office as she had been instructed. There was hardly anybody in the halls. Following the signs, she noticed how clean and shiny everything was. Then she remembered – it was the first day back from spring break. They had scrubbed the entire place in the two weeks while there were no kids.

She walked down a long hall, noticing the soft pastel colours of the walls and the combinations of posters and paintings everywhere. "This school is into arts and activism," she thought with a smile. She slowed by a wall of posters about climate change and the upcoming rally for nature with call to action messages all over them. She pulled out her notebook and wrote down the date of the rally and drew a big star next to it.

Her old school had focused more on football than art and nature, so this was encouraging and more suited to her views. There were three large glass display cases. One of them was full of trophies, won by the Orcas Lacrosse team, but the other two caught her eye when she went over to take a better look. There were masks and carvings like she had never seen before. A huge carved wooden eagle kept her enraptured.

"A local artist made that for us when he graduated."

Lou startled at the voice and turned to see who was talking to her. "It's beautiful. All of it is so nice." Lou said genuinely.

"Sorry to scare you. I didn't mean to sneak up on you. My name is Amy Dirkson; I'm the school counsellor."

She stuck out her hand and Lou smiled and shook it. "My name is Lou Dalrymple."

Amy looked delighted, "You are the new student from Nova Scotia! Welcome to Eagle Wind High School, we're so happy to have you here!"

At first, Lou was a little taken aback by the fact that she knew her by name and by the enthusiasm with which she was greeted. However, Lou sensed that this was probably how Ms. Dirkson said everything – with lots of exclamation marks.

"Well, come on into my office, it's just down the hall. Let's get your schedule and homeroom assignment. Then I'll give you a quick tour and walk you to your homeroom."

Lou felt a wave of shyness when she thought about walking into a classroom full of kids. They entered an office that was labeled with a handwritten sign that said 'Ms. Dirkson, Counsellor.' She had covered it in happy face and flower stickers.

Lou was looking around when Ms. Dirkson said, "Make yourself at home. Have a seat. Do you want some water, a cookie?"

Lou had figured her for a cookie person. They were the best kind of people, in her opinion. Lou smiled and said, "I would love a cookie."

Ms. Dirkson handed Lou a plate of cookies and then went to the filing cabinet. As she stood much shorter than Lou, she had to pull up a stepstool to reach into the top drawer. Ms. Dirkson was stout and had solid calves that she stretched to her maximum height to get in the file drawer even with the help of the step. She was dressed in a lemon-yellow spring dress with a flower pinned to her waist. She wore red kitten heels and big blue baubles for earrings. Chattering happily the entire time, she hunted for papers and files. When she found what she was looking for, she made a cheerful noise and firmly shut the cabinet drawer.

Carefully she backed down the stepstool and sat at her desk.

"Okay, Lou, it seems we have all your paperwork. All I need is your picture for the student ID."

They got a picture done and the papers all sorted out right before students started flooding the hallway. Ms. Dirkson ushered her out of the office and said, "By the way, you can call me Amy. All the kids do. Ms. Dirkson just sounds so stuffy."

As they walked, they passed more posters and carvings. Lou felt like she was in an art gallery, not a high school. Amy chattered on, but Lou was having trouble concentrating on what she was saying. Lou's stomach was in a knot, and her hands were sweating. This was it, the moment she had to suffer through: being the new kid. She took a breath through her nose and exhaled out of her mouth like her father had showed her when he needed to calm down.

As she was being toured around the building, Lou noticed the hallway getting more crowded with kids. Amy dropped her off at her homeroom and wished her an excellent day. "Now Lou, you can come and see me any time if you need something."

Lou smiled and gave a little wave before walking through the doorway of her new classroom.

Most of the students had already arrived and taken their seats. When Lou walked into the classroom and scanned for a seat, every kid turned to look at her. Lou's knees got wobbly as she spotted an empty seat right at the front of the class. As she sat down, she could hear whispering behind her. Lou panicked and her mind raced. "What are they saying?" she wondered. "Did I hear laughing?"

Lou started to sweat, so she started rifling through her backpack to find a pen to distract herself. Then, thankfully, the bell rang, and her teacher strolled in the door.

He put his briefcase on the desk and looked at every student one at a time, seemingly assessing them. When he finished staring down every student in the eye, he returned his gaze to Lou and said, "You are new."

Lou nodded, transfixed.

He continued, "I am Mr. Patrick. You will address me as Mr. Patrick, or Sir."

Lou nodded again, staring. She had never had a teacher with a booming voice like his. He was a very tall, imposing black man with thick glasses. His skin was a warm shade, and his voice carried like thunder. He wore a wool suit jacket, a tie and dress pants that already had chalk marks on them.

Then came the moment she had been dreading for weeks. "Well, stand up and tell us about yourself."

She was nervous but managed to be clear about her recent move. "My family just arrived from Halifax. I have a dog named Rocky, and I like to read." But then said something she hadn't meant to. "And my hobby is building spy devices."

Lou heard a few snickers but not outright laughter. She sat back down.

Mr. Patrick said, "That's interesting." He glared over his glasses at the kids who were giggling. When they stopped and looked sheepish, he took attendance.

Her morning passed with a few people smiling and saying hi and welcomes from teachers. Lou thought, "This is a little weird, but I guess it is a small school, so the teachers knew I was coming."

At lunch time, she found her way to the cafeteria. It was a large space that doubled as an assembly hall. There were giant murals on the walls. The back wall had a huge painting with crossed lacrosse sticks and a giant leaping Orca in the background. Eagle Wind Orcas was written in large black and red letters, with a list of championship wins that went on for years.

After Lou found a seat at a table by herself, she pulled her lunch out of her backpack. She pretended to be busy inspecting her apple, but she was sneaking glances around and checking out the other kids. A table full of seniors sitting in seats and on the table caught her attention. She was tempted to make a note that the furthest table at the back belonged to the older kids, but she thought better of pulling out her notebook just yet.

As she was staring at the seniors, the skateboard kid from the park came sauntering into the cafeteria, still dressed all in black and carrying his skateboard. He pulled back his hood and flipped his bangs out of his face. Then he greeted the other kids with shoulder punches and a wide smile.

"He does go to school here," Lou thought as she quickly started unwrapping her sandwich while trying to melt into her plastic chair. "Why am I being all nervous and shy? He wouldn't have noticed me yesterday anyway. Wait, why do I even care?" Lou was deep in thought with a pensive look on her face.

She didn't notice when somebody stopped at her table, waiting for her to look over. The boy cleared his throat and said, "Hi, you must be the new girl."

Lou jumped, startled. She looked to see who the voice was coming from and found a friendly-looking boy in wheelchair smiling at her.

"My name is Oliver, what's yours?" He stuck out his hand for a handshake.

Lou shook his hand and responded, "My name is Lou, I got here this weekend from Halifax. We live on Pine street. This is my first day." Lou was nervous and couldn't stop talking.

Oliver smiled, "Pine Street? That is not too far from my house! You would pass my place when you walk home." He put his lunch on the table and pulled his chair up. "Do you mind if I join you for lunch?" Without waiting for an answer, he latched the wheel brake and asked, "Why did you move here?"

It surprised Lou how friendly he was. She answered, "My mom got a transfer here for a new job."

"Cool," Oliver said. "My mom grew up here and I live with her. She knows everybody." Oliver seemed to make it his mission to make her feel at ease. It was working.

They started eating their sandwiches and Lou discovered her

dad had made peanut butter and jam. Lou noted that she would need to ask for more mature lunches.

She scanned Oliver over her bread and wondered if he was her age. He seemed small to be her age and thin. He wore a collared shirt and chinos; they were neatly pressed but seemed too big. He was blond with a smart haircut and a firm jaw. His lean hands moved precisely when he laid out his lunch on a paper towel. Oliver chewed a bite, wiped his mouth and said, "What grade are you in?"

Lou finished a bite and responded, "Ten."

"Yeah, me too," Oliver said munching. He continued, "Which homeroom are you in?"

Lou answered, "Mr. Patrick's."

Oliver smiled over his sandwich, "Me too. I was just late today, so I wasn't in class for homeroom."

Lou said, "Mr. Patrick did this thing where he looked each of us over. It felt like he was trying to read my mind."

Oliver chuckled a little. "Oh, he always does that. He says it is to make sure everybody is paying attention and ready to learn. And also, he likes messing with us."

Lou laughed at that. She was feeling better about her first day.

Oliver pulled out a small bottle and tipped four pills into his hand. He took them all at once with a gulp from his water bottle. The bottle had words printed on it that Lou squinted to read: "Fastest Wheeler North Island Summer Camp." Lou wanted to ask about it but decided against it.

When Oliver finished taking his pills, he explained, "Everybody wants to ask but they are shy about it, so I'll just tell you why I'm in a chair."

Lou stammered, "Um, er... you don't have... I mean don't feel..."

Oliver interrupted, "Don't feel weird about it. I'ill tell you and then you won't need to wonder." He packed up his lunch and put his backpack on the handles of the chair. He turned back to Lou and started his story. "When I was three, I got a tumour in my spine, and when they took it out, I mostly lost the ability to walk."

Lou listened attentively and noticed that he rattled off his history in a tone that was unemotional, probably because he told it so often.

He continued, "I still do physio a couple of times a week to keep trying to walk. I can take a few steps with a cane or a walker, but the doctors don't think I will ever be able to walk much more than that."

Lou, who never liked the idea of giving up, couldn't help herself. "If you can take a few steps, why do they say you won't be able to do more? We should research new tech that is available. I am good at finding cool stuff."

Oliver smiled. "Don't worry, I am not buying any of what they say. If I can already walk a bit, I'll be able to walk a lot someday."

They talked the entire lunch hour, and when the bell ending lunch rang, it surprised them that the time had passed so quickly. They made their way to history class and as they navigated the busy hall, Lou thought, "Oliver is so friendly, and he isn't one bit shy."

She smiled at him, but he was busy saying hi to everyone.

When they got to class, Lou pulled out her notebook and wrote another list:

First day of School:

    1. 1.Don't sit at the far back table at lunch. Seniors!

She tucked the notebook into her backpack and flipped open her history textbook.

CHAPTER FOUR

After school it was drizzling out, so Lou buttoned up her raincoat and set out down the stairs. She heard someone calling her.

"Lou! Wait up!"

It was Oliver with a waterproof cape over him and his chair rolling down the ramp beside the stairs. When he caught up, he said, "Want to see where I live?"

Before Lou could answer she spotted a galloping giant dog bombing straight at them. Laughing, Lou exclaimed, "Rocky! What are you doing here?"

Her enormous dog came skidding to a halt and shook the rain off himself. Oliver and Lou put their arms up to protect themselves from the spray.

"Is this your dog, Lou?" Oliver exclaimed.

As Rocky sniffed Oliver and his chair, Lou explained, "Yeah, he's mine, but I have no clue how he got here from our place, or how he knew where to find me."

Rocky decided Oliver was okay, nudging his hand with his nose to ask for a scratch. Lou chuckled, "He likes you." They set off down the street, chatting happily.

Oliver still looked a little stunned by Rocky's gigantic frame. "How'd he find you, and holy cow, how much does he weigh?" Lou smiled, "I don't understand how he figures anything out, but he seems to. You should see how fast he figured out the door handles at our house." She scratched Rocky's wet ear and chuckled, "Last time we weighed him, he was right around ninety kilograms." Oliver's mouth gaped and he shook his head.

As they turned the corner, Oliver pointed out a yellow bungalow with a ramp up to the front door. "That's my place. Do you want to come in for a snack?"

Lou glanced at Rocky who had sat on the pavement and was awkwardly scratching at his ear, spraying water on her pants. She stepped out of range of the splatter and said with a smile, "I'd love to, but I think your Mom would have a fit if you brought a super-sized wet dog home for a visit."

Oliver looked over at Rocky, who stopped scratching but forgot to take his paw out of his ear. Oliver considered the potential disaster of bringing Lou and her dog into the house. He agreed, "Yeah, I suppose you're right. Maybe you can come over another day?"

Lou suddenly realized that she might be making her first friend, and it made her happy. She smiled, nodding as she said, "I would for sure, but first I have to figure out how Rocky got to the school and if he plans to make it a daily pickup."

Oliver laughed, "Well, let me know tomorrow. I have a sweet parking spot at the back of our homeroom class. Want to pull up a desk and join me?" He looked hopefully at Lou, smiling when she promised to sit with him.

They said goodbye and Oliver wheeled up the ramp. Lou saw the front door open and a slight blonde woman greeted him. He looked just like her; it had to be his mom. Noticing Lou standing there, the woman waved hello. When Lou quickly figured out that she had in fact been staring, she realized it might seem rude.

She awkwardly waved at Oliver and his mother and turned to follow Rocky.

He had gone ahead and was waiting patiently for Lou to follow. When she caught up, she put her hand on his head and whispered, "Let's go home and you can explain to me how you found me, and when you learned to tell time."

Lou was taking in the details of every house and yard as they sauntered along the block. Movement caught her eye as she went by a run-down house that was no bigger than a cottage. It used to be painted blue, but now it looked more faded grey. Next to the front door was a large window and the dirty white curtains were closed, but the motion she had caught was the one curtain opening slightly with somebody peeking out. When she tried to look at the person in the shadows, they snapped the drapes shut.

"Huh, that was weird," Lou said to Rocky. He raised his ears a bit as if he agreed.

Lou slowed their pace to see more of the property, trying not to seem nosy. It was one of the largest yards on the street, and yet one of the tiniest houses. There was no car in the driveway, but there was a rusted baby carriage and some discarded garbage by the front door. Lou wondered why the person looking out the window had hidden themselves. She would have loved to stop to see if the curtains would open again and maybe catch a glimpse of the person inside. She knew better than to spy on people out in the open, so she made a mental note to write down what she had seen later on. Trying not to be too obvious, she turned her head back as they walked past the end of the little house's yard. The person didn't show themselves again.

Lou and Rocky arrived home and ran up the front stairs, bursting through the door. Her father had seen them coming and had old towels at the ready. Knowing what the procedure was, Rocky sat down on the doormat, waiting to be dried. He managed not to shake himself first.

Mr. Dalrymple praised their very wet dog. "Excellent fetching,

Rocky. You brought Lou home and didn't bring mud in. I think somebody deserves a cookie!" Rocky perked up his ears and thumped his tail. Lou hung her coat in the closet and was unlacing her boots.

"How was your day, Bunny?" asked her dad while he finished drying Rocky. "I want to hear all about everything."

Lou thought for a second before answering, "It was actually pretty great, Dad. I met a kid named Oliver, and we walked home together. He met Rocky, and I saw his house, and we are sitting together in homeroom tomorrow. He's super nice."

Her dad smiled and tousled her damp hair. "It's great to see you so excited!" Mr. Dalrymple went to the kitchen and Lou followed. As he pulled out yogurt from the fridge and put in a bowl, he said, "I'm so happy that your first day was good. Were you able to find your way around okay?" He put the bowl of yogurt in front of Lou and started hunting around for the cutlery drawer to get her a spoon.

Lou watched him muttering to himself as he searched until he found it. "I had no trouble getting around. It is a tiny school and there are gigantic signs for the class numbers."

As she tucked into her yogurt, Lou decided to talk to her dad about her new lunch plan. She considered her words carefully. Her father loved spoiling her, so she had to tread lightly and not hurt his feelings. "Dad, I was thinking, it might be time for me to make my own lunches for school. I know you have always gotten up early to get everything ready for me and Mom, but I think I can get lunch done myself."

Her dad thought about it for a second. "Sure Lou, of course you are old enough to take on that responsibility. I'll miss making your lunch, but it isn't about me; it's what you want to do on your own." Smiling, he added, "Your mother and I are always so impressed with all the things you can do. Your talent for building cool devices and inventions is always so amazing. I suppose making a lunch is not that hard by comparison." He chuckled at his own humour.

Lou decided that since their conversation went well, and her father didn't seem to feel rejected about lunches, she could press onward. "I was also wondering if I could ask you to get some other types of food the next time you do groceries?"

"Sure, what do you want?" he asked.

She gave him a list that included sushi among other items she considered more mature, things the older kids might eat. He added them to the grocery list attached to the fridge. "I'll see what your mother wants and do a proper shop tomorrow. We need to get ourselves supplied anyway."

Lou finished her yogurt and put the bowl in the dishwasher. "When are you going to start job hunting? Do you think you will find something fast?"

Flipping the dishtowel over his shoulder, Mr. Dalrymple answered, "The nice thing about being a bookkeeper is that they always need somebody to count the beans." He chuckled and then added, "I will probably start looking next week. I can't be a stay-at-home dad forever."

Rolling her eyes at the bean counter joke, she gave her dad a kiss on the cheek. "You'll find a great place to work for sure."

Lou and Rocky bounded up the stairs into her room and shut the door. Lou immediately vaulted onto her bed, tucking a pillow behind her back to lean on the headboard. She opened her backpack and pulled out her notebook. Grabbing her pen, she turned to her first day of school page to finish journaling about her day.

Rocky was standing in the middle of the room. He would do that sometimes; he would get tired and forget to lie down.

"Hey, Rocky!" she called.

The dog startled, waking up although his eyes were open. He noticed that he was still standing, so he walked over to Lou's bed, leaning up against the side of it and sliding down until he hit the floor.

"Nice work, Rockster, you probably made the kitchen ceiling rattle."

Lou went back to the list in her notebook. She tapped her pen against her lips and then started writing. She made some points about her teacher and the art in the halls at school. Then Amy got a mention with a flower drawn beside her name. She wrote about Oliver and noted some important points to remember about him. The word 'tumour' got a star next to it. She also wrote: Research Robotic Mobility Solutions – Exoskeleton?

She made a list about the little cottage she saw:

1. 1.Rundown and dirty but occupied
2. 2.Suspicious character looking out the window
3. 3.Broken objects scattered
4. 4.No car visible
5. 5.Potential shady activities: drug dealers/criminals storing stuff/puppy mill? (no barking)

When Lou had thought of all she could about the little cottage, she made notes about people and houses she saw on her walk home. She was ever vigilant and curious, always watching for mysteries.

She hesitated, and then at the very bottom of the page she smiled and wrote in small letters: 'Skater boy at school. Find out his name.' Just before she closed the book, she quickly drew a small heart. Then scratched it out and snapped the notebook shut.

Lou tucked the notebook in her backpack and noticed her phone in the side pocket. She had forgotten about it and hadn't asked for Oliver's number. Did he use Snapchat, or what? She would ask him tomorrow. She was just happy to have somebody to put in her phone besides her parents.

Skootching to the edge of the bed, she leaned over and gave Rocky an ear massage. He loved that best, which Lou knew because he would start a deep rumble as soon as she started. Then he would roll onto his back as she rubbed harder. His rumble turned into a dog song of pleasure until her hands got tired.

Lou blew a hair out of her face. "At least you're dry," she said, then crossed the hall to the bathroom to wash her hands, leaving Rocky on the floor snoring. She had heard her mother come in the door and careened down the stairs to greet her.

"Hey Mom, how was your first day?"

Mrs. Dalrymple took off her coat and hung it in the closet, turning to answer Lou. "It wasn't anything like my old job at all. It's the same company but very different here. I will tell you two about it over dinner." She gave Lou a quick kiss on the forehead before going in the kitchen to see what was for supper.

Lou and her parents had a lot to talk about over dinner. By the time they had washed up the dishes, they had all updated each other on the stories of the day. Mr. Dalrymple took orders for lunch supplies and asked if anybody knew where the shopping bags ended up.

As Lou's parents continued chatting about groceries and such, Lou went to her room to do some research.

When her father heard Lou's door click shut, he said, "Lou wants different food that she feels would be more 'mature' as she called it, so she can make her own lunches."

Lou's mother mused, "Well, she is in grade ten and wants to make a good impression on her new classmates." She grinned, "I don't know what more mature lunches might be, but I am sure Lou will put what she wants on the grocery list."

Back upstairs in her room, Lou pulled out her laptop and started trying to figure out who Jake and Calvin were and what they could be up to. She remembered their faces pretty clearly as they were on the little lake. She started by searching through local business websites and community events. Surely, they would pop up in pictures somewhere. As she scoured photo after photo she started wondering if this would be a waste of time. She rubbed her eyes, shocked to see it was past nine. No wonder she was tired. Her parents came in to say goodnight.

"Do you have homework already?" her mother asked.

Lou tore her eyes from the screen, replying, "No, I am just researching." Her parents assumed she was planning to build one of her gadgets, so they both kissed her head, patted Rocky and left the room.

Before closing the door, her dad reminded her, "Don't stay up too late, Lou. You're walking to school tomorrow, so you will need extra time."

Lou was already back looking at pictures, distractedly saying, "Okay, Dad, I won't."

Minutes after her parents left the room, she found it. There were Jake and Calvin dressed exactly the same way as when she had seen them on the little lake. It looked like they were standing off to the side of a building where people were getting their pictures taken. They were in the background, but Lou could see them making sour faces. They clearly had no idea their picture was being snapped.

Lou zoomed in on the sign on the building reading *Marine Antiques and Oddities*. She flipped to the page in her notebook where she kept her list for the investigation, making a note of the shop name. Then she kept scanning the picture, eyeing the van behind the two men. When she saw a decal on it, she squinted hard because it was out of focus.

"This is for sure their van, they are leaning on it with the door open." She zoomed in, finally making out the words *Speedy Local Seafood Delivery* on the van decal.

"That's what they do! It also explains why they were so dirty," she figured. She scribbled some more notes, and searched up the companies and mapped the addresses. It didn't do much good at the moment as she had no idea where to find them and how far they were. She made a note to inflate her bicycle tires as she was going to need wheels this weekend.

By the time she got everything written down, she was tired and needed to get to bed. It would not do to be exhausted on her second day. She had wanted to have some options for robotic mobility for Oliver tomorrow, but she would have to wait and do it after school the next day.

She still had to shower, brush her teeth, and let Rocky outside to pee. She considered just lying down and going to sleep, skipping her elaborate nighttime routine, but she knew full well that she wouldn't sleep a wink if she didn't do it.

Lou stood, putting her foot under Rocky's face and wiggling her toes. That was the best way to get him awake and moving, as long as it worked. It was not working this time. He moved his big head and dragged a slack lip across Lou's foot.

"I guess he's down for the night," she thought. Grabbing her pajamas, she had to force open and closed the jumbled drawer. She knew she would need to organize the mess at some point, but not tonight. Lou took a shower, and before she wrapped a towel around herself, she checked if her chest had grown in the last few days.

"Nothing," she said in a disappointed voice. Her mother had told her not to expect grand things for a bit longer. All the women in her family were late bloomers. She made a mental note to get a bra with foam in it; anything would help.

Her mother had also told her, "Sweetie, you are strong and slim, and you don't have the genetics for big breasts. It doesn't even matter. You shouldn't worry about what your body looks like. Just be healthy."

Lou had rolled her eyes at that, but it helped calm her worries.

For the next stage of her routine, she brushed her teeth one at a time, front and back; brushed her hair a hundred strokes; and put zit cream on her face. This took half an hour, and she did the same thing every night. Her strict routine was – in her mind –

essential to keeping herself disciplined. If she was going to be a spy and an engineer, she had to keep sharp.

Once she finished in the bathroom, she quietly returned to her room and turned off the light. She was careful not to trip over Rocky as she made her way to bed. He made a "GGRUMFFLL" noise and rolled over. Pulling her blanket up to her chin, she whispered, "Sweet dreams, Rocky."

CHAPTER FIVE

Lou was awakened by her alarm. She stretched out in bed, then reached over to her nightstand drawer, and pulled out her notebook. She made a note about a device she had been having trouble building but thought had figured out in a dream. She didn't want to forget that. Lou got herself ready for the day and went downstairs with Rocky. He hadn't been outside since dinner last night, so he was at the back-patio door in a shot, whining.

After letting him out, Lou started hunting in the fridge for breakfast. Her dad came in, greeting her warmly. "Hey, Bunny, you're up early."

Lou had a mouth full of grapes when she turned from the fridge. Chewing quickly, she mumbled, "I had to give myself time to make my lunch." She carried an unbalanced armload of food to the counter when she asked, "Where's Mom?"

Dad lent a hand, helping her put her precarious load of food down. "She had to go into work early today. I think it is going to be a big task just to learn a fresh job, so we will probably be dealing with your mom being at work long hours for a little while."

Lou nodded as she made a sandwich with ham and cheese and packed it in her lunch.

Rocky was at the back door carrying his food bowl. When nobody showed up with a bag of kibble, he started running his metal bowl along the patio bannister. Laughing, Lou said, "Okay, dude, we get it. You're hangry."

As she loaded kibble into the bowl, she asked her father about Rocky's surprise appearance at school the day before. "I forgot to ask you last night, how do you think Rocky found me?"

Her dad replied, "It was actually kind of weird. A few minutes before I was about to leave to pick you up, Rocky came to the front door and pulled your hat off the peg and dropped it. I couldn't understand what he wanted, but I figured he was hinting at coming along. I opened the door, and he shot out and raced down the road. I got in the van and followed behind him, driving in the direction he went running. Then I spotted you and your friend, and Rocky headed toward home."

Lou was gob smacked. "You were there?"

Mr. Dalrymple laughed. "Of course I was. I wanted to find Rocky, but I was not too worried because his sense of direction has always been legendary. I also wanted to make sure you were okay on your first day."

"You know I would have been okay, Dad," she said, sounding a little insulted. "I like walking, and now I have a friend to walk with, and Rocky." Lou had another question. "How did Rocky know what time it was?"

Her father scratched Rocky behind the ear and said, "You are the researcher. Maybe you can figure out how dogs know when it's time for their people to come home."

Although he was probably joking, Lou made a mental note to research that.

Lou was happy to have Rocky along when she waved goodbye to her father. He watched her leave from the front window. Rocky bounded to the sidewalk and waited for her to catch up, then together they set off for school.

When they turned the corner and walked for a bit, Lou scanned the little blue house. Nothing had changed since the day before. "Oh well, we will go by there every day so we can keep an eye on it," she said to Rocky, who seemed to agree.

As they lumbered on, they approached Oliver's house. He was on the front porch. When he saw her, he did a wheelie all the way down the ramp and pulled up to the sidewalk. He was blushing a little at Lou's shocked expression. "Hi Lou! Want to walk with me today?"

Lou exclaimed, "For sure! That way you can tell me how you do a wheelie down a ramp without breaking yourself!"

Oliver chuckled at her reaction. They set off to school, their conversation lasting the whole way to the school doors. When they got there, Rocky nudged Lou's hand and loped down the sidewalk heading home.

As Rocky headed off, Oliver muttered, "I don't think that will ever not be weird." Then they went inside.

Oliver invited Lou to sit at the desk beside his wheelchair. When the two of them took their spots in homeroom, Mr. Patrick made an announcement. "Okay people, settle down, I have somebody important for you to meet."

Lou looked at the young woman, wondering if she might be a new teacher or something. The first thing she noticed was her giant smile and her long black hair. Then she spotted her necklace; it was a beaded mask like the ones in the school halls.

Mr. Patrick continued, "This is Cecie Joe, and she will be working with us until the end of the school year as an Aboriginal Liaison. She will be assisting our Socials and History teachers. You can find her in the office next to Ms. Dirkson."

Cecie stood up as he finished his remarks. She was tall and confident. Lou immediately liked her. Cecie thanked Mr. Patrick before stepping to the front of the room. "Hey everybody! I'm thrilled to be working at the same school where I grew up. I'm a member of the Squamish Nation, and I currently attend university here in British Columbia. I am doing my degree in psychology with a specialty in Aboriginal counselling."

Lou's former high school didn't have anyone doing that job. The idea of it excited her.

Cecie continued, "During my internship here I will be working directly with First Nations students and filling in on some history classes. My door is always open for any student who needs to talk on any subject. You guys all look pretty smart. I can't wait to learn from you."

Lou and Oliver looked at each other. Their eyebrows went up, and Lou knew he was thinking the same thing she was. "She's cool, and we get to teach her stuff?" he whispered.

When Lou and Oliver headed to the cafeteria later, they saw Cecie in her office hanging posters. They stopped in, and Lou offered to help. They ended up eating their lunches in Cecie's office while they chatted and helped her get settled.

Lou asked Cecie about the classes she was taking for her degree, and Oliver questioned her about what she was going to be teaching. Cecie told them about growing up on the reservation with a large family, including a whole bunch of cousins. Oliver and Lou were super interested in Cecie's stories, specifically about her elders. Lou wondered what it would be like to have a big family around.

When the bell rang Cecie said, "Thank you so much for helping me get set up today. I hope you'll drop by whenever you feel like it. Also, tomorrow I'll be in your Socials class, so I'll see you then!"

Beaming with excitement, Lou and Oliver said goodbye and raced to their next class.

After school, Lou went to her locker and packed up. A few kids said hi, and the younger girl with a neighboring locker chatted with Lou for a bit. As Lou went to the front doors, she thought to herself, "This was a great day, and nobody has called me a freak yet. Bonus for me."

She smiled to herself as she walked outside. There was a cluster of kids near the sidewalk, and she went to see what was happening. She found Oliver and Rocky surrounded by curious kids. Oliver was petting Rocky, and when they spotted Lou, Oliver shouted and waved. Rocky wagged his whip tail so hard that he cleared a path through the kids as he whacked their legs with it. Poor Rocky always looked confused when he wagged his tail and people backed away. He couldn't figure it out.

Slowly, the kids dispersed after they were through swarming Rocky. There were remarks like "cool dog" and "so friendly," which made Lou smile.

Oliver explained, "Rocky was here waiting for you and the other kids wanted to see him. I knew he was nice, so I came over and joined in to tell them his name and that he's your dog."

Lou bent down to talk directly to the dog. "Rocky, are you going to walk me to school and pick me up every day?" Rocky sat down and lifted a paw up on Lou's leg.

Oliver chuckled. "I would take that as a yes."

As they walked towards Oliver's house, they heard the distinct sound of wheels on the cement racing up behind them. Rocky turned around to see what it was, and being protective, he moved to intercept a kid on a skateboard. By the time Lou realized it was *that kid* on a skateboard, it was too late. He veered onto the grass to avoid the giant dog and landed flat on his face. Lou was horrified, and shouted, "Rocky! Sit!"

Rocky lay all the way down, sensing he had done something wrong.

The boy picked himself up and brushed off his clothes, seeming unharmed. Lou rushed over, exclaiming, "I'm so sorry! He wouldn't hurt you; he is just big and always in the way."

Lou was mortified, but then the boy spoke. "No worries, it was my fault, I was speeding." He picked up his skateboard and checked it for damage. Turning, he sauntered over saying, "Hey, Oliver!"

He then looked closer at Lou. "You are the new kid, right?"

Lou found herself flushing, at a loss for words. She stammered a little and soon squashed down her nerves, finally managing to explain, "Yeah, our family just moved here last week. My name is Lou."

"Mine's Tyler," responded the boy as he swept his bangs off his face. Lou noticed that he had a bit of stubble on his chin and an earring.

She forgot to speak again, but Oliver saved her. "You should say hi to Rocky the dog. He's pretty cool."

Tyler bent over and gave Rocky an ear scratch. After a moment, he stepped onto the sidewalk, dropped his skateboard on its wheels, and said, "Nice to meet you and your dog, Lou."

As he rolled away he called out, "Later!"

Lou, Oliver and Rocky strolled down the street until they came to Oliver's driveway. "You want to come in, Lou?" he said hopefully.

Lou was trying not to be obvious as she stared at Tyler riding away in the distance, so she quickly turned her attention back to Oliver. She noticed his mother had come out on the porch. Smiling at Oliver, Lou said, "That would be great."

She turned to Rocky and instructed him. "Go home boy, I will be there later." Rocky looked a little dejected that he wasn't coming in the house, but he wheeled around and took off down the block.

Lou finished off by sending a text to her dad that she was going to Oliver's house before going inside. Oliver's mother was waiting for them with some cookies at the ready. When the silence stretched uncomfortably, she had to give Oliver a look. "Aren't you going to introduce me?"

Realizing his lapse, Oliver said, "Mom, this is my new friend Lou. Lou, this is my mother."

Lou smiled and waved a little wave, saying, "Nice to meet you, Ms. Bamberg."

Oliver's mother handed him a cane with a big hook on the end before replying, "So nice to meet you, Lou. Oliver talked about how you are new to the area. Amazing dog you have there. Oliver tells me he walks you to school and back every day."

While they were chatting, Oliver put the hook under his ankle and lifted his foot up onto his other leg with it. He was chatting with Lou and his mom, all the while taking his shoes off.

Lou watched him, amazed at what she was seeing. Without thinking, she blurted out, "How do you get them on again?" Belatedly, she realized that might be a rude question, but Oliver just rolled to the closet and pulled out another cane with a grabber mechanism attached to it. He showed it to Lou and put his shoe back on. Grinning, Lou asked, "Can I see it? I love gadgets."

Ms. Bamberg went into her office and left them alone. When they settled into the front room, Oliver went to get two cans of pop from the fridge. They ate the cookies happily and talked about their day. After a while, Oliver asked Lou, "Do you miss your friends?"

Lou had been dreading this question. She decided Oliver was kind enough to know her secret. She cleared her throat and began, "Oliver, I didn't really have friends at my old school. There was this group of girls who decided that my hair was too red, I was too tall, my feet were too big, and I was too loud. They made me feel bad all the time, so I hung out with teachers in their classrooms and helped them."

Oliver had been listening intently, which he always did. He was a good listener. When Lou took a breath, he said, "That bites. Those girls were mean, and it's good that you are here now. We don't have gangs of kids who bully people. Not that I know about, and I know everybody."

Lou immediately felt more comfortable with what she had just confessed to Oliver. Then she had a thought. "If you know everybody, why did you come sit with me at lunch?"

Oliver was finishing a last bite of cookie. He swallowed it before explaining, "I know what it's like to be different and I make it my mission to sit with people who are sitting alone. I saw you and knew it was your first day, so I wanted to welcome you to the school."

They talked for a while more about their hobbies and school. Oliver listed the teachers for Lou, telling her what they were like. "Mr. Patrick is my favourite, but the History teacher is so boring. I am glad Cecie will be helping in that class, she couldn't possibly make it any worse."

Lou's phone chimed; it was her mother's tone. She looked at the message and said, "Oops, supper's ready. I have to jet."

Oliver nodded his understanding. "Okay. Will you and Rocky pick me up again tomorrow?"

Lou stood up, got her jacket and backpack ready, and laced up her boots. "Same time, same place!" She grinned while opening the door. As she flew down the ramp she called, "See ya."

Rocky greeted her at her front door, wagging his tail so hard he sent the umbrella stand flying. Lou was picking the umbrellas up when her mom came out of the kitchen wearing her favourite apron over her work clothes – the one that said, 'Kiss the cook' on it. Mrs. Dalrymple surveyed the umbrellas on the floor and rolled her eyes before asking, "Did you have fun at Oliver's house?"

Lou nodded. "What are we having for supper?"

Her mother's tone turned serious, but with a sly grin she stated, "Gorilla toenails."

It was Lou's turn to roll her eyes. "You always say that, Mom!"

Her father was setting the table when she walked further into the house. "Hi, Lou! Go ahead and wash your hands; dinner is on. We want to hear all about your day."

They had Lou's favourite: lasagna. Between bites of dinner,

Lou told her parents about her day. She told them about Cecie and all the things she does at the school as a counsellor. Lou's dad said, "What a great education you will get in history and Aboriginal culture. You never got that in your old school."

Lou's mother stood up and began clearing the table. She agreed, "This school sounds great."

When they had all tidied the kitchen, Mr. Dalrymple asked, "Do you have homework?"

Mrs. Dalrymple nudged him. "Mervin, I'm sure she wouldn't have any homework yet."

Lou headed up to her room and was already halfway up the stairs when she called back over her shoulder, "No homework tonight."

Rocky was already lying on the floor inside her room. He lifted his head up and made a deep happy noise that sounded like he was mumbling. Lou loved when he did that because it was his greeting just for her. She patted his big head and flopped onto her bed. She pulled out the pack of licorice that was always in her nightstand and started munching on a piece. She had been looking forward to updating her notes and getting some research done.

Lou started by looking up robotic solutions for people with mobility issues. She spent a long time looking up everything from standing style wheelchairs to adapted segues and robotic exoskeletons controlled by the electrical impulses in the brain. Fascinated, she couldn't stop reading and making notes. She finally ended up with a list of the top products that might help Oliver walk. It satisfied her that she had dug up everything technology had to offer. Lou had always planned to be a mechanical engineer, but now that she has seen what biomedical engineering could do, she might reconsider her choice.

Flipping from the robotics research to her daily notes page, Lou wrote a few highlights of her day, which included going to

Oliver's house. Again, she wrote a note in tiny letters at the bottom of the page, "His name is Tyler."

She had planned to do more research on the men in the boat, but she was running out of energy. After she closed up her notebook, Lou let Rocky outside and followed her nighttime routine. When she got back to her room, her parents and Rocky were there waiting. Noticing the licorice wrapper poking out of the drawer, Lou's mother gave a disapproving look and shook her head.

Mr. Dalrymple decided to leap into conversation rather than let a long discussion about junk food get started. "We wanted to say goodnight and let you know that we are going into the city on Saturday. We have to get some furniture we need for the house and pick up Mom's car. Do you want to come along?"

This was a great opportunity to have some time to do what was on her list. After a moment of excitement at the thought, Lou answered, "No thanks, I'd like to get to know the area so I can figure out where everything is."

They agreed that furniture shopping would be boring for her and gave her permission to stay behind. As they left the room, Lou's dad said, "Goodnight Bunny," and closed the door behind him.

Lou gave Rocky a quick ear rub and turned off her light. Rocky was already asleep as he rolled onto his back. "Goodnight, Goofus," Lou chuckled.

CHAPTER SIX

The rest of the week flew by. Lou and Oliver spent lots of time together, and he introduced her to his other friends. He hadn't been exaggerating; he seemed to know everybody. They ate at a bigger table in the cafeteria (but not the one that belonged to the seniors). Lou kept an eye on Tyler and tried not to be too obvious about it. He would give them his usual wave as he went by on his skateboard after school, and Lou found herself looking forward to it.

The teachers started to assign projects and reading. Lou was always a good student, so she knew she could handle the new topics she was learning in class. She was enthralled when Cecie came into her history class and announced she was going to be teaching a three-weeklong section on world cultures, Aboriginal People of Canada, and other societies.

Lou was happy to finally have an interesting history lesson, reading ahead in their textbook 'Indigenous Peoples in Canada.' Every night she made notes for class the next day. She read to the part where the book laid out everything from residential school trauma to the land treaty process. There was a big section on Truth and Reconciliation that was a little more of a heavy read, but she wanted to be able to understand. She knew that Cecie would be covering her nation in Squamish, too. All week, Lou fell asleep with either a textbook on her face, or her notebook in her lap.

When Saturday rolled around, her parents left early, and she woke up to an empty house. There was a note on the counter when she got to the kitchen. It read, 'Have a great day, Bunny. Don't forget to do your chores and eat before you head out.' There was a ten-dollar bill under the note.

She and Rocky had breakfast, then Lou swept the kitchen floor and put in a load of laundry. When that was done, Lou tucked her phone and the money in her pocket and went into the garage. She searched for her bike among the boxes. Eventually she found it and, only by luck, spotted a box that had 'helmets' written on one of her mother's very organized labels.

Lou took the bike outside and noticed the tires were flat. She rooted around a bit and found the air pump. Rocky was sitting on the grass trying to catch and eat a moth while he waited for her.

Rocky caught something – but it wasn't a moth. He started panicking and bolting all over the yard. He stopped and smashed his mouth down in the grass and started rubbing his face back and forth, howling. Lou ran over just in time to see a very angry hornet fly out from under his lip. Rocky fell to the ground pawing at his cheeks.

Lou sat with him and checked his lips and mouth. He had a swollen lip, but he wasn't dying, although he tried to convince Lou that he was. She patted his belly and said, "How about we don't chase tiny angry things with stingers, huh?"

Rocky kept licking his lips to make the pain stop. He looked miserable.

When Lou was done comforting her very sad and injured dog, she went back to her bike and grabbed some tools to fill her tires and tighten up all the nuts. She oiled the chain and made sure her seat was adjusted to her height because she had grown through the winter. The blue paint had gotten chipped in transit, and it was a bit dirty. She made a face but decided she didn't want to spend any more time fiddling with her bike.

Securing her helmet, she said, "Let's go, Rock, we're exploring today." Rocky loved running alongside Lou's bike, and he was already on the sidewalk waiting before she turned her bike around. He was over his insect trauma and was ready to go.

Lou rode by Oliver's house with Rocky running alongside. She saw his mother in the garden. Ms. Bamberg noticed them and smiled, waving as she said, "Hi Lou!"

Rocky stopped and gave a friendly bark, and Lou waved back. She knew Oliver had gone to a softball training camp that weekend. He was trying out for a wheelchair softball team with kids from everywhere. Lou hoped he would get chosen. He really wanted to play on that team.

Lou had her backpack filled with snacks, her notebook, and some of her spy gear, just in case she might need it. Inside was also a drawn a map of her top priorities of places to check out. Mostly, she planned to find and conduct surveillance on the antique store and the seafood delivery company.

She had figured out the general area of Squamish on the map. There was a big highway cutting through from north to south. On the east side of the highway were cliffs and mountains. (The biggest cliff was called The Chief. Lou had made a note to hike to the top at some point.)

The west side of the highway consisted mostly of the downtown and some small suburbs. Lou had thought she found out where she made a wrong turn the other day after seeing it on a satellite image. She also found the little lake, and the park. Beyond the city limits were industrial areas with manufacturing and forestry trucks that loaded trees onto barges.

Further to the west was Howe Sound, which led out to the ocean. A peninsula jutted out from the mainland into the sound. At the far tip of the peninsula was a container terminal serviced by tugboats. Lou had read with interest about the large cargo barges moving in and out all day. She thought it sounded cool and wondered if she could see some of that from on her bike.

She navigated her way to her first stop on the list, the antique shop. Lou found its location made more sense to her now. She had wondered why it was in a more industrial area at the edge of town. The shop was in a big, run-down, converted two-story house; the store was on the bottom and it had what looked like a residence upstairs. Then she spotted the sign from the picture she had found. This was it!

Walking around the side, she found a shady spot for Rocky. She leaned her bike against some garbage cans, saying, "Rocky, stay and guard." Rocky wasn't going to bite anybody that would take her bike, but most people wouldn't try if they saw him. She took her helmet off and hung it on the handlebar.

Inside the store, it smelled both musty and vaguely of sea spray. Having lived in an ocean city before, she was comforted by the smell. As her eyes adjusted to dimmer lighting, she saw how cluttered everything was. She walked through the tight aisles thinking, "This is a lot of ship stuff. But what were the two guys I saw on the lake doing in the pictures in front of this place?"

Lou was always putting theories and connections together but she couldn't figure out what the men in a van that delivered seafood would have been doing there.

At the back of the store, she saw a long counter, one that looked like a shelf from an old ship. It stretched across the entire back wall. There was an old cash machine and piles of papers. Behind it, there was a small, bent old man smiling at her. "Well hello, dolly, what can I do for you today?"

Lou continued to look around and take in the many items. She tore her eyes away, making eye contact with the old man. "Hello sir, are you the captain of this ship?"

The old man snickered at the cheeky smile on Lou's face when he answered. "Yes, I am the owner, the name's Sam. They call me Old Sam because I'm an antique myself." He chuckled at his own joke like he had just thought of it. Lou figured he has probably told that one for years. She found him charming and smiled warmly.

Sam continued, "Want to look around, or is there something in particular you need? I have portholes from old ships, huge ropes, every kind of brass attachment you can imagine and a million other interesting things."

Eyes wide, she replied, "You sure have a lot of cool stuff. I see the marine items, but what are the oddities?"

The old man smiled, gesturing to a doorway with a curtain covering it. Lou followed him. When they walked in, he flicked on the lights.

The contents of this compact room were astonishing. There were glass cabinets and display cases everywhere. Some items were behind glass and locked, and others were displayed on counters and shelves. She tried to figure out what she was looking at.

Seeing her confusion, Sam explained, "This is where I keep the special oddities I have collected over the years." His voice was full of pride, and Lou could see he loved these incredible and strange items.

Unprompted, he started listing his treasures. "This is part of my taxidermy collection - real butterflies from the 1800s in a frame."

Lou was enthralled. "These are so neat," she said while trying to figure out what the weird ones could be.

Sam could see that Lou was a willing audience, so he unlocked some cabinets and began picking things out to show her. He knew she wasn't going to buy anything, but her reactions made him happy.

He showed her a box of vampire fighting supplies and explained, "These are of unknown origin, but they are very old. I wish I could remember where I got this one. I even have a piece of paper about it, but I can't find that either!"

Lou picked up a heavy cross covered in gems and admired it. She asked, "What would this be worth?"

He thought for a second, seeming to struggle with a memory. "That kit is going for about $10,000."

Lou's jaw dropped, and she put back the cross, deciding not to pick up the wooden stake.

Next, he picked up a strange looking device and offered it to Lou. Holding it carefully she asked, fascinated, "What is this?"

He explained, "It's a 1940 ECT Therapy Unit Medical device. You put the mask on your face, and it's connected to the machine by wires. The thing looks frightening, so I haven't tried it. I don't really know what it is supposed to cure, really."

Lou saw a price on it of $1,200. She was shocked at the values of these oddities. She was also surprised that this room had no security cameras.

Old Sam rummaged around, clearly looking for something specific, but he wasn't finding it. Wanting to be helpful, Lou finally said, "If you can tell me what you're looking for, maybe I can help?"

He scratched his head as he answered. "I had a cast iron bust of a man. It was in this cabinet... at least I thought it was. I must have sold it and forgotten."

The shelves were dusty, except where items had sat. Spying a clear space, she asked, "What was in this spot before?"

Sam looked closely before answering, "That is where I keep the Ophthalmophantome from the 1900s." Getting agitated, he muttered, "I would certainly remember selling that. It was priced at $8,000!"

He started pacing. Lou quickly looked around and took stock of the other clean spots along the dusty shelves. There were more than a few spots where things had been but were now gone. Lou was surprised that he could lose track of items of this value. The more he paced the more Lou was sure there was something else worrying him about the missing items than just misplacing or forgetting them.

Sam left the oddities room and began frantically flipping through papers at the counter, muttering, "I am sure I didn't sell that thing."

The phone rang, and he answered it. He talked for a minute about a brass bell from an old tugboat that he said he would find for the customer. Sam hung up the phone and looked lost in thought, forgetting Lou was there. When she cleared her throat, he looked startled. "Oh, yes, where was I? Yes, I have to find the bell from that boat. Now where have I left it?" He had forgotten what he was talking about and focused on his new task.

Lou spent an hour chatting with Sam after they searched for and found the brass bell. He was happy for the help but had entirely forgotten about the missing items from the oddities room. He was thrilled to talk about the store, but when he found out Lou was new to town, he was delighted to tell her the history of Squamish.

Sam and Lou made fast friends, and as she was leaving, she decided that he seemed a little lonely. They said friendly goodbyes, and Lou resolved to visit him again. He was a nice man, and she was convinced more that ever that he was being robbed without noticing.

Outside the store, the sunshine was so bright it made her squint. As Lou rounded the corner to get her bike and wake her dog, a van pulled up in front of the store. Automatically, she glanced over her shoulder at the sound of the engine turning off and did a double take. Hushing Rocky and telling him to stay, she crept around the corner to get a better look at the decal on the van, which said 'Speedy Local Seafood Delivery.'

CHAPTER SEVEN

"Rocky, it's them!" Lou whispered frantically. Rocky didn't know what she meant, but he could tell it wasn't good, so he stood up straight.

If Jake and Calvin had been paying attention, they would have seen a redheaded girl peeking at them around the corner of the building. However, they were busy arguing and didn't see Lou as they walked towards the store.

Lou needed to know what they were up to. Frozen, she stayed to watch what they could possibly be doing inside the store – and most importantly, where they were going next – hardly daring to breathe in case she attracted their attention. She kept reminding herself that they had no idea who she was and wouldn't have any reason to be concerned if they saw her. But still, she didn't want them to see her face if she could help it.

When Jake and Calvin were close to the front door, Calvin split from Jake's side and began walking around the side of the building. "Where's he going?" Lou wondered, but she stayed put until she saw Jake walk into the front door of the shop. As soon as he stepped inside, she darted down the side of the building to see what Calvin was up to. She reached the back just in time to see him look around suspiciously before opening the back-entrance door and slipping inside.

Lou was desperate to see what was going on inside, but all the windows were too high for her to see into. She gave up looking and gathered her bike and helmet instead. Looking at Rocky, she instructed him to lie down and stay until she returned. She made sure he was out of sight from the front of the store before walking her bike out to the front dirt parking lot and right next to the road. She set up her bike stand and tucked her hair up inside the helmet. Then she zipped up her hoodie and waited.

It wasn't long before Lou saw the front door open. She bent down, pretending to do a roadside repair on her tire. She watched through the spokes of her tire. Jake, emerging from the store, glanced her way but otherwise paid her no attention as he approached the van. She was pretty sure he couldn't see her face from that distance.

A minute later, she watched as Calvin dashed from behind the building and then jumped into the van. He was carrying two bags with obviously heavy objects in them. Lou whispered to herself, "Calvin must have stolen those items while that Jake guy distracted Sam!" Suddenly, all the dots connected in Lou's head as she nearly shouted, "That's what they were sinking in the lake!" Her mind started spinning. Could that be it? Are they sinking stolen items into the lake? Why would they hide them there?

The van slowly turned around in the parking lot and headed back in the direction it had come. Before they got too far, Lou could see an address on their back windows. She made a note of it in her phone and called for Rocky. He ran across the parking lot to catch up to her, excited that they had a mission.

Lou's mind was racing, and her heart was pumping, trying to catch up to the van. She followed from a distance for a while but eventually lost them around a corner. She had no idea what road they had turned onto, but they were for sure out of sight, so she stopped in an industrial parking lot for a break. She pulled out her water bottle and a collapsible dog bowl and poured a drink for Rocky. As she took a long swig of water herself, her brain was moving fast. "What do you think, Rock? Where could they be headed?"

After a moment of thought, she figured they probably had deliveries to do, as they would have picked up their seafood in the morning. If that was the case, they wouldn't be going back to their company address. The more she thought about it, the more she was convinced they would be headed to the lake later in the afternoon to sink their newly stolen treasures. "What else could have been in the bags?" she wondered, but then decided it was for sure things they slipped out from under the old man's nose.

If her calculations were right, they would need to fetch their boat and fake fishing gear before heading to the lake. This meant she had some time to get snacks and get to the lake before them in order to find a hiding spot with a good view. She took a quick look at her map to locate a grocery store.

Lou stashed the food in her backpack when she and Rocky set out toward the lake. Rocky was looking like he needed his late afternoon nap and wasn't running very fast anymore. This was a busy day for a dog who normally spent most of his time on the sofa.

When they arrived at the lake, nobody was there. This gave Lou the chance to select the ideal surveillance spot. She decided that there was no way to tell where they would sink the bags, so she found a spot where she could see most of the lake. She walked around to the other side of the small beach and scoped out the tallest grass as close to the water as she could get.

Lou laid her bike behind their hiding spot where it wouldn't be noticed. She stamped down the grass in a circle that would fit them both, but not be noticeable by anybody on the lake. She sat beside Rocky who was already setting himself up for a big nap. He was stretched out and shifted around for maximum comfort. Lou sat next to him and started pulling things out of her backpack.

First, she grabbed snacks, which included pepperoni sticks. Rocky opened one eye to see if he might get any. Seeing his look, Lou unwrapped one stick and gave him half before she had the other half herself.

As she chewed, Lou unpacked her notebook, binoculars, a small bag of supplies, a tent peg, duct tape and an old cell phone with a broken screen. She set everything down on a plastic tablecloth with a pattern of ribs and chicken on it. Frowning at it, she made a mental note to get herself a more sophisticated mat to keep her devices on.

After she was organized and Rocky had scoffed down his third pepperoni stick and gone to sleep, Lou set about getting her surveillance operation in order. She didn't know if they would actually come today, but she wanted to be ready just in case. She was happy to have a new cell phone she could use for video and audio recordings. She had an older one at home that she used sometimes, but this one was better. She double checked that the phone battery was fully charged and then taped the phone to the tent peg and tested it.

She needed to be able to start the video recording of the suspects from her hiding place in the grass without being seen. After a bit of thinking, she had an idea. She began digging through the small bag of miscellaneous items and pulled out some twine, a clothes peg with a spring, and a rubber eraser. She took out the jackknife that was always in her pocket and started to work on her idea.

After about fifteen minutes, she made a satisfied sound and stretched her back. She had taped the phone horizontally to the tent peg. Then she stuck the clothes peg and eraser together and secured the clothes peg to the back of the phone. She tied the twine to one arm of the clothes peg and tested the spring. She heard the click of the phone taking the photo. It worked, and everything stayed together. She quickly turned the phone to silent mode.

Now that it was assembled and working, Lou reached out of the grassy area and stuck the tent peg in the ground, setting the camera on wide-angle. She checked the recording and adjusted the peg to the right spot and backed into the grass, then she unrolled the twine that was tied to the clothes peg and tested that it would actually fire up and record when the eraser touched the button. Satisfied that all would go well, she sat and waited to see if her theory was right.

Lou and Rocky spent the rest of the afternoon in their hiding spot. Lou was beginning to wonder if her parents were home yet and was thinking about packing up her gear for the day. Then she heard the crunching of tires on gravel and the creaking of a rusty trailer. She looked across the lake and saw the white van backing down the beach with a boat trailer. Lou's heart jumped into her throat. "It's Jake and Calvin!" She silently congratulated herself for getting it right. She watched for a little longer, and then got herself into position to catch them in the act.

As they got into the boat and paddled out onto the water, she saw Calvin pulling out the black bags from the cooler they used before. Peering through her binoculars, she could see the bags had heavy items in them, similar in size and shape to the ones Calvin had carried out of Sam's shop.

Lou spun the dial on her binoculars, trying to bring the scene into focus. When Rocky suddenly started woofing, she nearly jumped out of her skin. She whipped around to silence him, but he was still fast asleep and dreaming. "Nice timing, dude," she muttered. In response, he twitched his leg and knocked over Lou's water bottle. It was not very loud, but the men looked around. Thankfully, they weren't able to tell where the sound came from.

Lou settled Rocky and went back to observing the action. Jake and Calvin had loaded the boat into the water and were setting up their fishing rods while Lou pulled the twine to start the phone recording.

Occasionally a person walking or jogging would pass by the trail that came near the little beach. When the men saw somebody coming, they would pretend to fish. When nobody was around, they began arguing like the other day.

Calvin glared, his voice gruff as he asked, "Jake, this is our last time, right?"

Jake answered, "We won't be back here until we need to get the stuff out of the water."

Lou could hear everything they said, so she hoped the camera mic would pick it up too. A gust of wind came up and turned the boat around, so now their backs were facing Lou just as Calvin dropped the bags. Jake pulled out the notebook and wrote down the location of the bags, and they quickly paddled back to the beach. They had stopped arguing and said nothing as they left.

Once they were gone, Lou grabbed the phone and quickly checked the video. The voices weren't clear, but the video showed them dropping something. "Perfect!" she thought. She packed up her bag and put on her helmet. Checking her phone, she saw there was a message from her dad. *"We're home now Lou, please be here by five. You should be helping with dinner."* It had been 4:30 when the message came in; now it was 4:55. Fortunately, she wouldn't be too late if she hustled.

She rousted her sleepy dog, and they sped away home. The whole way, Lou's mind was racing. Had she really seen what she had suspected? Were they going to steal more things? Why were they hiding Sam's items or other ones too? Lou often suspected conspiracies and such, but they rarely were what she thought. Somehow, though, this seemed different.

Lou and Rocky arrived home a few minutes after five, but Lou's parents weren't very strict about time. She saw that her mother's car was in the driveway along with the van. Lou parked her bike in the garage and burst into the house to find her parents were already in the kitchen cooking. "Oh, that smells good!" Lou said.

Her mother turned around and smiled at them. "Oh good, you're back. Wash your hands and set the table, please."

Mr. Dalrymple greeted Lou as he stood beside Rocky and scratched his ears. The dog leaned hard against him, and Lou's dad had to brace himself to take the weight. Rocky then slid down to the floor, rolled over and made it clear that a belly scratch would be in order. Mr. Dalrymple laughed a little and gave a very thorough scratch to the happy dog.

Lou was vibrating on the inside but wanted to remain calm. She hadn't yet figured out exactly what she had seen or how she could explain it, never mind what was on the recording. She didn't want to just blurt out her theory about a crime to her parents, so she played it cool.

Catching up with her parents as she was setting out the dishes, Lou asked, "So, did you get furniture?"

Lou's mother seemed very happy with their day. "Once we got over our shock about how much more things cost here, we found some really nice items on sale. You will see this week when they are delivered. What about you, what did the two of you get up to?"

Lou had been prepared for this question. She didn't want to tell them what she suspected quite yet because she still had to organize her thoughts. So she answered, "I decided to figure out where things are, so we were exploring all day. There was this really cool antique store, and I found a lake where we had a picnic. We never found the dog park, but we will go looking again. I think I know where it is now."

Mr. Dalrymple perked up. "What kind of antiques?"

Lou described the store as best she could, but it was hard to describe exactly how bizarre this place was. After she finished, her dad said, "I would love to poke around a store like that!"

After dinner, Lou rushed to her room to make notes on the day. She unloaded her bag, took the duct tape off the phone, and plugged it in. She spent the rest of the evening writing out detailed notes about the store and a timeline all the way to Jake and Calvin's departure from the lake. She read all the pages back to herself, making corrections along the way. After watching the video over and over, she made a second set of notes emphasizing the exact details. Because she had noticed that the audio recording was not as good as what she heard live, she made notes on what they said, too.

It was getting late and Rocky needed to go back outside. There was a gorgeous sunset, so Lou decided to go for a quick stroll with him and catch the end of it. Her parents were in the den watching TV. They barely glanced up when they saw her go in the kitchen to grab a poop bag for their walk. Lou waved the bag, and her father gave a military salute. "We are going to bed soon," he called after her. "Please don't be too long."

The night air was chilly and fresh. She spent her walk checking out her neighbours' lit windows and thinking about how she was going to deal with this situation on the lake. The walk cleared her head and gave her some insight into the people in her neighbourhood. She loved seeing how other people lived. She had a whole section of her notebook entitled 'Night Windows' where she diligently made notes on what she saw. Lou called it a hobby, but Oliver called it stalking. She smiled to herself at that.

After Lou and Rocky's walk, they came back to a quiet house. Her parents had gone to bed. As she brushed her teeth and finished getting ready for bed, Lou thought hard about her next steps. Suddenly, she stopped halfway through her brushing because an idea popped into her brain. "I have to tell Oliver! He'll have some ideas about all this and maybe help me figure out what to do next."

Having decided on a plan of action, she went to bed and fell asleep instantly.

CHAPTER EIGHT

L ou came downstairs for breakfast to find that Rocky was already outside. Her parents were in their yardwork outfits, and her mother was putting on sunscreen. "Good morning, Bunny, did you have a good sleep?"

Lou nodded, stuffing her mouth full of dry cereal. Her mother reminded her, "We all have chores today. Do you want to help your dad with the raking, or me with the flowerbeds?"

Lou finished chewing before she answered. "It depends... which one will be finished sooner? I was hoping to go out again today."

Mr. Dalrymple grinned. "Well, you know your mother can spend hours gardening, but I should be done pretty quickly."

Lou snapped her fingers before pointing at her dad. "I'm your helper, then."

Her mother rolled her eyes and stepped outside.

Before Lou got dressed and grabbed the rakes from the shed, she quickly sent a text to Oliver. "*Hey, are you back yet?*"

He responded right away. "*Ya!*"

Lou messaged back that she would be done by two o'clock and asked he if wanted to hang out. He answered, "*Sounds good, meet at my place and then we'll head out.*"

When Lou was finished helping her dad, she and Rocky headed over to Oliver's place. She rode her bike but then wondered if Oliver would want her to walk if they ended up going out somewhere. She hadn't thought about this challenge when she left the house and felt annoyed with herself.

As she pulled up, Oliver's garage door was open. To her surprise, he was sitting on a stool working on a bike.

She squeezed her brakes, slowing to a stop just outside the garage. "That's so cool! It has hand pedals!"

Oliver was wiping the bike with a rag, "Yeah, it's a heavy-duty trail bike. The three tires have to be exactly the same inflation or it runs unevenly. It's fussy, but when it's properly calibrated it runs like a dream."

Lou inspected every inch of it and commented, "This thing is an engineering marvel."

"Dad got it for me last year. He likes to ride with me when I visit him in Vancouver. I was just getting it ready for the road." Lou had known Oliver's dad wasn't living with them, but he didn't talk about him a lot. She changed the subject.

"I need your help with something. I was thinking we could grab an ice cream and I can tell you the whole story and see what you think, if that's okay?" asked Lou.

Nodding his agreement, Oliver shifted himself from the stool to the bike easily. Lou handed him his helmet, and they left.

Oliver led her along a street full of small stores and restaurants. Lou was trying to take in all the places, memorizing which ones she might want to visit. They pulled up to Oliver's favourite ice cream shop and got their ice creams at the little drive-through window.

Lou explained, "I brought Rocky here the other day. I probably didn't notice the drive-through window because I came in the front door."

Oliver responded, "This place had a drive-through before anybody else thought of it, and they make their own ice cream."

Lou made an impressed face as they found a picnic table across the path at the park.

Oliver had put his cone in a cup holder on the bike, and when they settled in, Rocky thought maybe Oliver would share. He sat beside Oliver and looked back and forth between the boy and the ice cream. Oliver laughed. "I don't think so, boy; it isn't good for you."

Lou dug around in her backpack and found a treat for Rocky before pulling out her notebook. Rocky found a grassy spot, made a mess of drool while chewing his treat, and then keeled over onto his side for a nap. Oliver laughed, saying, "I think he was already asleep when his head hit the ground!"

Rifling through her notebook, Lou nodded and said, "He usually is." She found her latest collection of notes so she could refer to them. Next, she pulled out the phone she had used to record the events of yesterday. She tied her hair back in a ponytail and set her shoulders square. "I have something to tell you, Oliver, and I want to know what you think of it."

Oliver knew Lou well enough already to know that when she tied her hair back, she was dead serious. He popped the last bit of cone into his mouth and said, "Hit me."

Lou went through every detail of what she was calling *The Sinking Crime*. Oliver listened respectfully, asking some questions here and there, but most of the time he was concentrating hard. Lou could see that she made the right choice in telling Oliver. He had an open mind, whereas most people she had shared her theories with teased her — or worse, disregarded her.

When she finished talking, Lou handed the phone to Oliver and hit the play button. He watched the video, backing it up once in a while and squinting. When it was finished, he turned the phone off and handed it back to Lou. "That's bananas!"

He said it in such a way that Lou was sure he believed her. She appreciated Oliver a lot more in that moment. Her eyes wide, she exclaimed, "I know, right?"

Oliver pulled a water bottle out of his backpack and took a big swig. He wiped his mouth on his sleeve and looked her in the eye, "So, what are we going to do about it?"

Lou already had a plan in mind. The first thing she needed to do was show Oliver all the key locations. "Let's go to the antique shop and I can show you what it's like, and then we can go to the lake."

They set off to the weird store, chatting about their theories the whole time. But when they arrived at the store, it was closed. They read the sign on the door that said, "*Open when I wake up, closed when I need to sleep. When I have had enough, also closed. Plus, Sundays.*"

Lou smiled, because she could picture Sam saying something like that.

They used this stop for a water break and gave Rocky some in his collapsible bowl. Since there was nothing more to be done here, they decided they should head to their next stop, the lake. Thirst quenched, they wheeled off again with Rocky following behind.

The lake and trails were much busier today. They stopped their bikes down near the beach so Oliver could see where Lou had filmed from and where the little boat had been launched. Oliver was thinking hard as he took in the scene. "Do you think this is deep water? I mean, would a person who knew where the bags are be able to find them?"

Lou had already looked up how deep it was. She answered, "Maybe. In summer, when it's warmer and the water level goes down, a good swimmer could dive to the bottom. But I'm not sure how easy it would be to find the stuff, though, the water were this murky. Even if you could find the bags, they looked really heavy."

They both sat silent for a while, deep in their own thoughts on how they could find what was stolen from the antique shop.

Lou broke the silence. "Wait! Maybe we don't need the

evidence. Maybe we could bring what I have to the police and they could drag the lake!"

Oliver agreed enthusiastically, "Good idea, those items have gotta be worth a fortune. It would be a big score for the police to find the stuff and arrest those selfish jerks."

They talked about what bringing this to the police could mean, and Lou realized that she should definitely tell her parents before pursuing it further.

Oliver asked, "What do you think they'll say?"

Lou thought for a moment. "I really don't know. They've always been good about my hobby and sleuthing, but this is different."

Oliver agreed, asking if she wanted him there when she told them. She shook her head. "They haven't met you yet, so it would be weird. I'll tell them tonight and update you in the morning."

They agreed on the plan and started back for supper.

Lou and Rocky continued home after they dropped off Oliver. Supper was already on the table, so Lou carried her backpack in and put it under the table when she sat down. Her mother gave her a questioning look but kept eating. When they were almost done, Lou announced, "I have to talk to you guys about something important." She started unloading her notebook as her parents looked at each other, their concern evident on their face.

Her dad said, "Lay it on us, Bunny."

Lou took a breath and started from the beginning. Her parents listened and looked at each other occasionally. Lou couldn't tell how they were reacting, so she pushed on. When she was finished explaining, she played bits of the video for them. "I think they're stealing from old Sam's store and hiding the things to come back for later."

The Dalrymples looked at each other, each hoping the other one would speak first. Her dad lost the eyeball challenge. He cleared his throat. "Lou, sweetheart... I'm worried that you even got yourself involved in something like this in the first place. You can't investigate what might be serious criminal activity; you're fifteen. Besides, although your sleuthing is really good, there could be a million explanations for what you saw. You witnessed something, we don't know what, and frankly it's not your job to fix it."

Lou's mother nodded her agreement. "I would think that the store owner would have reported any theft to the police. Don't you?"

Lou was frustrated. "That's just it, Mom! The owner looks like he is losing his memory. He doesn't seem to know what has sold or what should be in the shop anymore, never mind realizing that something has gone missing."

Despite her efforts, Lou could tell they weren't convinced. Lou silently packed up her stuff, fighting back tears. Frustrated, she went to her room to figure out a Plan B. Rocky followed behind, nosing the door of Lou's bedroom open before coming in.

He crawled up on her bed, stretching out so he ended up taking up most of it. Lou grumbled, "I am not that upset, Rocky. I don't need your full-on hugging sympathy. You always get on the bed when you think I am crying, but I promise that I'm not right now."

Rocky looked at her with his sweet droopy eyes and put his head on her stomach. Rocky knew she was upset and was having none of it.

As he drifted off, he could hear her watching the video over and over, muttering to herself.

❖

The next day, Lou decided she needed a new plan for what to do about the thieves. She grabbed a cereal bar for breakfast, said a terse goodbye to her father before he could ask her anything, and she and Rocky were out the door.

As they approached Oliver's house, he wasn't outside yet. She sent him a text. *"You coming or what? We're going to be late."*

He answered right away. *"Chill your shorts, I'm putting my shoes on."*

Lou grinned and entertained herself by picking small burs off Rocky's head, making a face as she did so. "What were you rolling in this morning that got you all these nasty things?"

Rocky made a little noise, the dog equivalent of*: how should I know?*

Oliver came rolling out showing off his signature wheelie down the ramp. He didn't even say hi, launching straight into questions. "So, how did it go with the parental unit?"

As they began walking, Lou told Oliver that she got nothing from her parents. She complained, "They usually support me, but I could tell they weren't buying that what I saw was a crime. They just kept talking about reasons that I had made a mistake even getting involved." She glanced at Oliver, her face set in a determined expression. "Oliver, I saw this happen. Now there's a little old man who will never realize he is being ripped off unless somebody does something about it!"

Oliver stopped, putting his hand on her arm. "Lou, you aren't wrong. We just have to figure out how to get somebody to believe this is happening."

Lou huffed in frustration. "I know, but I feel a little out of my league. I have figured out lots of stuff before, but this is more serious."

They continued the last few steps towards the school where a group of kids in their grade had seen the conversation... and Oliver holding Lou's arm. They called out in a teasing voice, saying things like, "Hey Oliver, way to go, snap up the new girl!" and "Hey Red, smooch smooch smooch."

They didn't know that Lou had plenty of experience with this kind of teasing. She pulled herself to her full height and raised her voice. "Oh, grow up. Can't you chuckleheads find something interesting in your own lives to talk about."

As she was walking away, she got angrier just thinking about it. She spun around and turned back to the tallest boy, pointing her finger in his face. "Me and Oliver are just friends, although that's none of your business." She lowered her voice and threatened, "So this is the last time we want to hear anything snotty out of your face, ever! Got it?"

Oliver and Rocky had backtracked, taking up their positions on either side of Lou.

But she wasn't done yet. "AND what makes you think it's open season on the new kid? Don't have enough braincells to come up with new insults for the other kids you bully? Jeez man, what is wrong with you?" Lou watched the surprise roll across their faces, shocking both the tall kid and his group into silence. She decided she had made her point, so she spun on her heel and started to walk away.

Rocky added a deep growl to the conversation. Then turned around and kicked up grass and walked away.

It was safe to say that the group was not expecting any of that. As they looked at each other to decide what to do next, Lou heard skateboard wheels coming up behind them. She turned to see Tyler skating toward where they were standing. As he got closer, he called out, "Hey you guys, how's it going?"

As usual, Lou was frozen around Tyler, so Oliver stepped in. "Lou was just shutting down these fine folks hard."

Tyler laughed and addressed the group. "Are you guys pretending to be the imperial rulers around here? What is wrong with you, picking on the new kid?"

The group of kids was shocked that Tyler defended Lou. They nudged each other and looked down at their shoes, trying to keep a bit of pride.

Tyler turned back to Lou and Oliver. "They're just being jerks.

I think between us and your horse-sized dog, we put them in their place. They won't try it again, and if they do, tell me."

Lou mumbled thanks as she watched Tyler walk away. Oliver leaned over, whispering, "Lou, where did that come from? No braincells? I can't believe how fast you shut them down, and now I might be a little scared of you myself." He smiled widely and laughed at her blush.

She adjusted her backpack and stated proudly, "I've seen this kind of thing before, and I was experimenting with a new response. I think it worked."

"You're some kind of smart." Oliver laughed as he went into the school.

Lou went to her locker, replaying the whole scene in her mind. As she pulled her books out, it struck her. "Tyler called me the new *kid*." *Kid* was not how she wanted him to see her, and it made her stomach drop.

Oliver pulled up beside her, "Come on Lou, hurry up, we don't want to be late for homeroom!"

She hardly paid attention to the first class because she was trying to figure out how she felt about the kids who were teasing her and Oliver. She didn't want to label them as bullies right away. That would just start the whole thing all over again and she wanted to leave it behind. Then she took a deep calming breath. She decided that they knew Oliver, and she was his friend, so she would give them another chance to grow up and be decent. She had a little self-satisfied smile on her face when Oliver gave her a random thumbs up. She liked Oliver, but it was different with Tyler; he made her nervous.

Oliver and Lou had lunch together, and they were joined by two kids from their grade. Stacy and Caden introduced themselves to Lou when they asked if they could join in at the table. Because Oliver already had a mouth full of sandwich, Lou answered for him. "For sure!"

They chatted, but Lou could tell they were nervous and had

something to say. They gave each other looks, before finally Stacy spoke. "We were outside the front of the school this morning."

She paused, fiddling with her bracelet. "We thought what you did was cool. Those guys aren't so bad, but they love bugging kids they think won't fight back."

Oliver replied, "A few of them are friends of mine. They think they're funny, but they cross the line sometimes. Lou set them straight. They won't cross her again." He chuckled and then stuffed a whole muffin in his mouth.

Stacy glanced between Lou and Oliver with a curious look in her eyes. "But actually, are you guys a thing?"

Oliver had swallowed his muffin, so he answered. "No! We aren't. Besides, her dog doesn't let her date." He cracked himself up with that remark but stopped laughing when his eyes shot open as he looked over Lou's shoulder.

All the kids in the cafeteria were looking at the same thing. Behind Lou was a wall of windows. As she turned around to see what everybody was looking at, she slammed her hand over her mouth and exclaimed, "Seriously?"

At the window, on his hind legs, was a two-meter-tall Rocky. He had been licking the window while he was waiting for Lou to come out.

Lou exclaimed, "That dog!" watching in horror as a kid opened the exit door. Rocky came running in. His plan was to come in and tear around the cafeteria greeting kids, or at least knocking everything over in his efforts to reach Lou. She shouted, "Stop, Rocky! Sit!"

He obeyed, but he was going so fast he skidded for the last bit and came to a stop in front of Lou. Now everybody was watching, and laughter started to break out. Lou was mortified, but she had to deal with Rocky first. She marched him to the exit and pointed to the road. She commanded, him, "Rocky, you are three hours early. Go home and pick me up later."

A much sadder dog reluctantly stood up and slumped away.

The laughter continued, but it was mixed with remarks like, "Did you see the size of that doggo?" and "Does he have a saddle?" and "Cool dog."

Lou went back to her table to more chuckling and saw Oliver using his napkin to wipe tears of laughter running down his cheeks. He suggested, "Rocky is so famous now, I bet the lacrosse team will make him their mascot."

Lou joined everybody, breaking into a laugh. She no longer felt embarrassed by Rocky's performance.

CHAPTER NINE

After lunch, Lou and Oliver were on their way back to class. Lou was complaining about her parents. She had only gotten more frustrated as the day went on. They hadn't thought she should get involved in the situation at the lake, but she couldn't let it go. She didn't know what to do.

Meanwhile, Oliver was trying to come up with a suggestion. Then it dawned on him. "Maybe you could tell another adult, someone who might see it your way, or at least listen?"

Lou muttered, "Getting a second opinion would be great, but who could I trust with this? I don't really know any other adults." Oliver shrugged. He was out of ideas.

As they sat in history class, lost in their own thoughts, Cecie came in to teach a segment. This made Lou and Oliver's day; Cecie was their favourite, and her teaching was so interesting.

For today's class, Cecie focused on the royal proclamation of 1763, which established the recognition of First Nation rights in Canada. Lou was riveted, making notes furiously in her history binder. As class ended, Cecie reminded the students, "Remember, my door is always open for help with your history or socials assignments, or really anything else you want to talk about."

Lou and Oliver looked at each other, both with raised eyebrows. They were thinking the same thing. Cecie would hear them out at least! They quickly chatted, agreeing that at lunch tomorrow, Lou would bring all her evidence to Cecie to see what she thought. Oliver offered to come too, which made Lou happy. She patted his shoulder and said, "You're an okay guy, for somebody who memorizes Shakespearian insults and all."

Oliver clutched his chest and pretended to die from Lou's remark. They both had a laugh and went to their next class.

After supper that night, Lou put her evidence together, making sure it was in chronological order. She thought about Oliver and smiled, really liking their friendship. They had spent a lot of time together in the last month since she moved to the area. She knew Oliver had plenty of friends, but he always seemed to have time for her. Then she started to wonder how he fit in time with his other friends when it seemed like he was always with her.

Thinking back, she remembered what he had told her about his close friends. They were into sports like lacrosse, rock climbing, hockey, and skiing. He couldn't join them in a lot of those sports, and probably got left behind a lot. Suddenly, it made sense that he had a lot of time for her lately, and Lou couldn't help feeling bad for him. She made a mental note to ask him when he would find out about his softball try-out. Lou admired his determination and felt lucky to have such a good friend.

The next day, Lou and Oliver went to Cecie's office at lunch. They brought her a muffin as an offering because they knew they would take up her whole lunch hour.

Cecie welcomed them in, looking surprised when they ominously closed the door. Understanding it would likely be something serious, she put the paperwork she had been doing aside and gave them her full attention.

"Well, hello you two," she said, trying to make them comfortable.

"Hello, Cecie," they both mumbled, looking decidedly nervous despite Cecie's welcome.

Cecie decided to face their nervousness straight on. "Whatever you are going to tell me, I promise you I will do my best to help with no judgement."

Lou breathed a little easier. "Thanks, Cecie. I need to tell somebody what I saw, and I didn't know who else I could turn to. You always say we can bring anything to you."

Cecie nodded. Lou quickly laid notes, diagrams, and her phone on the desk. When she was ready, she began telling her story. Cecie sat forward in her chair and didn't interrupt. She just listened and nodded. As Lou finally showed her the video, Cecie watched it with a furrowed brow, clutching her necklace.

When Lou was done, she switched off the phone, sweating a little. Cecie sat back in deep thought, her face as serious as Lou and Oliver had ever seen it. After a minute, she said, "Wow Lou, that is a heck of a story. Thank you for trusting me with it. I respect what you have told me and will try to help you work out the truth of the situation, no matter what it ends up being."

Lou breathed her relief at being heard. She looked over at Oliver, who grinned and gave a thumbs up. Cecie moved on to her next question. "Have you told your parents about all of this?"

Lou nodded, saying, "I told them the whole story plus I showed them the evidence, but I think they thought it was just another one of my conspiracy theories. I don't think they even came close to believing me. They were more concerned about my being in danger or something."

Cecie responded, "It's understandable that they would be

worried about you. I would be too, Lou. Do you think you should let it go or is your gut telling you otherwise?

"Lou would keep going until she gets grounded," Oliver jumped in. They all chuckled.

Cecie suggested, "Lou, I think I should talk to principal Sheppard about this. He should know that you brought it to me. Sam is well known and loved around here. After that, we can see where we go from there."

Lou was nervous, but all the support Cecie had given her reassured her. "Okay," she mumbled.

After that conversation, Lou finally felt hopeful that her concerns were being taken seriously.

After lunch, Lou and Oliver went back to class and anxiously waited for Cecie, who had rushed to tell principal Sheppard about Lou's findings, to report back.

Cecie recounted most of Lou's story and told him about the highly suspicious video. It turns out that Principal Sheppard was also familiar with Sam and his store. As an antique fan, he went to poke around there often. The principal did not doubt that someone might easily fool Sam, and it is possible items were disappearing. Cecie was saddened by this, but glad Lou's instincts had brought it to light.

Principal Sheppard called Lou's parents and talked about how he felt her allegations were worth bringing to the police. Cecie offered to take Lou down to the station, with their permission, to file a report. Lou's parents were shocked but quickly agreed to meet Cecie and Lou at the police station.

The bell rang; Lou had been in gym class, which was now over. She was still red and sweaty when Cecie waved her into her office.

Cecie started right into it when Lou sat down in one of the chairs in her office. "I just wanted to give you an update about my conversation with Principal Sheppard."

Lou's eyes went wide, she blurted, "Did he believe me?"

"Yes and, lucky for us, Mr. Sheppard knows Sam, and agrees he has started to become forgetful. He said that he wasn't surprised that people with bad intentions would find Sam and take advantage of him."

Lou answered, "And Sam seemed like such a nice man. It makes me sick that he's being ripped off."

Cecie looked thoughtful and sighed, "The more I think about it, the more sad it feels."

Lou shifted in her seat. "I just want him to be safe in his store. He has been there forever and lives alone above it in a big apartment. He is the only one in that building most of the time."

Cecie nodded and continued to explain, "Principal Sheppard called your parents and suggested the police should at least have a report on it. I'll take you over to the station and go in with you so I can give Principal Sheppard's view and support you."

Lou was stunned and asked, "When?"

"Your parents are meeting us at the police station now."

"Then I'd better grab my notebook!" Lou was already halfway out the door.

Cecie and Lou arrived at the police station and waited in the parking lot for her parents. Lou sent Oliver a quick text to update him and told him that she would call him later. She turned off her phone and turned to Cecie. "I'm nervous, I've never been in a police station before."

Cecie responded with comforting words as she always did. "You can do this, Lou. Having courage is being scared and doing the scary thing anyway. You will be fine. Just tell the story in as much detail as you can."

Lou pulled the folder marked 'Evidence' out of her backpack. Although Lou felt a little better, by the time her parents pulled in, the full weight of what she was about to do hit her. She took a deep breath and stepped out of Cecie's car.

She was glad to see her parents. Lou's mother got out of their van and went straight to Lou. She looked concerned, asking, "Are you okay, Lou?"

Lou answered, "I am nervous but fine. I have all my notes and everything."

Mr. Dalrymple extended his hand and said, "You must be Cecie Joe. I am Lou's father, Mervin, and this is her mother, Roberta." Cecie greeted Lou's parents politely as they headed to the front doors.

When they were through the double doors, they saw a large reception desk with an even bigger police officer talking on the phone. Lou almost walked right back out; she was so stunned by this huge man in a uniform. He had a square haircut and a forehead so big you could hardly see his eyes. It made him look mean.

Hanging up the phone, the officer looked up to see who had come in. Seeing them there, his face lit up. He stood up quickly, coming out from behind the desk smiling. "CECIE!" he shouted as he gave Cecie a bear hug, picking her right off her feet.

Lou was now officially confused.

Cecie introduced the man. "Lou, this my Uncle Bobby – I mean Constable Robert Joe."

The giant man shook Lou's hand, her small palm disappearing completely in his bear sized paws. "Good to meet'ya, Lou. What can we do for you?" Lou's parents smiled and stood back.

Cecie spoke first to help Lou break the ice. "Lou has something to report that might be a police matter, and her parents and I are here to support her." Lou nodded agreement, holding up her folder of papers.

Officer Joe smiled at that and turned to find somebody among the officers working at desks behind him who might be free. "Yo, Lansing, can you talk to this young lady?"

Constable Lansing stood up, calling, "Over here, girls. I'll take your statement."

Lou thought he looked slightly annoyed, but it just might be his face. He escorted them into a little room with a table and interview chairs and then went to get extra seats for her parents and Cecie. While he was out, Lou arranged her notes on the table.

Officer Lansing came back with folding chairs and set them up in a row behind Lou at the back wall. Then he sat down across the table from Lou and pulled out a notebook and pen. Lou began describing her story from the beginning when she first saw the men in the boat behaving suspiciously. She laid the events out in detail but was rattled a little when she noticed the officer not taking any notes. By the time she was describing the store, he had put his pen down. When she finished the story, and it was time for the video, he had closed his notebook. Lou started the video, and he watched it, moving the phone closer and further, seeming to be trying to see something.

He shut off the phone and handed it back to Lou. "I am glad you are a responsible and vigilant citizen..." Lou had a sense that he had said this a million times before. "But I didn't see them drop anything in the water but fishing lines. And as for old Sam and his store, he has been selling his dusty old stuff around here for ages. We have never had a report that anybody stole from him."

Lou could see that her case was losing ground. She glanced at her parents; they didn't look too impressed with the officer either.

Cecie jumped in to help, "Constable Lansing, Lou has witnessed some sketchy behavior. At the very least, should somebody not check with Sam?"

He looked at Cecie and then Lou, seeming to ignore the question completely. "We don't have the time or the resources to send people chasing down hunches."

Lou spoke up, "But it's not just a hunch." She was trying not to raise her voice. It was no use. He stood up to indicate the meeting was over and went to open the door.

Lou gathered her papers, now wondering if she had been

seeing things. How was it that an officer didn't think the video and other evidence was suspicious? She wasn't mad, exactly, more confused about how she could have been so wrong about all of it. Suddenly, the intercom in the room clicked and an authoritative voice echoed loudly, "Officer Lansing, please bring your interviewees into my office."

Lansing looked surprised and took a moment before he sighed and grumbled something about eavesdropping under his breath. He led the way to a large office down the hall with a sign on the door that said 'Sergeant Preston.'

As everyone filed in, a woman in a sharp police uniform stood up to greet them. She was tall and had short grey hair and ice-blue eyes. She had sounded a little scary to Lou over the intercom, but when she smiled, she wasn't so intimidating.

Sergeant Preston introduced herself and shook everybody's hands. Then she asked to see Lou's folder and said, "I heard some of your story, Lou, and I appreciate your bringing it to us." She flipped through Lou's notes.

There was a polite silence in the room as the Sergeant scanned a few pages. Lansing stood at the back of the room and fidgeted.

"Can you show me the video that you played for Constable Lansing, Lou?"

Lou set up the video and played a few key segments. Sergeant Preston watched it intensely. When she was done, she adjusted her glasses and declared, "You have a point here, Lou. You made the right call; it looks pretty suspicious. Do you mind if I hang on to your phone and notes?"

Lou nodded, "I could make more notes if you want, I remember all of it."

Sergeant Preston smiled, "I think all these pages will do. You are very thorough. We could use more officers like you, and we might just offer you a job someday." She looked over her glasses at Constable Lansing and stopped smiling. She continued, "I will look these over in the next few days. I will let you know if we need anything else."

Lou had a pile of questions, but she decided that asking the police how they would conduct their investigation wouldn't go over well.

Cecie and Lou's parents provided their contact information and other details before they made their way out of Sergeant Preston's office. When they turned to wave goodbye, the door was closed firmly, and they could hear a raised voice from the office.

In the parking lot, Lou and Cecie said goodbye, and Lou hopped into her parents' van. As she put on her seatbelt, she decided she would gloat a little, "I told you it was something criminal."

Back in the office, Sergeant Preston sat behind her desk and gestured for Lansing to sit down. She barked, "What makes you think they weren't dropping things in the water?"

Lansing answered casually, "In the video, their boat was in a spot where you could have seen them dropping things off the back. I didn't see that happen."

"So, no possibility that they could have dumped something you couldn't see off the other side?"

Nobody at the precinct was too keen on Lansing; he wasn't very bright. Sergeant Preston had been there as long as he had, yet she had a record of solved cases twice the length of his. It was a part of why she was now his boss and was considered a formidable one at that.

Lansing looked dumbstruck and flushed with anger. He was not expecting this. Stammering he said, "Not likely. Besides, what do you think would be worth stealing from that dusty old place?"

Sergeant Preston kept her eyes locked on his. She demanded, "I want you to go over there and ask for a list of his stock, and what it is worth."

He sneered, "Sam wouldn't have an inventory list or anything like that. It is just a bunch of junk. He's a senile old coot."

Sergeant Preston thought to herself, "I have to remind Lansing how to do his job far too often."

When she was done scolding him, she handed him Lou's evidence and phone and said, "Set up a file number and a formal report. I want it on my desk by noon tomorrow." Lansing nodded and moped out of her office.

Sergeant Preston thought, "Lou is one sharp kid."

CHAPTER TEN

The next day, Oliver, Lou, and Rocky headed to school. They chattered happily about their plans for the summer, how much they felt done with school, and how lame their gym teacher was.

"I swear the guy has worn the same jogging shorts since 1972," said Oliver.

Lou looked at him and quipped, "And how would you know about what jogging shorts he wore back then?"

Oliver stopped rolling his wheelchair and started tapping on his phone. In a few seconds he came up with a picture of a page out of the Sears summer catalogue, 1972. The shorts were a different colour but exactly the same, and just as short.

Lou laughed, "You would know where to find that picture. If those shorts are anywhere near that old, we'll have to be ready for a fabric disintegration mid-class."

They carried on, laughing, as Rocky barked at crows along the way.

As they approached the school, they spotted a police car. Lou was instantly curious as to what was going on. She told Rocky to head home, and they went into the school. As Lou was unloading her lunch and books into her locker, she heard her name being paged.

"Lou Dalrymple, please report to the Principal's office."

Lou's stomach sank into her feet, her mind racing. "What did I do? Is Rocky at the windows again?"

When she walked into the Principal's office, she saw Cecie, Amy, and Sergeant Preston already there. Amy stood up carrying Lou's counselling file as she came over to whisper, "Don't worry Lou, you haven't done anything wrong, the officer just wants to talk to you, is that okay?"

A bit relieved, Lou nodded, and they all sat down. Principal Sheppard began, "Lou, Sergeant Preston is here to give us all an update on her progress."

Sergeant Preston started, "We've been in touch with Sam and have looked through his inventory."

Lou blurted, "Did you see what I meant about the missing items in the oddities room?"

The Sergeant nodded and answered, "Yes, you were right that there were items that disappeared. Thankfully, Sam was able to look up what he was missing and how valuable they were."

They spoke for a little while longer to get the details right. Sergeant Preston looked over her glasses, scanning her notes quickly, before she raised her gaze to Lou. "It seems like you did a very detailed investigation and I commend you for it."

Lou was thrilled with the best compliment anybody could give her. "Thank you, Ma'am." Lou flushed.

Cecie and Amy stood up to walk Lou back to class. They all exchanged goodbyes, and Lou left the office walking on air. Both counsellors were chattering to Lou about how amazing it was to get this senior officer looking into it. Lou almost didn't hear them; she was on her own planet.

❖

When Lou got home after school, she took Rocky for a long walk to clear her head. She was too tired to drop in on Oliver. She would see him in the morning on their walk to school.

When Rocky was starting to lag behind, Lou decided they would head home. It was supper time anyway and she very much hoped her parents had dinner ready.

Lou and Rocky came through the door and the house smelled of Dad's homemade pizza. He was just pulling it out of the oven when her mother said, "Good timing sweetie, we were just about to text you."

They grabbed their slices and sat in the living room. Lou swallowed a huge bite of pizza and said, "The Sergeant came to school today to give us all an update. It was cool."

"Anything more than we already know?" asked Lou's mother.

Lou, still chewing, said, "Not much really, but I think when they visited Sam, they saw how easy it would be to steal from him."

Over the next few days, Lou heard nothing from the police. She was overwhelmed with kids at school asking her about the cop and the serious-looking meeting. Thankfully, Sergeant Preston had advised her to keep it simple when people asked her about her report.

Sergeant Preston had said, "People, and maybe even the media will want to know the details if word gets out. All you need to say is that you found something and turned it in to the police. That will keep you from having to answer questions you shouldn't be."

Lou took her advice seriously because she didn't want to do anything that could mess up the police department's work. She was tempted to go down to the lake or even check up on Sam, but she had to resist. She didn't want to draw attention to those areas.

She held off until the next Saturday, but when she still had not received an update, her curiosity won out. Lou set Oliver a text, "*Heading to the lake, you in?*"

He was quick to respond, *"Yup. I'll be ready in a few minutes."*

She and Rocky went over to pick up Oliver, and they rode their bikes to the lake.

As they approached the path that went down to the little beach, that's when they saw police cars in the parking lot and on the trail that led to the lake. There was something going on at the beach, too.

They stopped so Lou could pull out her binoculars and take a closer look. She almost dropped them when she saw Sergeant Preston on the beach holding up a piece of paper, turning it until it was the right orientation. Lou focused in as best she could. She whispered, "Oliver! That's my diagram!"

As they shared the binoculars, they watched the police's inflatable zodiac boat launch. Sergeant Preston had a radio in her hand, instructing the officers in the boat where to go. One of the officers was wearing a wetsuit and dive gear. Lou had her eyes locked on the action. She asked Oliver, "Is that lake super deep or something?"

Oliver was intently watching too and answered, "It isn't very deep, but you couldn't really snorkel to find something at the bottom. That's probably why they have the diver."

Lou couldn't believe what she was seeing. They spent another half hour watching the zodiac slowly navigate the lake. The diver followed along and then would go under every few feet. Oliver was having his turn with the binoculars when he whispered, "They found something!"

Lou grabbed the binoculars and looked. She saw the diver lift something up. It was hard to distinguish what they were holding up out of the water and loading into the boat because it was so covered in wet weeds. Then she saw it, a black bag, and it was heavy. As they were loading the object into the boat, Sergeant Preston put the radio to her mouth. Lou couldn't hear what she said, but she signaled a police car parked on the other shore and made big circles with her arm all around her head.

Lou and Oliver figured out pretty quickly what she was doing. The car she was signaling flashed up its emergency lights and pulled in front of the road, blocking all access to the lake. Two officers, including Constable Lansing, started putting yellow tape all around the access points to the lake. The tape said, "Do Not Enter–Crime Scene."

Lou and Oliver looked at each other wide eyed and nodded. They started to turn around as subtly as possible so they wouldn't be seen. Lou whispered, "Rocky, sneak!" The giant dog crawled on his belly next to Lou as all three of them retreated to the main path.

As they backed away from the scene, Lou mentioned, "I bet they put police tape around the area because they don't want the public coming to the lake."

Oliver agreed, "The police might be there all day."

When they were clear of the scene, they couldn't contain their excitement and decided the occasion called for an ice cream. They sat at the park next to the bike trail and ate their double scoop cones, chattering excitedly as they analyzed every moment of what had gone on. Would there be arrests? Would Sam get his stuff back? Would there be a trial?

It was dark when they eventually headed home, and they decided they would meet up again tomorrow and go back to the lake.

On Sunday morning, Lou was getting ready to go meet Oliver when she heard her mother on the phone. She eavesdropped because it sounded important, and also because that is what she always did. It was Sergeant Preston. Lou heard clearly what she said. "We have some results from your report, Mrs. Dalrymple. We need Lou down at the station this morning."

When her mother told her, she ran to her room to grab her

bag and notebook. Her father had heard so he was putting his shoes on. Lou found Rocky napping, but he opened one eye, then put his head back down. Her mother had been in the garden when the phone rang so she changed out of her muddy pants, and they all hopped into the van.

As they entered the station, Lou saw it was as bustling as any weekday. Constable Joe wasn't there, but Constable Lansing was. Every inch of his desk was covered in piles of paper, and he didn't look happy about it. Sergeant Preston led the way to her office and said, "Lansing, those files need to be checked, every one of them!"

Lou caught Lansing's eye, giving him one of her signature smirks.

They continued toward the office, and Lou startled; Sam was sitting at a desk, and an officer seemed to be interviewing him. Sam didn't look well. He was in a stained cardigan and his sparse hair obviously hadn't been combed in a while. He had a short scruffy beard. All of him, from his clothes to his hair and skin, seemed grey. He also looked confused. It made Lou sad.

When they all sat down in her office, Sergeant Preston got right to it. "Lou, I have to ask you, would you be able to identify the men you saw at the lake?"

Lou blurted, "Are they being arrested? Was I right about what was going on?"

Mrs. Dalrymple put her hand on Lou's leg, saying, "Lou, please answer the officer's questions. They are important."

Lou realized she was letting her curiosity get away from her and tamped it down. She answered respectfully, "Yes, Ma'am. I saw them from further away at the lake, but much closer-up coming out of the store. I'd recognize them for sure!"

Sergeant Preston asked very seriously, "Are you certain these two men on the lake were the same ones at the store? I am sorry to ask you again, but I have to be sure. You may need to testify as an eyewitness.

Lou was stunned, "I would be a witness, like in a court?" Her mind was racing. They were using her notes and evidence! She refocused on the gravity of the question and nodded her understanding.

The sergeant scanned an official-looking document and asked, "I know you have told the story many times, but I just need to check a few facts with you. Is that okay?" Lou nodded. She continued, "At any time while you were watching the men on the boat, do you think they could possibly have seen you?"

Lou's stomach knotted up. It suddenly dawned on her that they could have easily come closer to where she was hidden and seen her and the camera she had set up. She could have been in danger for real. She answered, "No, I made sure Rocky, and I were deep in the grass."

Sergeant Preston wrote some notes and asked, "I want you to think back hard, Lou. Did you see anybody else on or around the lake while you recorded them?"

Now Lou was surer of her answer, "No, Ma'am, I am absolutely positive nobody else was there. I was watching to see if they had anybody else there helping them, and they didn't."

"One more thing, Lou," Sergeant Preston closed the file, leaning forward, her fingers intertwined, looking very serious. "I have to remind you that what you did, although incredibly helpful, was also dangerous. We can't have teenagers potentially getting in the crossfire of criminal activity. By all means, report what you see, but leave it to the police in the future."

Lou started to object, "I tried, but the Constable didn't listen..." The withering look on Sergeant Preston's face made her reconsider saying anything else. Lou slowly realized what was being said to her. She should have reported it before she set up surveillance by herself.

Then she remembered something she wanted to know. "Is Sam okay?"

Sergeant Preston frowned. "He is upset, and we have had to

explain it over a few times, but you were right. He had no idea that the items were even missing."

Lou and her family were dismissed with thanks and they walked out of the police station. Lou was unusually quiet. She had some thinking to do.

❖

The next week was a flurry of activity in Squamish, but of most interest to the community was the arrest of Jake and Calvin. It was the talk of the town for days. There were even news stories in the local papers. Lou was overjoyed and proud of herself.

Enjoying the revealing of the crime, pretty much as she had laid it out to the police, Lou clipped every article in the paper, and printed out the online stories. This one would get its very own scrapbook. As time went on, she kept looking for a mention, any mention of her name. It didn't show up anywhere.

Sergeant Preston did a TV interview with reporters on the front stairs of the police station. She mentioned being grateful for "the help of citizens of Squamish who greatly assisted in bringing these thefts to a stop."

Lou was disappointed, but she knew that as a minor, her identity would have to be protected. Still, she would have liked some investigation brownie points.

As it is with news stories, they are quickly taken over by some other breaking news. After a few days, the crime was mostly gone from the websites and far below the websites' feature stories.

She was enjoying a bit of fame in her school; rumours travel fast. Everybody wanted to know the details, which she mostly shared. She had been asked to leave out certain parts because the criminals would be going to court. Saying too much could wreck the case against them if she let the wrong thing slip.

It made her laugh that everybody wanted to know what Rocky

did to help. She didn't have the heart to tell them that he mostly slept through everything.

One of the last news stories Lou saw, said that the criminals pled guilty and were going to jail for a long time; there would be no trial. Lou was happy that she wouldn't need to testify after all.

Kids approached her and congratulated her on her bravery for a few days. Although she was proud of herself, it dawned on her that she had been reckless putting herself in the situation in the first place. She decided that in future she wouldn't leave herself vulnerable like that.

A week later, Oliver asked Lou to come over on Friday evening for supper. She agreed happily and then checked with her parents. They smiled, and her dad said, "We'll drive you."

Odd, thought Lou. She normally walked, but she quickly forgot about it.

Friday night came, and her parents were ready to go somewhere. They were dressed up. Lou was about to ask why when Rocky started throwing his food bowl around. She fed him quickly, and they left. Her mother was carrying a dish of squares, so Lou asked, "Are you going to a potluck or something?"

Mrs. Dalrymple smiled, answering, "Of a sort, yes."

Strangely, Lou's parents parked the van in front of Oliver's house and followed her to the front door. Before she had a chance to ask what they were doing, Oliver was at the front door waving madly.

She stepped into the house and there was a living room full of people there yelling "SURPRISE!"

Lou looked confused, so Oliver pointed at a banner covered in balloons that said, 'LOU #1 SUPER SLEUTH!!'

As she looked around, Lou was agog seeing who was there. She saw Oliver had invited some of their friends from school, and even Cecie was there! She hardly recognized Sergeant Preston dressed in her regular clothes. Lou waved at her because she didn't know what to say.

Then her eyes landed on a stooped figure seated on the couch. It made her tear up. Freshly showered and in a new cardigan, holding wilted flowers, was old Sam.

CHAPTER ELEVEN

The second week of May brought an explosion of flowers and blooming trees like Lou had never seen before. The tourists were trickling into town already. Spring was longer on the west coast, Lou noted. Back east, the seasons seemed to change faster.

Lou decided to take her bike to school because Oliver wasn't going to be there. He had a specialist's appointment in Vancouver and would be gone all day. He was nervous because he had an MRI scan of his spine and was hoping it would show that the tingling he had been feeling in his legs might be a good sign. Lou hoped he would get good news.

As she rode to school, Rocky loped along beside her, narrowly missing a telephone pole because he was focused on a nearby cat. Lou snickered at him and called out, "Don't you even think about messing with that cat! He would take a chunk out of your nose, buddy." Rocky gave the cat a last look and decided to keep on moving. But not before he gave the cat the stink eye and kicked up some grass with his back paws.

While locking her bike on the rack, Lou saw Cecie's car coming into the school parking lot. Lou sent Rocky home and then stopped to wait for her. They chatted about the weather and nothing in particular as they strolled to the school entrance. A warm May day tended to make people slow down and savour the moment, and that is what they did.

It had been a couple of weeks since the celebration party of Lou's investigation, and everything was getting back to normal. Lou watched Cecie as she spoke. She felt a wave of gratitude come over her and smiled. Cecie had supported her no matter what anybody else said, and Amy had been super nice about the whole thing too. She was feeling more at home all the time. Her new life seemed to be turning out better than she thought it would.

Cecie seemed to read her thoughts, asking, "Have you wrapped up the last month of drama in your mind?"

Lou gave that some thought and answered, "Mostly, I suppose. I'm still worried about old Sam, and I'm glad I won't have to testify."

Cecie stopped before opening the front entrance door and put her hand on Lou's shoulder. "You did a good thing, Lou. If something happens and you ever have to testify, I'll be there for you. Deal?" Lou had a lump in her throat from relief and gratitude. She wiped her nose on the back of her hand and hugged Cecie hard.

Oliver sat in the waiting room, scratching a small line into the frame of his wheelchair with a penknife. There were many other lines on there already - one for every doctor's appointment. The fact that he was in a chair made him sad some days. He was an optimistic person though, so as he scratched today's line into the black paint, he thought, "Maybe today will be the day I get a better prognosis."

The doctors had been watching for small indicators of healing, and there was reason to have hope in what they found. Oliver had to believe if he did the physiotherapy he had been assigned, he just had to get better. He couldn't let himself think that he would never be able to walk again. If he did, he felt he wouldn't be able to live his dreams. However, he didn't share those sad thoughts with anybody.

He looked at his mother and smiled. She always drove him to his many appointments and made sure he didn't skip a single physiotherapy session, ever. She was also the one who told him she was sure he would someday be able to walk again, but if not, he would have an amazing life, anyway. That always made Oliver feel better because he knew it was true.

The doctor came out to the waiting room and smiled at Oliver. "Come on in, lad, let's get you sorted so your ma can take you for ice cream."

Oliver and his mother followed the doctor into his examination room. He had been treating Oliver since he diagnosed the spinal tumor. Nobody knew more about Oliver's challenges, and the doctor wanted Oliver to walk again just as much as anybody.

The questions were always the same. "How have you been feeling since I last saw you? Have you been taking your medications? Have you felt anything unusual?"

Oliver perked up on that last one. "Actually, I have had some weird tingling in my legs. Especially at night."

The doctor nodded. "Well, that makes some sense based on your MRI results. I was going to let you know that the scan caught some more nerve activity that wasn't there before. You have had an increasing amount in the last two years, which is why you can take an assisted step or two. I can see more action in the scan now."

Oliver couldn't help getting his hopes up, although many people had told him not to. The two people in the room with him, his mother and the doctor, had never told him anything other than he could do it. The healing process would just take time.

They talked about all the important appointments and scans coming up in the summer. When they were done and leaving the building, Oliver turned to his mother and asked, "When we come to Vancouver for appointments in the summer, could Lou come with us? Maybe we could go do something fun after the appointment?"

His mother replied quickly, "Of course we can." Then she paused, looking like she had something to say but wanted to consider it first. She finally decided to ask. "So, what is going on with you and Lou anyway?"

Oliver shrugged. "We're really good friends, she has my back and I have hers. I think we have friend-zoned each other. I have lots of friends, but I have never known anybody like Lou. I don't want to wreck it."

After a moment, he continued, "Besides, she's not my type."

Oliver's Mother made a serious face and said, "Oh you have a type, do you?"

Oliver blushed.

She continued, "I really admire your maturity, kid." She tousled his hair, and they headed for the ice cream shop.

On Saturday morning, Oliver decided to invite a gang of friends to a backyard party. His mother went out and bought hotdogs and pop. In the afternoon, everybody showed up, including Lou and Rocky. Lou was carrying a shopping bag full of potato chips and dog treats. She knew the other kids would want Rocky to perform his party tricks, some of which would require food motivation.

They arrived at Oliver's house and Lou helped set up the food, lawn chairs, and games that people had brought. They spent a great day laughing and joking around. Lou noticed Oliver was a whole other person when you put him in a crowd. He was the life of the party, and Lou was happy to listen to his stories.

As always, Rocky was a hit with his tricks. One girl stacked potato chips on his nose and made him hold still. When she said, "Okay," Rocky flipped the stack of chips in the air and caught every one of them in his mouth. There was a round of applause for that one.

The party wrapped up around nine in the evening when the food ran out. Everybody said their goodbyes and left but Lou stayed to help. She looked around to see if anything else needed cleaning up. When she saw her work was done, she tied a knot in the last garbage bag and put it in the can. Oliver had gathered up the empty chip bowls and wheeled up next to Lou. "Thanks for helping out, Loubaloo."

Lou grabbed her backpack and answered, "You're welcome. I had a lot of fun."

Lou waved goodbye to Oliver and followed Rocky down the sidewalk. He had had a big day with all the attention and tricks, so she was not surprised that he was dragging himself home. Lou suspected that Rocky helped himself to some unauthorized snacks from the buffet table. He looked a little sugar-shocked and his tail was droopy.

The pair arrived at home and joined the Dalrymples in the living room. Lou had an idea she wanted to run by them. She had already planned her strategy on the way home, so she launched straight in. "You know that Oliver has a ramp in the front of the house for his wheelchair, right?"

Her parents both said yes, but they could sense there was more to this conversation. They were right.

Lou continued, "You also know that he can only see his friends at school, outside or at his house, right?"

They both nodded.

Lou took a deep breath and then went for it. "Oliver is my

best friend, and I would like to have him over sometimes, but I can't because he isn't able to get up the stairs. Not easily, anyway." She went on, "I was wondering if we could get a ramp for our house so Oliver could come over."

Mr. Dalrymple, totally ignoring the question, said, "Oh don't worry, he can come over. I will just carry him up the stairs."

Lou's eyes went wide. She had to point out the flaw in that logic without upsetting her father. "Dad, how do you think I would feel having somebody carry me because I couldn't walk?"

Lou's mother answered for him. "You would feel uncomfortable and humiliated." She looked over at her husband to make sure he got the point.

Chastened, Mr. Dalrymple replied, "Okay, Lou, I understand. This is a big ask though, your mother and I will have to discuss it."

Lou nodded her understanding, but she had one more point to make. "I get that, Dad, but Oliver doesn't have any friends who can host him. We have to go to the mall or whatever for a bunch of us to get together. I would like to have him over to our house with a ramp he can get up by himself. It would make him feel more included, I think."

Having made her final argument, she said her goodnights and went to her room. Rocky didn't even get up from where he had flopped out on Mrs. Dalrymple's feet. Lou was not surprised; he was pooped.

Fifteen minutes later, Lou came flying out of her room waving a piece of paper. Her parents saw her arrive in the living room bright red and sweating; her hair matted down where she had been leaning on her hand. She had eraser crumbles on her shirt.

Lou was breathless as she declared, "I figured it out, you guys! I have a design for a ramp that will work for Oliver, and it tucks away when we don't need it!" She was already moving things off the coffee table to spread out her papers. She sat on the floor and started explaining how a ramp could work on the back deck with a few hinges, handles and pistons. Her parents looked at each other over Lou's head, having a silent conversation with their eyes.

When Lou finished explaining her design could work, she sat back on her heels and made her most compelling point. "If I was in a chair my whole life, wouldn't it make all the difference if somebody made a ramp for me?"

Her father looked at the design and stroked his chin. Meanwhile, Lou's mother asked some questions about everything from materials to construction, which Lou answered.

Finally, Mr. Dalrymple confessed, "I've never done a project like this before."

Lou responded, "I can help Dad, we can do it together. And Mom is a great painter, we could do it in a weekend."

Lou's mother brought up the cost of the materials, but Lou was ready for that question. She flipped over her paper and pointed out the final figure she had calculated on her budget sheet. Then she pulled money out of her pocket. "That's half of it - all of my birthday money. I will get a job this summer and pay for the rest if you want me to."

Her parents looked at each other and shrugged. They knew they were beat.

"I guess we're building a ramp" Mr. Dalrymple declared with a smile.

When Lou came home from school on Friday, they went out to buy the materials for the ramp. They worked on it all weekend. By Sunday night, they were sitting on the back deck eating takeout pizza and admiring their perfect stow-away ramp, painted to match the house. They toasted each other's talents with their icy-cold pops.

Lou's dad observed, "That was a flawless design, Bunny. Very impressive that you thought of the two-way hinges. That made the whole thing work!"

Her mother, already groomed and dressed again without a single spot of paint in her hair, agreed. "You are some kid."

Lou could not have been happier about all of it, but she was particularly pleased by her parents' recognition.

Lou was busting a seam with excitement to show Oliver what they had built. She spent Monday after school sweeping the driveway and making sure everything was ready. Rocky was having a hard time figuring out the ramp. He knew how to do stairs, mostly anyway. He often tripped up the steps and slid back down. But this ramp thing was a whole other challenge.

As Lou was getting everything ready, Rocky kept trying to go up the ramp. He would forget where to put his paws and fall forward and slide down the ramp, dragging his lips along the length of it. When he finally made it up, he wanted to go back down.

Lou observed this and called out, "Rocky, just give it up, man. This is not your thing; you're too big and clumsy."

As she said it, he started down the ramp, immediately lost his footing and his back legs went out from under him. He slammed down on his bum and rode the ramp like a slide. When he hit the bottom, his back legs grabbed on the pavement and he did a full somersault. He sat up and looked confused about how he had gotten there.

Lou went over to give him a scratch. "I love that you keep trying anyway."

Rocky flopped out in the grass; he was done with his efforts for the day.

Lou sat on the deck and texted Oliver, *"Hey O. Do you want to come and see something cool in my backyard tomorrow?"*

He responded right away. *"What is it?"*

Lou grinned and wrote back, *"You'll just have to see."*

Oliver sent back a GIF that was a gnome jumping up and down and sticking out its tongue.

The next day, Lou could barely contain her excitement. Oliver

118

sensed her enthusiasm and kept trying to get the secret out of her. She was not budging. When Lou set her mind to something, it stuck.

After school, as they approached her driveway, Lou grabbed the handles on his chair. Oliver never liked people doing so without permission, but he knew the driveway and path leading to the backyard was loaded with pebbles and was not exactly accessible. As he was trying to talk Lou into telling him what the surprise would be, he noticed there were no pebbles. In fact, the whole driveway had been swept clean. He let her keep pushing him because it was Lou.

When they rounded the corner of the house and approached the deck, Lou snapped Oliver's brakes on and flew over to what looked like a big piece of wood. Oliver had no idea what it could be. "What are you showing me?"

She cracked a wide smile and started moving the ramp into position. The pistons and hinges creaked a little, but everything unfolded exactly as it should and landed as a perfectly sturdy ramp.

Oliver gaped, and for a change, couldn't find the words. Lou stepped in. "It's a ramp, so you can visit me, Oliver."

Still mute, Oliver's eyes welled up. He tried to hide it by looking down and wiping his eyes with his sleeve. He finally found his words, and when he looked up to speak, "Lou, this is the nicest thing anybody has ever done for me, like ever."

Lou had tears in her eyes too.

She considered hugging him, but decided he might not want a hug. Then she pulled herself back from awkward thoughts and punched his arm instead. "You're a cool friend, Oliver, and I wanted to be able to invite you over."

To break the moment, they decided to inspect the ramp. Oliver asked Lou to put it away and set it up a few times so he could check out the details.

Lou explained, "I designed it, and me and my parents built it last weekend."

Oliver asked a dozen questions. As he was taking his inaugural trip up the ramp, Lou's parents brought out lemonade.

Oliver and Lou chattered away on the patio, with Mr. and Mrs. Dalrymple watching them through the window. Lou's father put his arm around his wife and said, "That kid is something else, isn't she, Roberta?"

Lou's mother kissed his cheek and agreed, "We did a good job with that girl."

CHAPTER TWELVE

O ver the next two weeks, as every student tracked the countdown to the end of school, Oliver spent a lot of time at Lou's place. The novelty of being able to access a friend's house easily was irresistible. Oliver's mother had even started to send food with him to contribute to the dinners he was mooching from Lou's parents.

He and Lou had a legitimate reason for spending almost every afternoon and sometimes evening at her house. Exams were coming, and they were study buddies. The Dalrymple living room was a mess of notes and charts. Lou's parents would deliver cookies, snacks, and encouragement. Mr. Dalrymple checked on them to see if they needed anything and said, "I'm so impressed with you two; you are taking your exams very seriously."

Oliver looked up with a cheeky grin, blowing his hair out of his eyes. "That's because we have a bet about who will get the best overall average mark."

Lou was chewing a cookie and nodded in agreement.

Mr. Dalrymple laughed as he went back to the kitchen. "You guys are something else."

Lou was well and truly settling into her school and her new town. She was getting more familiar with everything and everyone, and she was happier than she ever remembered being. She was getting to know more people, and although she and Oliver were pretty much a unit, she now had some nice girl friends to hangout and explore the shops with. There was no sign of the bullying she had been so worried about. That now-famous incident when she barked back at the group of kids seemed to have done the trick.

What she loved most was how big a fan group Rocky was collecting. Everybody knew his name and would come and give him an ear scratch when they were walking anywhere. They finally found the dog park, and he was a big hit with the other dogs and their people. When Rocky would run at his top speed, the other dogs would get caught up in the excitement and run along beside and behind him until he finally flopped down in the middle of the park and just let the other dogs run around him.

Lou would watch these shenanigans and when it was time to go, she would walk into the melee to fetch her dog. Sometimes she had to retrieve a young puppy or two off of him. He would lie down, and when the youngest pups in the park got tired, they would climb up on Rocky and settle in for a nap.

On the second to last Monday of school, Oliver and Lou arrived at school to find Cecie and Amy having coffee and chatting in the counsellor's office. As they peeked in the open door, Amy welcomed them to join in. Lou and Oliver found spots to sit as Amy asked, "How are you two coping with exam time?"

Lou piped up, "Really well. We study together, and I think we're nailing the material."

Oliver grinned, agreeing, "She's right, we have it down cold."

Amy chuckled at their confidence. "Okay then, I am not going to worry about either of you."

Cecie sat forward in her chair. "So, how excited are you for the end of the school year?"

Lou spoke up, "I think it'll be great to have time to keep exploring, but I think I should get a job this summer." She realized what she was about to say was awkward but said it anyway. "My dad hasn't been able to find a job yet, so I'll have to save up my own money if I want to buy anything new."

Amy saw Lou flush a little at her confession, and in her usual way, she chirped, "Don't worry about your dad, he will get a great job soon." Looking over her glasses, Amy toasted Lou with her coffee cup. "You are pretty smart, Lou. I think you'll find something that suits your talents. There are lots of places hiring for summer jobs. This place is full of tourists in the summer."

Cecie nodded in agreement as Amy rifled through her desk drawer and made a satisfied sound as she found the pamphlet she was looking for. "Here is a list of employers in the area who hire young people. I just updated it last week, and there are links to their websites. You should start applying now though," Amy said with a rare serious tone.

Lou looked over the piece of paper while Cecie asked Oliver about his plans for the summer.

Oliver was excited to tell her. "When I made the softball team, the league also offered me a job as an assistant coach for a new junior rookie team right here in town. It isn't a lot of hours, or much money, but it'll be fun."

Amy and Cecie were very excited for Oliver. They knew he would be a great inspiration to younger kids with challenges.

As the morning bell rang Amy pronounced, "You guys will be great at anything you set out to do."

Lou and Oliver waved as they flew out the office door to get to class.

At lunchtime, Lou sat with the usual table gang. They were all chattering, but Lou was distracted and not paying much attention. Tyler was at his usual place, sitting on the table and laughing with his friends. When he was in the room, Lou would get flustered and it only got worse if he said hi to their table on his way by. She often got mad at herself because it was unlike her to struggle with words. She could always rely on being able to come up with something to say, yet she was practically mute when Tyler was around.

Oliver knew her well enough to know where her gaze was fixed. He just shook his head, chuckling quietly at how she didn't seem to be aware there were people talking all around her.

After school, Rocky picked Lou up as always. They were walking home alone because Oliver had softball practice. Lou was lost in her own thoughts, but then she heard the signature sound of rolling wheels approaching from behind. She quickly checked her shirt for stains, wiped her mouth and thought about tying her hair up. She decided against it, because why should she care? It was frustrating, as she realized she did care. A lot.

Tyler approached Lou and stopped, kicking up his skateboard to walk beside her. "Hey Lou, where's your boyfriend?" he said grinning with a twinkle in his eyes.

Lou was determined not to be awkward, but the words slipped out of her mouth before she could stop them. "How would I even know? And besides, he is NOT my boyfriend!"

She immediately regretted her words. She sounded way too defensive, and the last thing she wanted to do was to end the conversation.

Thankfully, Tyler didn't seem offended. He carried on with what he wanted to say. "I was wondering what you are doing Saturday night?"

Lou's entire inner workings suddenly caught fire. She stammered, "Um...nothing." It didn't sound casual, but at least she didn't start a verbal flood which she would not have been able to stop.

If Tyler noticed her bright red face, he didn't show it. He continued, "I am supposed to babysit my little cousin that night, but I have a date. My parents said I have to find a sitter if I want to go out."

Lou's hopes deflated as he said, "You do babysit, right?"

She tried to sound like it was no big deal and blurted, "Yeah, I took my babysitter course." Lou immediately realized that she sounded awkward and was mad at herself for not coming up with something cooler. Then she noticed she hadn't answered him. "I can babysit for sure."

Tyler smiled, "Well, that's good to know. Give me your number and I'll text you with the details." He pulled out his phone, and when he had typed in her number, he said, "I owe you one, Lou; you're a lifesaver."

Lou smiled weakly and mumbled, "Sure."

Tyler rolled away and left Lou on the sidewalk, staring after him. When he was out of sight, a hot tear rolled down her cheek. Rocky leaned against her hard and she snapped at him, "Go home, Rocky! I don't want to be comforted."

Rocky sullenly walked away toward home. Lou was left alone with her unhappy feelings and anger. "What was I even thinking? That he would ask me out. Cripes, why did I even get my hopes up? He's older and so popular, and I'm a fifteen-year-old nerd!"

Lou arrived home to an empty house. Rocky was curled up on the front porch and didn't lift his head to greet her. Lou was still grousing about letting herself be hurt. She sat down next to Rocky and gave his big wrinkly head a soft scratch.

"Sorry, Rock. You didn't do anything wrong." Neither did Tyler, she thought to herself.

Rocky instantly forgave everything and put his head on her lap. They sat quietly together, just being still and thinking their separate thoughts.

Later that evening, Lou's parents came home with groceries and served dinner on the deck. Lou didn't feel like food – or company, for that matter – so she excused herself and went to her room. She really wanted to feel better but didn't quite know how, so she flipped through her notebook for inspiration.

She kept turning pages in her notebook until she found a particular page she had forgotten. It was titled "Modification and

Repairs List - Spy Devices" and she knew this not only needed to be done, but it would make her feel better too.

One at a time, she worked on the items. The first was easy; she just had to repair her periscope. She had made it last year, but it was getting ragged, and one of the mirrors had come loose. She took some tape off the old cardboard foil dispenser and readjusted the mirror, testing the mirror angle until she could clearly see something around a corner. She put fresh tape on it, and once declaring the periscope usable, she checked it off her list.

The next item was more complicated: it was her attempt at a coffee cup stealth camera. It was the perfect tool for catching pictures of things and people without detection, but it needed a modification and repair. She took the mechanism out of the reinforced cardboard cup and pulled it apart. It was supposed to work when a marble rolled back and hit the camera button on the inside, taking a picture, when she tipped the cup up and pretended to take a sip. She had already bought the heavier steel ball it needed and replaced the too-light marble. She also replaced the lens and mechanism with newer ones from the old phone she had. When that was working, she installed a micro digital storage card and sealed it all up.

Over the course of the evening, she worked on the devices that needed fixing. She started with her recording device hidden in a book. She installed a button in the spine of the book so she could turn the device on without opening the book. Her pen with a firecracker in it was still dry and ready to go. Her teddy bear with a camera in one eye was wrapped in a bag. She opened it up and tested the camera. It still worked, and all she had to do was download the mini-cam app on her new phone to control it remotely.

As she examined a few of her other devices, she made a list of supplies she still needed. Satisfied and tired, she snapped her notebook closed. She put away her collection of gear and went to get ready for bed.

She was just about to crawl into bed when she remembered to call downstairs for Rocky. "Hey beast, it is time for bed!"

There was thumping all the way across the house and up the stairs until he almost barreled into her as she held the door open for him. She smiled and said, "You fell asleep in the living room again, didn't you?"

Rocky didn't seem to understand the question, but he quickly licked her hand to let her know all was well. Then he laid down.

Lou crawled into bed and remembered something she forgot to write on her list. After adding the item, she stopped to look at the next blank page as she was about to close the book. She didn't really want to write what happened today, but she knew it was always better to journal than ignore something that mattered. With her pen poised over the page she knew she had to be honest with herself about why she was so upset. Finally, she wrote in small but deliberate letters, "I thought I could be his date, but he doesn't see me that way." Then she closed the book and put it down. That was enough gut punch of reality for the moment. She felt better after having written down her feelings and fell into a deep sleep.

When Saturday night came, Lou rode up to Tyler's address and put her bike at the side of the house. There was a basement light on, and without meaning to, she saw Tyler. This was clearly his bedroom. Lou saw him fussing with his hair, dressed in a nice shirt and jeans. She knew this was not the kind of spying she should be doing, but she had to drag herself away from the window.

She walked up to the front door and noticed a girl coming

down the pathway from the road. The girl clicked her car remote, and it beeped.

"This must be the date." Lou thought with a twinge of jealousy.

The girl gave her a confused look, and then her eyes lit up with realization, "Oh, you must be the babysitter!"

Lou tried to sound mature and hopefully a bit older. Lou had never seen this girl and figured that she didn't go to their high school. Lou had dressed in an outfit that she thought would make her look more mature, but it didn't – not compared to this girl. Tyler's date had on high heels and a sophisticated black dress that hugged her waist.

Lou noted miserably that she would never be as steady on heels as this girl was. She had a short blonde bob and wore chandelier earrings. Lou guessed that they were headed out somewhere nice. Tyler's date didn't knock. She opened the unlocked door and headed straight inside. Lou snapped out of her thoughts and followed the girl in, mumbling that she was in fact the babysitter.

Tyler greeted them both, his date with a kiss, and Lou with a hello. The pair were eager to leave, so Tyler gave Lou some quick instructions, and they were out the door.

Lou took out her laptop and set it up on the dining room table. She checked on the sleeping toddler, already in bed for the night, and started to look around. There were pictures everywhere, and lots of them were of Tyler. So many of him rock climbing and skiing. He didn't seem to have a brother or sister and did a lot of travelling with his parents. There were pictures at the Eiffel Tower, the Neuschwanstein Castle in Germany, and a family selfie taken while riding The London eye.

Lou thought his vacation stories must be so cool.

She came across a picture of a much younger Tyler holding a skateboard with a set of broken wheels dangling from it in one hand and his other arm in a cast. He was making a mock pouty face and Lou smiled. She wished even harder that she looked like the girl he was taking out tonight.

She poked around a little more before going into the kitchen to get a glass of water. On the counter there was a plate of cookies with a note tucked under it. "Thought you might like these. – T."

Lou grabbed a cookie and decided that when she eventually chose a boyfriend, he would have to be sweet like Tyler.

Lou sighed and settled in to write a final paper for English. She and Oliver were both doing the assignment this weekend, planning to review them for each other Monday at lunch. Oliver was good at language and Lou was excellent at finding logic gaps and grammar errors. Between the two of them, they got better marks than if they went it alone.

Lou was nearly done with her essay when Tyler's parents pulled in the driveway. His mother loaded Lou's bike into her van and drove her home. Lou could see where Tyler got his black hair from, and his mother's smile looked just like his. Tyler's mother was very friendly and paid Lou well. Lou thanked her for the job and the lift home. Tyler's mother rolled down the van window, calling out, "Tyler spoke highly of you when he said you were willing to come."

Lou nodded her thanks, then unloaded her bike and waved goodbye as Tyler's mother drove off.

When Lou got upstairs, her parents were already in their room. She got herself prepared for bed, stepping over Rocky who remained firmly asleep. "Heckuva guard dog you are," chuckled Lou.

He snorted a little and rolled on to his back. Lou had one more thing to do before she could go to sleep. She opened her notebook, flipped to a fresh page and wrote, "Requirements for future boyfriends." She made a ten-point list that included "knows how to bake cookies."

Then, feeling a lot better about the whole Tyler thing, she closed her notebook and slept for twelve hours.

CHAPTER THIRTEEN

A wave of excitement filled the building during the last week of school. Most of the seniors were thinking about prom and summer parties because they were done with their exams. On Wednesday morning, Lou and Oliver had just finished their English final. As they walked out of class, they were bickering.

Lou insisted, "Catawampus is not a real word, Oliver!"

Oliver looked incensed. "It absolutely is, Lou! I used it in a sentence to describe the state of the characters on the book report question."

As they walked, Lou looked up the word on her phone. When she discovered she had lost that argument, and it was in fact the same meaning as the word "askew" or "messy," she gave in with an exaggerated bow. Oliver enjoyed his victory very much.

The two of them were looking forward to leaving school to soak up the sun on their walk home. Lou was rummaging for an apple when Oliver asked, "Are we studying today?"

Lou nodded and kept chewing. As they went by Cecie's office, they saw her packing a box on her desk. She looked distracted and kept picking things up, not putting them in the box and placing them back on the desk.

Lou knocked softly on the doorframe and said, "Hey Cecie,

what are you doing?"

Cecie looked up, surprised to see Lou and Oliver at the door. Her eyes were slightly red, and there was a crumpled tissue on the desk. Cecie spoke in a sad tone, "Oh hi, guys. I'm glad you dropped in. Today is my last day, my contract is over."

Oliver exclaimed, "So you aren't going to be back in September?"

Shaking her head, Cecie responded, "It was a one semester internship for university, and it wasn't meant to be a long-term assignment. Honestly, I didn't think it would be so hard to leave."

Lou was shocked. She hadn't understood that Cecie's job was short-term. Lou scanned her mind searching for a solution. "Can't you apply to be a teacher here?"

Cecie smiled sadly and answered, "I wish it worked that way, but it doesn't. I would love to work here, but I still have another semester of university to do."

Cecie resumed filling her box and said, "But don't worry. I have a job waiting for me right here on the coast, so I will be here, just not in this school. I'll be working for the local Health Services Department. It's my dream to make people's lives better, and I'm being given the chance to do it."

Oliver and Lou were impressed with Cecie's plans, but sad to see her leave. Lou asked, "Are you going to be here this summer?"

Cecie answered, "Absolutely! I have a summer job here." Cecie looked at Lou's face and clued into what Lou was getting at. "If you want to phone me, Lou, I can give you my number." Based on Lou's smile, Cecie knew she had it right.

They exchanged numbers and hugged goodbye. It was pretty hard on Lou, since she had developed a deep trust of Cecie and was very sad to see her leave.

Oliver and Lou saw Rocky waiting for them in the schoolyard as they came out the front door. He was stretched out and relaxing as a couple of younger girls were sitting with him rubbing his belly. Oliver commented, "Rocky is the most popular guy around here. The ladies love him." Lou rolled her eyes and went to extract her dog from his fan club.

With their final exams coming to an end, Lou and Oliver were in great moods and talked about summer plans all the way home. Lou's top priority was to get a job, and Oliver's was to sleep in every morning.

On the last day of school, they cleaned out their lockers and said goodbye to their teachers. They poked their heads into Mr. Patrick's room to wish him a nice summer.

He waved them in, saying, "I have something for you two." He pulled out a pair of books from his creaky old briefcase. "You will be pleased to know I will be your English teacher in September."

Lou and Oliver were careful to arrange their faces not to look intimidated. He was a demanding teacher, and now he was giving them summer homework.

Mr. Patrick smiled, pleased with himself, as he handed them their respective books. "Don't get your shorts in a knot about a little summer reading. This is not a punishment; it's an opportunity."

They both looked down at the titles of the books and broke into huge smiles. Lou was assigned to read a book called, "A Technical Guide to Building a Time Machine" and Oliver's was titled, "Top 100 Shakespearean Insults." They looked at each other with wide eyes, wondering how Mr. Patrick knew them so well.

Mr. Patrick snapped his briefcase closed and said, "Oliver, we will be diving deep into Shakespeare's plays next semester, and I think you will appreciate them better knowing what these phrases mean. He was a master at burying scathing insults in long monologues. And Lou, I think you could use something more challenging to plan and design, so maybe this will give you something to think about this summer."

Both Lou and Oliver flipped through their books, excitedly chattering about them, forgetting Mr. Patrick was in the room.

He pointedly cleared his throat and the kids snapped to attention. They thanked him profusely. He picked up his pen, dismissing them. "Now get on out with yourselves and be ready to impress me when you get here in September."

When they were finally clear of the school grounds, Lou, Oliver, and Rocky were giddy about everything summer had in store for them. Oliver and Lou were getting silly and couldn't stop laughing. Rocky was just happy because they were. He didn't really know what they were talking about, but he jumped all around them the whole way home anyway.

After all the students had left the school, Amy Dirkson was tidying up her office. She carefully put her plants into a box, speaking to each one as she picked it up. "Well, haven't you grown this year?" She picked a dried flower off the next one. "You are coming to my house for the summer, my geranium friend."

What Amy didn't notice was Cecie leaning against her door frame, smiling. When Amy saw her, she jumped. "Oh, Cecie, I didn't see you there. You must think I am a loon talking to my plants!"

Cecie moved a pile of files from a chair and sat down. "I read somewhere that talking to your plants makes them healthier."

Amy nodded, picked up another plant, and breathed on it. "Carbon dioxide does it every time."

Both women chuckled before settling into a conversation about the school year. The topic of Lou came up in their conversation. They revisited the whole drama with the police and the crime and agreed that Lou was an exceptional girl with a great future ahead of her.

Amy confessed, "I was a little worried about how easily she could have been seen or discovered by those two guys."

Cecie nodded. "I know she could have gotten herself in a

world of trouble. I am really impressed about how quickly she clued into old Sam's memory issues. That was really smart."

Cecie's comment reminded Amy of something. "I heard that the police department contacted a social worker to talk to Sam. He has always been determined to run that store forever, but maybe now he will accept some help."

They continued chatting while Amy loaded boxes. When the topic again turned back to Lou and Oliver, Cecie smiled and shook her head. "I don't know what those two are going to get up to this summer, but I hope Lou's detective agency is closed for business."

Amy laughed as she gave Cecie a knowing look. "Don't count on it."

Lou and Oliver decided that they had spent enough time inside during the school year. They had thought about putting together their summer plans that evening, but decided they needed to blow off some steam first.

They both grabbed their phones and started texting with the gang. An hour later, most of the grade ten class arrived at the BBQ pit at the local park. Armed with a cooler of pop and bags of marshmallows, Lou, Oliver, and Rocky arrived. Music was already pumping through speakers, and there were multiple super competitive frisbee games already underway. One boy who was sitting on the grass with a group, spotted Rocky and called out, "Hey Rocky, want a treat?"

Rocky's ears perked up and Lou saw the look in her dog's eyes; he very much wanted a treat. She tried to grab his collar, but it was too late, he was galloping toward the kid holding up a chip. Lou grabbed Rocky's tail, but all she managed to do was get herself dragged along behind the dog, so she had to let go.

Rocky barreled down on the boy, who suddenly realized his

mistake. He threw the chip behind him. Lou yelled, but all Rocky saw was a chip flying behind a now-scared boy.

Recognizing what was about to happen, all the kids threw themselves to the ground and hoped for the best. Rocky got to the group at full speed, still focused on the chip. He made a flying leap over the top of all their heads. He nailed a four-paw landing behind the boy and picked up the chip, swallowing it whole.

Smacking his lips, Rocky turned around to see if there were any more chips.

The kids immediately began howling about the crazy jump, arguing about how high he went. Lou marched over to Rocky, wagging a finger at him. He plunked down and sat, listening to her intently. Or at least it looked that way.

Everybody settled back to their conversations after they fixed their rumpled picnic blankets. Lou made Rocky lie down, but he crawled in sneak mode over to the kid with the chips.

Lou gave up and went to sit with Oliver. "That dog listens so well, but he loses his mind over chips. I am glad nobody panicked when he charged at them."

Oliver grinned, chewing a marshmallow and said, "That, my friend, was catawampus."

Lou rolled her eyes and stuck her tongue out at him.

The group of kids got larger as more elaborate food and bigger speakers showed up. They had a fire going in the BBQ and there were some boys showing off their skateboard skills. Lou looked around and felt happy and relaxed.

The skateboard kids on the cement path stopped their tricks to talk to somebody walking along the path. Lou looked over to see why they had stopped and saw who joined them. It was Tyler.

Lou's first thought was, "What is he doing here?" As far as she knew, no one had invited him.

Then she decided he wasn't there on purpose, he just rode by and happened to spot the other skaters. She kept watch as Tyler showed the younger kids some tricks and then stood back to watch them give them a try. "He's teaching them," Lou thought to herself.

By then, most of the other kids from the party were also watching Tyler. When he picked up his skateboard to leave, his fellow skaters invited him to join the party. He shrugged, following them right to the group where Lou was sitting.

There was a buzz among the girls as he approached. It made Lou realize that she wasn't the only one who thought he was cute. She tried not to stare too obviously, forcing herself to turn her head. Then she heard, "Oh hey, Lou, I didn't know you'd be here!" and suddenly Tyler was sitting on the ground next to her.

She forced herself to not be awkward, so she answered, "Hey." She wanted to play it cool, as if the most popular guy in school would normally sit with her.

He swept his hair off his face and tucked his skateboard behind his back. "Thanks for helping out with the babysitting, you saved me."

Lou smiled, saying, "It was no trouble and I was happy to help."

Lou and Tyler chatted for a while. Different kids came to join them, cycling into the spaces as others left. At one point, Oliver came to offer a bag of chips to them. Tyler was happy to dig in. They told animated stories about Rocky, the local skateboarding community, and reviewed all the teachers. Tyler had just graduated and knew all the best stories from his years at high school. They had a lot to talk about.

It was getting close to Lou's curfew, so they started to pack up their blankets and clean up the garbage. Other kids had been slowly drifting off as well. Lou scanned the park to make sure they hadn't left anything behind. Her mind replayed the fun time she had with her new friends that night. She smiled to herself, when she realized she had made her way around to all the little groups of kids and was welcomed at them all. She never imagined that she would fit in so well, and so fast.

Tyler helped Lou and Oliver tidy up, and when they were ready to leave, he said, "Thanks for letting me hang. See ya!" and sped away on his skateboard.

The sound of Tyler's wheels departing woke Rocky up from a deep sleep. Lou shook her head as her sleepy dog walked over. He had fallen asleep on a marshmallow and it was stuck to the side of his face. Oliver cracked up as Lou removed the gooey mess.

Rocky tried to eat it, so she chastised him, "You've probably had a whole bag of these already so you can forget it." As they went up to the path and started for home, Lou threw the marshmallow in a garbage can and enjoyed the walk home with her two best friends.

The park was a bit of a distance from their neighbourhood, so they both sent texts to their parents that they would be home soon. Oliver put his phone in his pocket. "I figured I better send Mom a text before she blows my phone up calling me because I am three minutes late."

Lou could relate. "Same with my parents... You know what we should do? We need to renegotiate our curfews for the summer. We are both almost sixteen."

Oliver eagerly agreed. "Another half hour or what?"

Lou considered how successful they would be in this. "That sounds reasonable, but we should ask for an hour, though. I read about it in an article about negotiation techniques."

Oliver stopped and gave her a look. "You read some weird stuff, Loueesha."

Once they had agreed to a time they would request, and what they would agree to if they got resistance, they were satisfied with the plan. They moved onto other topics and were almost at Oliver's house by the time they finished making a list of what activities they wanted to do this summer.

They walked the rest of the way in comfortable silence. They were both getting tired and Rocky was dragging his feet. As they approach Oliver's house, Lou said, "Check ya later," and headed home. Rocky gave Oliver's hand a quick lick and caught up to Lou.

When Lou answered all her parents' questions about the party, who had been there, and why the side of Rocky's face was sticky, they hugged her goodnight and she went to her room. Rocky slept through the rough washcloth cleaning that Lou did to get sandy marshmallow goo off his face. He farted loudly and put his paw over his face. Lou stood up and stared down at him. "All partied out, dude?"

It was late, but she wanted to make a few notes from her and Oliver's conversation and summer plans, and of course the party.

She wrote:

Summer Plan

- get a job
- find ocean inlet and see whales
- explore everywhere
- check on old Sam once in a while

The most important note was a detailed account of the party. "It was so much fun," she wrote. Then she continued to list the names of the kids that were there, and what would be important to remember about them. Jada: does dance. Stu: collects exotic fish. Douglas: plays dungeons and dragons. By the time she had exhausted her memory she had a solid list of memories. She drew hearts beside the names of people she liked right off the bat.

A single note at the bottom of the page said, "Best night ever. New friends!"

Lou closed her notebook and placed it on her nightstand with a satisfied and tired sigh. She gave Rocky's rump a pat and turned off the lamp. Drifting off to sleep, she found her mind replaying her conversation with Tyler. She decided he was really a nice guy. Not because of his popularity, but despite it.

That was the last thing she remembered crossing her mind.

CHAPTER FOURTEEN

With school over, Lou had lots of time to ride her bike and hang out with Oliver and her other friends. She spent the first week of summer dividing her time between doing fun things and looking for a job.

At her age, there were limited jobs she could get. She looked online using Amy's list and sent resumes by email. The smaller businesses would have to be done the old-fashioned way, a paper resume delivery.

She dropped off her resume at several places that she could get to on her bike that might hire her. She would have loved to work at the police department, but she was told with great kindness that she would have to be a bit older first.

One day, when she had an envelope full of resumes in her bag, she decided to see what businesses were on the south end of town. It was a bit farther to bike, but not that hard to get there. She went by the yacht club and industrial buildings. There were a few businesses on her way, and she stopped into any she thought she could work at.

Last summer she had a fast food job and had very late shifts. Lou's parents always picked her up, but she could tell her shifts made it hard for them to get up and go to work early. She was determined to work a day job she could get to on her bike this summer.

When she turned the corner onto Logger's Lane, things started to look familiar. Then she saw Marine Antiques and Oddities. She couldn't figure out how she ended up here, but when she checked the map on her phone, she saw that she had taken a long, roundabout route. She pedaled over to the store to see if it was open. When she pulled up to the front of the building, she saw the door was propped open and spotted old Sam was trying to reach something on a shelf and muttering to himself.

Lou took off her helmet and called out, "Do you need me to reach that for you, Sam?"

Sam turned his head with one hand still reaching for something with a blank look on his face. It was clear that he was struggling with her name, and maybe even to recognize her. Then his eyes lit up. "Lou dear! Yes, yes please, I need that rope and the box behind it."

Lou smiled at Sam as she came into the store and climbed on a wooden chest to pull down what he needed. He shuffled off the counter at the back of the store and set the items down.

Sam then sat comfortably on his stool and turned his attention to Lou. "Thank you so much dear, I probably would have fallen on my keester trying to balance on a stepladder." He took a handkerchief out of his sweater pocket and wiped his forehead.

Lou smiled and asked, "How are you doing these days?"

Sam looked at her with watery eyes. "I'm okay, I suppose. It was so terrible what happened to me that I think about it quite a bit. It has made it hard to keep the business going. I am so tired every day."

He shrugged his shoulders to pull himself out of that thought. "Never mind me, what brings you here, girl?" His smile was affectionate and warm.

Lou hopped up and sat on a big box. "I was dropping off my resumes at places that might hire a student for the summer."

Sam put his lips together in a line and made a noise of understanding. Without further comment, he got up and walked around behind his counter.

Lou just waited because he often left rooms or did random things in the middle of a sentence. She peered into the oddities room and noticed it now had a new glass door on it. She hopped down off the box to go and read the sign on the door. It said, "Request key to access this area. Video surveillance."

Lou had a question about it as she walked back to the counter where Sam was fumbling with a handful of money. He handed her the bills and a fistful of coins. "How fast can you count it?"

She looked at him, wondering what this was all about. He pulled a stopwatch out of a drawer and said "GO!"

He started the watch, and Lou scrambled to grab the bills and start counting. She didn't know why she had to do this, but she loved a race so she counted as fast as she could. When she was done, she declared, "By my count, $245.93."

He took it back from her and counted it himself, very slowly. When he was done, he put the money back in the cash register. "Right to the penny." Before Lou could ask about it, Sam handed her a $20 bill. "Make change for a $14.36 item."

Lou walked over to the cash drawer, pulled out the change and handed it to Sam. She asked, "Is that right?"

Sam counted it and declared it correct. He slowly put the cash back in all the right slots. Lou decided not to distract him with any questions until he was done. When he closed the drawer, Lou took her chance, jumping in before he asked her to do another weird task. "Why did you ask me to do that, Sam?"

He sat back down on his stool, trying to organize his thoughts. Lou knew to be quiet when he did that. She looked at his sweater; it was the one he wore every time she saw him, same holes, same stains. It made her feel sad, but the way Sam was, this cardigan was probably just his favourite. She smiled a little at the thought.

Sam finished composing the right words. He explained, "I've been running this place on my own for a long time, Lou. I am starting to have trouble keeping up with everything. I finally got a person in to secure the important stuff." He gestured to the oddities room, and continued, "I have been thinking about getting some help around here for quite a while."

Lou began to realize what he was saying. She interrupted him, as was her typical way when she got excited. "I can help with the store, Sam! I can do a lot, and you would be able to relax and..." she trailed off because he was laughing. She hesitated for a second. Maybe she was wrong and that wasn't what he was going to say.

Sam wiped the tear out of his eye with his sleeve. Still chuckling, he said, "I see I have made the right choice, my dear. You can be my new assistant."

Lou was stunned. She wanted to leap over and hug him. She held herself back, deciding she needed to get more serious and professional and do some negotiating.

She cleared her throat and stiffly said, "I am prepared to consider your offer. What are the hours? At what hourly wage?"

Sam sat up straight, echoing her formal tone. "I would pay you what you think is right and need you here from noon to closing time Tuesdays, Wednesdays, Thursdays and some Saturdays."

Lou realized he was making fun of her trying to sound mature and broke into a laugh. Recovering, she said, "I'd be happy to take the job, Sam, and those hours sound great!"

They spent the next hour having tea and talking about the store, its history, and what it takes to run everything. Lou had grabbed her notebook from her backpack and listed anything that could possibly be important. When she looked over the tasks he listed, she pointed her pen at him and said, "How have you have been doing all of this by yourself?"

He nodded and shrugged. "It's been forty-five years; I wouldn't know what else to do with myself."

Lou saw the logic in that, but she also knew she could help. "I'm up for it. When do you want me to start?"

He looked at a dusty calendar on his desk, saying, "How about Tuesday?"

She shook his hand and replied, "I'll be here, and I won't let you down."

He picked up the calendar and passed it over to her. "Can you write your name on the day you start, and what you want your hourly wage to be? I might forget what we agreed to."

Lou did a quick calculation for inflation based on the wage she made at her last job and wrote it down. He didn't even look at it. "I will see you Tuesday then."

Lou checked if he needed her sooner, but he declined, so they said goodbye and Lou sped away on her bike. She looked back and saw he had flipped the sign to 'closed' and was locking the door.

Lou pulled up to her front yard and dumped her bike in the grass. She was running up the stairs, taking off her helmet, when Rocky spotted her through the front window. He stood on the sofa licking the glass with excitement. Lou saw through the window that her Mom came running into the living room to save a vase from Rocky's excited tail.

Filled with excitement, Lou burst through the door. Rocky leapt off the couch and bounded to greet Lou, and her mother sat down on a chair, still clutching the vase to her stomach. Lou's Dad came out of the den and said, "What's the ruckus?"

Lou got Rocky under control before she replied. "I got a job, you guys!"

Lou's Mother carefully put the vase down before turning to

look at her daughter. "That's awesome, Lou! Where are you working?"

Before she could answer, Mr. Dalrymple raised his arms over his head and cheered, "Fantastic, Bunny!" He ran over to her and wrapped his arms around her, spinning her in a circle. Rocky wanted to play too, so he just spun in circles until he fell over.

They were all laughing and excited. Her dad pulled her further into the house. "Let's go in the kitchen and you can tell us all about it."

When Lou told them about her day, and all the places she dropped off resumes, they looked impressed.

Lou's Mom said, "So you got a job the same day you brought in a resume?"

Lou realized that was exactly what happened and smiled, confessing, "I got a job at old Sam's store."

Her parents didn't say anything at first, giving each other a worried look. They quickly composed their faces. Lou's father asked, "What's your job going to be exactly?"

Lou started listing off all the things Sam needed help with. She also told them what passed for an interview, which was counting money. Mr. Dalrymple was impressed. Being an accountant himself, he respected accurate numbers. Her parents began to feel better about her new job.

They talked more about Lou's day and how much she would be paid. Lou added, "And I only work afternoons, because that is when Sam runs out of energy."

Her mother nodded with understanding. "I could use a Lou in my office; I run out of steam around four myself."

They discussed how Sam was doing and she told them about the new secure room for the oddities.

Lou had another thought. "He also has a camera system monitoring that room."

Mrs. Dalrymple seemed pleased with that news. "That's good, he needs a way to protect his rare items."

Lou reassured her confidently, "I'll make sure all his surveillance gear is running properly."

Her mother smiled. "Oh, I have no doubt you will."

Lou sat at the kitchen table while her parents were making dinner. She sent a text to Oliver giving him the big news. Oliver wrote back, *"NO WAY! Actually?"*

She smiled at her phone and sent a message back. *"Come over for supper and we can talk about it after."*

He responded, *"Be right there."*

Lou answered, *"Okay!"*

She turned to her parents and asked, "Hey, can Oliver come for dinner tonight?"

Her mom didn't stop stirring what was in the pot on the stove. "He's on his way over, isn't he?"

Lou smiled and nodded. Her dad confirmed, "He's welcome anytime."

After dinner, Oliver and Lou were on kitchen clean-up duty. Lou's parents went outside to relax on the deck and tried not to worry about the sound of roughly treated dishes in the kitchen. Oliver was loading the dishwasher, asking a bunch of questions about Lou's new job.

"What kind of stuff are you gonna to be doing?"

Lou answered, "Well, from what I figure, it'll be a bit of everything. All the stuff in the store is jumbled and has no price tags and he hand-writes receipts."

Oliver considered what he was going to say. He finished loading the dishes and turned his chair to face her. "You know, my grandpa has a garage that is jumbled and dusty like that, and my mom suggested she could help him clean it and sort out what he didn't need. He had a hairy fit, dude, seriously."

Lou raised her eyebrows and Oliver continued, "He was not having any of it. He said he always knew where everything was and didn't like people touching his stuff."

Lou got his drift. "So, you think Sam might not want me to do everything I thought needed doing?"

Oliver shrugged. "He has been running that place for a lot of years. He might be like my grandpa and get all weird about it."

Lou thought about it as she pulled out a box of cookies and offered it to Oliver. "That is good advice, Mr. Brains. When did you get all grown up?"

Oliver stuffed a cookie in his mouth whole and took two more out of the box. When he had the cookie halfway chewed, he opened his mouth wide.

"ARGH! Gross, Oliver!" Lou punched his arm lightly and Oliver laughed at her reaction.

They moved into the living room to discuss the serious matter of their social time with friends and where they would bike to. The first priority was to coordinate the free time they would have now that Lou had a job. Lou had her schedule all worked out and helped Oliver figure his out. He was looking forward to working with younger kids and teaching them how to manage their different abilities as they play softball. He loved the sport and hoped to pass that on to others.

They watched a movie until late that night. When Oliver was ready to leave for home, Lou offered, "Do you want Rocky to walk you home?"

Oliver looked at her with a question on his face. Lou explained, "Rocky knows his way and will make sure nobody bugs you. He knows what to do." Rocky seemed to know that he was going for a walk because he got up from his nap in the living room and sat by Oliver's chair.

Chuckling, Lou patted Rocky's head. "I think somebody's already decided he is walking you home."

Lou watched Oliver and Rocky get to the bottom of the ramp.

When Oliver waved goodbye, Lou said, "See you tomorrow!" Next, she put on a more serious tone and called out, "Rocky, guard!"

Oliver didn't quite know what to make of that, but Rocky seemed to, and he led the way as they went down the driveway.

A little while later, Rocky appeared back on the deck wanting to come in. Lou gave him a big ear scratch and had him sit. She went to the cookie jar with a picture of a dog on it and grabbed a treat. "Good job, Rock, you're the best dog ever."

Rocky finished his treat in seconds and decided it was time for a belly rub. He leaned on Lou's legs and slid onto the floor. She laughed. "It's a good thing I am always ready for your leaning on me. You would knock me over if I didn't see it coming."

Rocky had no response; he was in a belly rub trance. When she got tired, she called, "Come on, you big goofball. It's time for bed."

They went up the stairs and Lou left Rocky in her bedroom and went to do her nighttime routine. As she stood brushing her teeth, she could hear Rocky snoring from across the hall.

She put on her pajamas and stepped over her sleeping dog to get to her bed. She rolled her eyes and muttered, "You sound like a chain saw, dude."

Rocky rolled onto his back and farted. Lou quickly pulled the covers over her head and groaned, "Ugh, nasty, what have you been eating?"

She closed her eyes and dreamed of antiques that oddly, smelled bad.

CHAPTER FIFTEEN

L ou and Oliver wanted to make the most of the weekend before they started their summer jobs, so they met up at Lou's house early Saturday morning. After convincing Rocky to stay home and lounge in the backyard, they set off on their bikes armed with backpacks full of snacks. The plan was to get Lou more familiar with the areas outside of their neighbourhood. Oliver was the designated tour guide, and he was good at it. Lou was impressed at Oliver's knowledge of the entire area.

When they stopped for water, she asked, "How do you know so much about pretty much everything?"

Oliver chugged his water before answering, "In the wintertime, I like to read local blogs and learn cool stuff. You would be amazed at the history and nature around here."

Lou nodded as she looked at the map on her phone, trying to pinpoint their current location. "Where are we going today?"

To keep Lou on her feet, Oliver said slyly, "Just follow me, I have an idea." He cycled off, leaving Lou to follow his lead.

Lou was up for anything new, so she was happy to follow Oliver around. They left the paved road and ended up on a groomed trail with hikers, walkers, and other bikes. Everybody seemed to be out that day. They pedaled for three kilometers according to Lou's phone before they stopped for another water break and so Oliver could rest his arms a bit.

Concerned, Lou asked him if he was tired. He replied, "A little, but where we're going is not much further. I'm fine, I've done 20km on this bike."

Lou looked impressed. "So, it isn't harder for you to bike on this trail than the pavement?"

"The three wheels make it a more comfortable ride. I just need to rest a bit. By the end of the summer, I'll be faster than you," Oliver answered.

Lou laughed, saying, "I'll bet you an ice cream you still won't be able to beat me."

Oliver pointed at her. "You're on! You will be buying me a triple scoop. Count on it."

When they next stopped, they were in a big parking lot between a highway and a massive cliff face. They found a spot to rest and took off their helmets. Lou looked up at the glistening cliff.

Oliver was eating a cereal bar and when he was finished chewing his bite he pointed, "Can you see all the little dots on the rock face? Those are climbers."

Lou grabbed her binoculars out of her backpack and cleaned the lenses. "You know, I saw this place when I was researching the city before we moved here. I actually spent a lot of time looking at the trail pictures and all that too. I loved the network of trails, and that you could see the Chief and the ocean from almost anywhere. What I didn't know was how massive the mountains would be in real life." She kept looking through the binoculars and focused on the rock face as she spoke. "Those climbers are fearless!"

Oliver reclined on his bike and chuckled. "Oh yeah. And obsessed. Some of them sleep in their cars and climb all day." Then just as Oliver was about to speak again, a van pulled up beside them, taking the last parking spot near a trail. Four people jumped out of the van, hauling ropes over their shoulders. They chattered excitedly, pulling more and more gear out of the van, including giant backpacks with dozens of carabiners clinking noisily as they moved.

"What are those things?" asked Lou.

"You mean the metal things?" Oliver asked. "They hook onto the climber's ropes and anchors to keep them on the cliff safely."

Lou shook her head a little and quipped, "Well they sure do need a lot of them!"

Oliver smiled and drank a big gulp of his water.

As they watched, many more people headed to the trail. One young woman with dreadlocks and tattoos passed them on her way to the base of the Chief. She gave them a thumbs up, saying, "Right on!" and kept walking with her load of gear. Oliver and Lou didn't know what to say back, so they just waved awkwardly. They looked at each other and giggled.

Oliver chuckled, "Climbers have their own language."

Oliver decided he was starving; Lou agreed they should find a shady spot to eat lunch. They scanned around and spotted a picnic table under a tree. Lou watched Oliver unload his lunch bag. She commented, "Is that some kind of magic bottomless bag? Your lunch has more items than our family's grocery order!"

Oliver answered in his usual way. He opened his mouth full of sandwich and made a face at Lou.

They hung around for a little while and ate their lunches, watching the people come and go. They shared the binoculars back and forth to watch the climbers reach the tops of their ropes.

After packing up, Lou declared, "Rocky is going to start wondering where I am; we should get a wiggle on." They both pedaled onto the trail, and because it was Lou and Oliver, it became a race.

❖

The next day Lou was getting her gear together to explore a new trail but got a text from Oliver. *"Can't go riding today. My bike blew a gear on the way home, and my mom has a list of chores for me to do."*

Lou answered, *"Okay. The parentals bought a gazebo kit and want me to help build it anyway, so talk later?"*

Oliver answered, *"Well at least it'll be fun to hangout in when it's done! Text ya later."*

Lou put on her working clothes and headed outside. Her parents were already in the backyard, surrounded by wood, and were on their hands and knees, looking at a giant blueprint. Lou rolled her eyes and walked over to them. She had a feeling about how this project would end up. Her parents would bicker all day about how to best build the gazebo.

Rocky had already found his spot under a bush and all Lou could see were four long legs sticking out. "I guess he's having his post-breakfast nap," Lou commented, interrupting her parents. They looked at the dog and then went straight back to scanning the blueprint. Lou could see they were concentrating hard and already sweating before the first post was nailed.

Mr. Dalrymple stood up and put his pencil behind his ear. He walked over to Lou, put his arm around her and kissed the top of her head. Smiling, he said, "I'm so glad you're here, Bunny. This gazebo kit is more complicated than we thought, and we could really use your builder brain."

Lou's mother tossed her pencil and laid on her back in the grass, defeat written on her face. "What were we thinking, Mervin? We are not handy people. We build one wheelchair ramp, and all of a sudden we are contractors?"

Lou laid down beside her and put her arm over her mom's stomach. "I did some wood framing in trades class, Mom. Maybe I can help?"

When her mother was ready to give it another try, they climbed to their feet and got back to work. Lou's father figured out how to build the frame that the gazebo would sit on. Lou's mother was making progress on the roof construction. It would go on top of the gazebo frame after being built on the ground. Lou hoped they could lift it.

Rocky had woken up and was just randomly carrying around large planks of wood and dropping them in a pattern only he could figure out.

Mr. Dalrymple chastised him. "Rocky, stop dragging the wood around, you are getting teeth marks in it!" Rocky paused, a giant plank of wood in his mouth, and let it roll out of his jaw and onto the ground.

Then Lou saw his eyes light up and focus on a smaller board. He picked it up and before she could say anything, he stared tearing proudly around the yard with his prize. In Rocky logic he figured he wasn't allowed the big piece of wood, but the smaller one was okay.

Lou commanded, "Rocky, drop it!" The board fell to the ground and she rescued it, wiping the drool off. She told him to go lie down so he slumped back under his bush, grumbling.

Lou was pretty good at taking a blueprint and figuring out what pieces went where. She searched for the right ones and handed them to her parents to nail. The Dalrymple family made a good team. When they tackled a project, everybody contributed.

They worked all day, and by the time it was finally finished, it was almost dark. They ordered pizza and ate it in their new gazebo. As Lou chewed on her third piece of pizza, she was busy designing a ramp for the gazebo in her head.

It was a beautiful day when Lou looked out her window the next morning. "Not bad for a first official day of summer," she thought and wandered downstairs.

"There's something special about summer, isn't there? You

don't have to go to school and your alarm isn't set," said Mr. Dalrymple as he poured two coffee mugs.

Before Lou had a chance to answer, her mother came flying down the stairs with her briefcase, papers hanging out of it. She grabbed the coffee mug that Mr. Dalrymple had at the ready, took a quick sip and said, "Good luck with your day, honey." She took a second look at him and sighed as she put down her briefcase, "Mervin, you look rumpled." She straightened his tie and collar and patted it, satisfied that he looked professional. Turning to Lou, she said, "Have a great day of fun before you start your job."

She grabbed her bag and gave Mr. Dalrymple a kiss on the cheek. She put on her shoes at the door and called back, "I had better scoot now, I don't want to be late." She blew them a kiss on the way out the door and was gone.

Lou turned back to her dad, and they both shrugged. "Your mother is an amazing woman, Lou, and when she gets focused on something, she is like a laser beam until it's finished." Then his eyes lit up, and he smiled saying, "Like somebody else I know."

Lou laughed and seemed surprised to notice that her dad was in a suit. "Why are you all dressed up?"

Her father looked uncomfortable, pulling on his tie to loosen it a bit making it rumpled again. Lou thought his jacket looked like he had borrowed it from a much larger man.

He answered, "I have a job interview this morning. I am not sure it will be as good as my last position in Halifax, but it is worthwhile to go to every interview you are offered." Lou nodded as she chewed on a piece of toast. She hoped he would get a job because he had been pretty bored lately.

Her dad leaned against the counter taking a sip of coffee. "Are you going biking with Oliver today?"

Lou finished chewing her last bite of breakfast. "Nah, he has a coach's meeting today in Whistler." Her dad made an "ah" noise and busied himself with tidying. But since the kitchen was already spotless, Lou knew he was only doing it to keep himself busy, so he wouldn't worry about his interview.

Lou stood up from the table, crossing the room to put her plate in the dishwasher. "Don't be nervous Dad, you will rock your interview." He smiled and gave her a hug.

After her dad left, Lou packed up her backpack and loaded snacks into the extra pocket. She checked that she had Rocky's water dish and his treats. Her notebook and pen secured, she popped her phone in her back pocket and got her bike out of the garage. They sped off on their adventure. Rocky was running circles around her bike all the way down the road.

Lou decided to take a different route for a change and went west. She wanted to see whatever she could of the ocean and was determined to spend the day watching for whales or whatever else would catch her interest.

Lou had researched quite a bit about local whale-watching tours. Considering Squamish sat at the end of an inlet that led out into the ocean it made sense that whales would hang around the area. Lou also found out that Squamish had a big commercial fishing dock. She had also been surprised to see a massive container terminal with huge docks and cranes out on the far tip of the peninsula on her maps. The local Squamish website said that a lot of cargo went in and out of that terminal, including huge containers full of cars and heavy equipment. She was most interested in seeing whales though.

Lou coasted along a bike path she discovered would lead down to the waterfront. Rocky was lagging behind, so Lou hollered at him, "Rocky what is so interesting in those shrubs?" She turned her bike around, and by the time she got back to where Rocky was, all she could see was his tail. He had crawled off the path and under the bushes. At first his tail was wagging, but then it stopped. Lou opened her mouth, about to tell him to get out of there, when he howled and frantically tried to back out of the bushes. After struggling to get clear, he plopped down and sadly looked at Lou. "Rocky, what did you find?" She saw his nose had a nasty scratch on it and was bleeding. Lou always came prepared, so she pulled tissues and water out of her bag to clean him up. She was about to scold him about his curiosity when Rocky's attacker came strolling out from the bushes. Lou looked at Rocky and hooted, "A *cat?* You know better than messing with cats, dude. What were you thinking?"

As Lou cleaned up Rocky's nose, the long-haired grey cat strolled up near Lou and sat down and started grooming itself. Rocky stayed sitting but tried not to make eye contact. Lou addressed the cat, "Aren't you the bold one? Pick on somebody your own size." The cat stood up, fluffing its tail, and walked away. Rocky watched it go and gave a quiet *woof*. "Yeah, way to scare the cat, tough guy," Lou said, chuckling.

She gave Rocky some water, and as he was snout deep in his bowl, said, "Let's not tangle with any local critters again today, huh?" Rocky knew she was speaking to him, so he pulled his snout out of his water bowl and looked at her. As she glanced back at him, all the water he had been drinking came pouring out from his lips. He had simply forgotten to swallow. Then he shook his head.

Lou jumped back, but it was too late. Rocky soaked the entire front of her shirt and shorts. She was shocked at how completely wet she was. "Rocky," she groaned, "could you please, for once, not shake your head with a mouth full of water? Swallow then shake, we have gone over this!"

Looking confused, Rocky put his face back in the bowl and finished drinking. Lou dried herself up, and they carried on in their quest to find the dock and the whales.

Hopping back on her bike, Lou pedaled off. Rocky stayed close, glancing back once in a while to make sure he wasn't being followed by that cat. Lou's thoughts had turned to their destination. "Do you suppose we will be able to see some Orca pods from the fishing dock?" she asked Rocky.

As they made their way to the spot where Lou figured the dock would be, she recited list of facts about Orcas and Squamish to Rocky. He wasn't interested, because he was once again busy sniffing every shrub and fire hydrant.

Lou rolled her eyes but talked to him anyway, starting her lesson on whales. "They used to be called killer whales, but they are now known as Orcas. There are only seventy-four of them left who live around here permanently, but other pods come and go. They can eat an eleven-hundred-pound sea lion, and swim fifty-six kilometers an hour. They are expert hunters for their food."

Rocky perked up when he heard the word food. Lou chastised him, "Don't look so excited, dopey. Those whales would eat you in a second." Rocky seemed to get what she meant and looked like he might be concerned. Lou laughed. "Don't worry, we aren't going for a swim today."

When they got to the dock, they saw a huge pier where boats of all sorts were tied up. Lou pulled up to a fence, parked her bike, and took off her helmet. She walked out onto the pier, amazed at the number of whale-watching boats that were tied up. She started taking pictures of their signs, thinking she might try to talk her parents into taking a tour.

At the far end of the dock was another connected dock with fishing boats tied to it. She kept strolling checking out the boats. When they got near the end of the long dock Rocky marched ahead and sniffed a big net drying out on the pier. He launched himself into it, rolling on his back. Horrified, Lou yelled, "Rocky NO! You'll come home smelling like fish. Mom will kill us!"

As Rocky wriggled around on the net, he got himself more and more tangled in it. As Lou was trying to get him untangled, she heard somebody laughing. "Aye, your dog is havin' himself a good roll there, missy."

Lou looked up and saw a man standing on a boat in dirty overalls and rubber boots with an unlit cigar in his mouth. Lou panicked and squeaked out, "Sir, I'm so sorry, my dog is wrecking your net!"

She continued frantically to untangle Rocky, but just made it worse. It was dawning on Rocky that he couldn't get out and started to struggle. Then he had the idea to outrun the net and tried to sprint away. He fell down over and over and was getting very near to edge of the dock.

The man put his cigar down and stepped onto the dock. He reached up to grab a big hook on a cable attached to the boom on his boat. Leaning over, he hooked it into the net. Rocky was still struggling but getting tired. Lou was desperately trying to drag the net with Rocky tangled in it away from the edge of the dock.

The man went back to his boat and flipped a switch. A machine whirred to life and started lifting the net. The cable didn't even strain when Rocky and his net were lifted right off the ground. The boom swung around to the middle of the dock, safely away from the edges, and stopped.

The man watched the net and the cable as Lou was trying to figure out how Rocky was going to get himself out of there. The man reassured her, "Don't ya worry, he'll be fine."

Rocky did not look fine at all. He was almost upside down, with both ears and one paw sticking out of the net. His eyes were bugged out in panic and when he realized he was off the ground, he started howling.

Lou reached up and put her hand through the net, petting his nose to calm him. "He's not used to being picked up," she said weakly.

The man slowly lowered the net down onto the dock. Rocky had given up struggling and seemed resigned to his fate. Grabbing a big knife, the man began to cut away the net, eventually getting Rocky clear of his trap. The big dog slid out of the net and landed on the dock with a 'thunk'. Rocky didn't quite know what to do with this situation, so he just sat there looking stunned.

Smiling, the man scratched Rocky behind the ear. "That is a

mighty fine dog you have there. Not too bright, but at least he doesn't bite." He gathered up the net and unhooked it from the boom. "You never know when you need a good rigging knife close by." Tucking the knife away, the man went to sit down on the bench at the edge of the dock by his boat and resumed chewing on his cigar.

After she settled Rocky by her feet, Lou found her voice. "I don't know how to thank you for saving my dog!" Lou was practically in tears. "He could have ended up in the water if you hadn't been here." Then she pulled herself up and gathered her wits. "It might take me all summer, but I will pay for your ruined net."

Slapping his knee, he laughed long and hard. When he wiped the tears away with his sleeve, he said, "Oh don't you worry about my net, it was headed for the dump anyway. That thing would not have lasted another season. I was just drying it out. Besides, I haven't seen anything that funny in ages!"

Rocky had been sniffing the net carefully, in case it had plans to jump up and trap him again. He gave the net a *wuff* and then turned around and made like he was kicking dirt on it. He walked over to Lou and sat beside her.

Slowly, Lou and Rocky recovered from their dramatic introduction to commercial fishing on the west coast. The man offered them water, and they sat together on the workbench on the dock. Lou thought the man looked like a very tall grandpa with his cap and curly hair. She noticed that his skin was weathered, and his full beard could use a trim. He seemed happy to have company, even if it was only a girl and a howling giant dog.

"What kind of fish do you catch?" Lou asked him.

He gazed at the water as he replied. "Well, none at the moment." He continued sadly, "There are usually more salmon to catch, but there aren't many in this water this year. The Government isn't letting the commercial fishers go out."

Lou processed that for a minute. "So, what are you going to do?"

He thought before replying. He didn't know how much of his business plan would interest a teenager, so he kept it simple. "I'm looking at options, but I might be able to make a go of it as a whale watching tour boat. Problem is that it costs a lot of money to convert one of these boats."

Lou looked at him, but her mind was busy thinking of ideas for how he could redesign the boat. She started developing a blueprint in her head.

When Lou remained quiet, he continued, "Even the whale-watching business isn't a sure thing when the salmon are low. The Orcas don't come as much because they don't find enough food."

Lou nodded to show she was listening intently.

The man looked back out over the water; his expression grim. "There are a lot of commercial fishers heading to other locations temporarily, and they may not come back. Everybody knows Howe Sound is mostly dried up."

Lou had a million more questions and wanted to ask for a tour of his boat to see how it worked, but she thought she had better come back another day. They had taken up enough of his time already. Lou limited herself to a few more questions, unable to resist finding out more about the salmon and why they were low. He was kind and answered them all.

The wind began to pick up, Rocky got restless. Lou had been sitting cross legged on the dock. Pulling herself to her feet, Lou said, "Thank you so much for saving my dog and answering all my questions. I learned a lot today." Then she realized she had another question. "My name is Lou, what's yours?"

He put down his cigar, surprised to note he had talked more with Lou than anyone else in a while. He said, "They call me Tank."

"Because your boat is called FishTank?" she blurted out.

Tank laughed. "Jeez, you're some smart girl. That is indeed how I got the name!"

Lou felt awkward asking but pushed forward anyway with one more question. "Why do you have an unlit cigar in your mouth?"

Tank confessed, "I haven't smoked a cigar in fifteen years, but I can't seem to think without having one in my lips." Lou nodded and chuckled a little. He smiled, saying, "Come see me anytime my boat is at the dock." He scratched Rocky's ear, and they said their goodbyes.

Lou headed back down the dock towards her bicycle, calling, "Come on, big dog! As Rocky stood up, he navigated his way around the net carefully and growled. He was warning it not to try that monkey business again. But when the wind moved the net, he tucked his tail between his legs and ran to the top of the dock howling *yipe, yipe, yipe* the whole way.

Turning back, Lou waved to Tank one last time before pedaling to where Rocky was waiting for her. She stopped to scratch Rocky's ears. "I know you're still offended about being picked up off the ground like a chihuahua or something, but you're safe now. Next time, don't roll in something just because it smells good!"

Lou and Rocky slowly headed home. They turned the corner onto the street where Lou had seen the little blue house with the mysterious person behind the curtain. Over the last while nothing much had changed anytime she saw it. Until today.

It was being torn down.

Lou braked hard. By the time Rocky noticed, he was down the block. He came running back to see what she was looking at.

Meanwhile, Lou was taking a quick inventory in her head. The old broken carriage was still sitting by what used to be the front of the house. But now there were other broken things being loaded into dumpsters on the front lawn. There was a team of people wearing construction hardhats all over the house, tearing off shingles, siding, pulling out windows and taking off the front door.

Lou was startled when she saw a massive bulldozer waiting to knock the whole house down. She was beside herself with curiosity. "What happened to the person at the window? Did they move or were they evicted? Were they drug dealers?" Lou's mind was spinning with all the possibilities.

Eventually Rocky got bored with the whole house destruction thing and started pawing at Lou's leg. "Ouch!" Lou cried. "You need your nails cut!" But she got the message. With a last quick look back at the house, she saw a big truck pull in to take away the dumpsters. She pedaled home, still cooking up theories about the house and who might have lived there.

CHAPTER SIXTEEN

L ou sat up with a start. "Crap, it's Tuesday, and I'm going to be late!"

It was her first day at her new job, and she was disoriented, having no idea how late she had slept. Glancing at the clock, she saw it was only eight o'clock. She flopped back down and breathed a sigh of relief, remembering her start time was noon and that she hadn't actually overslept.

Rocky had slept through her scare, so when she got up, she stepped over him and left her room. He was still tired from their big day at the dock. He had probably had nightmares about the scary net.

Lou got herself ready for the day before wandering downstairs. Her parents weren't home, so she scrounged around the fridge for some breakfast. She found a note on the counter.

"Good morning, Bunny, I had to go into Vancouver and won't be home until supper. Have a good first day at the store! Love, Dad." Lou smiled, hoping he was off at another job interview.

Looking at the time, Lou figured Rocky had slept for about twelve hours; he would need to eat and go outside by now. She took the stairs two at a time and walked into her room.

Rocky was on his back and had pulled her comforter down

from her bed and over himself. She couldn't help but laugh because this was funny every time he did it. He would never dare steal her blankets until she was gone, though. He knew better than to take them off her. Lou chuckled and nudged him. "Alright, blanket thief, it's time to get up."

Lou spent the morning writing in her journal about her exciting day at the dock, trying to remember all the details she had discovered. Her to-do list ended up pretty long by the time she finished listing all the topics she intended to research. She was already interested in salmon migration and orcas, but now she also wanted to know how to convert boats from one type to another. She felt sure Tank would let her help. She made a few diagrams and labeled them.

Lou ate an early lunch and put a snack in her bag. Rocky had been outside in the yard all morning, and now he was passed out on the deck. Lou looked out the back door. "Hey Rocky, you coming inside?"

He lifted his head and opened one eye. He could tell what she wanted, so he answered by putting his head back down and breathing so deeply that his lips fluttered.

She rolled her eyes, saying, "I'll take that as a no." She put his water bowl outside and filled it from the hose. She scanned the yard to double check that the gates were closed and locked. Rocky liked to go on walks by himself, but he wasn't allowed to when no one was home.

When she was sure all was set and secure, she locked the front door and hopped on her bike to go to work.

❖

When Lou pulled up to the store, she found old Sam was outside trying to straighten a sign above the door with a broom. He was on a small stepladder, teetering dangerously. She called, "Sam don't move! You'll fall!"

After dropping her bike, she ran over to try to steady him. She held onto the ladder with one hand and his calf with the other.

Still holding the broom above his head, he remembered. "Oh yes, it's Tuesday and you are here to work." He made a final adjustment to the sign and climbed down, grunting. "The old bones aren't what they used to be, Lou."

As Lou helped him put away the ladder, they chatted about the weekend and what the plan would be for the day. When they got to the back counter, Lou noticed he had brought out a second stool, and she smiled at that.

The phone rang constantly. Sam would put down the receiver and go to find whatever object the customer was asking about. Then he would come back and try to answer the question. Often, he would forget what he had been asked, and had to go back to look again once the caller reminded him. It was hard for Lou to watch Sam struggling.

As the day went on, she started a list of jobs he needed done – some by her, and others by a professional of some sort. It was very obvious to Lou, even on her first day, that Sam needed a lot of help. The place had always been a jumble of items, but now it was dusty as well. The back counter was covered in stacks of paper, an old-style cash, and mechanical calculator complete with a worn lever. Lou had only ever seen these before in a museum. They were antiques that he still used daily.

Her list included everything from dusting and sorting items to asking Sam about maybe getting portable phones and a computer. After Sam gave Lou a tour of his system on how the shelves were organized, she felt surer of where she could find things. It wasn't quite as jumbled as she first thought now that she saw how his brain worked.

She made notes as he was speaking and explaining where he got his items and who his sources were. Anytime Lou had an idea, she wrote that down too.

As the afternoon went on, she remembered what she asked,

"Sam, who came and installed the glass door and security cameras?"

He looked deep in thought and then he brightened. "That nice lady, Sergeant Preston, came by with a business card for somebody who she thought could help me. I called him and he had it all fixed up in a day."

"That was a good idea, I'm sure that nobody wants a repeat of that incident," Lou replied. Sam nodded; his expression serious. He was clearly thinking about it as he shuffled papers on the counter.

They finished the day off at five when Sam flipped the "open" sign to "closed." He locked up while Lou retrieved her bike and put on her helmet. Digging around in his pocket, he pulled out an envelope and gave it to her.

The front of the envelope had a note that said, "Lou pay - five hours." When she opened it, it was full of cash. Lou didn't know what to say.

Sam explained, "I figured out the sum for every day, and here is the first shift's pay." Lou thanked him, but it got her wondering if this was how he was going to pay her all summer. It seemed odd.

She waved goodbye as he walked up the stairs on the side of the building to his apartment above the store. Lou winced a bit as the stairs creaked and moved when he stepped on each one. She shook her head and started worrying about him in earnest.

Lou had a lot to think about during her ride home. She realized how hard it was becoming for Sam to keep up with the daily functions of the store, never mind filling his orders. Those thoughts were still running through her mind when she walked into her house.

Rocky startled out of a nap when she came in, scrambling to

his feet with no grace but lots of enthusiasm. Lou had seen her father's van in the driveway, so she shouted, "Hi Dad, I'm home!"

Rocky was leaning hard on her legs in his excitement, so she just gave up and sat on the couch to be greeted. When Rocky was done having his ears scratched, he slid down to the floor and laid on Lou's feet.

Mr. Dalrymple came down the stairs doing up the buttons on his cardigan. "Hello Louisiana, how was your first day at work?" He kissed her on top of her head, nearly tripping over Rocky who was now lying on her feet.

"Dad, don't call me that!" she said, ignoring his question. "How many nicknames can you possibly come up with? You know Oliver does it too now!"

Smiling, he said, "Ok, Louisa, I apologize. But you should know, I have a bunch of them."

Lou rolled her eyes and decided she would just ignore his teasing.

Rocky started to lick the carpet for some reason, so Lou nudged him. "Never mind the carpet. How about getting off my feet?" Rocky stood up and went to the back door to be let out. Her father followed her into the kitchen, as she went to let Rocky outside.

Knowing that her dad was curious about her first day at the store, Lou pulled some juice out of the fridge and poured them each a glass. Then she sat at the table with her father.

"What kind of antiques does Sam have?" he asked. Lou explained that the main room in the store had a lot of old ship and sailboat stuff. The back room was where Sam kept the oddities. "Those items were the ones the thieves took, right? You said that they are now protected by the glass door? Did he ever get back the items the thieves took?"

Lou nodded over her juice glass and said, "Oh yeah, Sergeant Preston brought them over herself. They are all back in the oddities room and it's locked now. I wrote price tags for all of them today. They are worth a bunch of money." Lou's dad nodded distractedly as he mulled over everything she had told him.

Lou remembered the note from this morning and that her father had been gone all day. "What were you doing in Vancouver today?"

He gulped down the last of his juice before he responded. "I had another job interview."

Lou smiled. "Wow, that's great Dad! How do you think you did?"

He answered sadly, "Oh, I did just fine, but I figured out I probably won't take a job in the city. The drive was really long, the traffic was terrible, and I'm pretty sure I can get a job around here."

Lou was concerned. "Does Mom know?"

He shook his head. "No, not yet, but I know she had hoped I could work locally, so she won't be too disappointed."

Lou gave his hand a squeeze across the table because he looked tired and defeated. She felt sorry for her dad every time a job didn't work out. He squeezed her hand back and said, "Besides, if I'm far away, how can I look out for you every day, Bunny?"

She got up and grabbed her lunch bag out of her backpack and as she went by her dad, she kissed the top of his head. "You know I can take care of myself, but I love that you still want to look out for me."

As she unloaded her lunch bag, she found the cash Sam had given her for the shift. Turning to her father, she asked, "Is it normal to get paid cash at the end of every day when you have a job? I know that's not how you and Mom get paid, but I was wondering if some bosses still do that?"

Mr. Dalrymple didn't even try to hide his surprise. As an accountant he knew full well that nobody should pay cash to employees. Shaking his head, he answered, "I bet he hasn't had employees for a very long time. It's old school and is simply not done anymore."

"Yeah, I thought it was kinda weird."

"I'm willing to bet he has his own system of tracking all the money, but I think it must be pretty unconventional," Mr. Dalrymple reassured her.

Lou chuckled. "There is a lot of unconventional in Sam's world."

"Just let him pay you the way he is used to. But make sure you take note of the hours you work every day and what he has paid you," her dad instructed. "He might accidentally forget one day."

Lou nodded her understanding as she headed up the stairs. "I am going to shower all this dust out of my hair, then I can come help with dinner."

The next morning, Lou's parents were out when she got up. She was awake early and felt the need to get out for some fresh air before going to work at noon. Rocky wasn't interested in leaving his sunny spot on the patio, so Lou hopped on her bike by herself and went to see if Oliver was around. Sadly, he wasn't home and didn't return her texts.

Lou had finally figured out that she could navigate anywhere by seeing where the Chief was. Her area of town was in the shadow of the Chief until about noon every day. When the sun moved further west, her house and her neighbours all got sunshine. She pedaled around some more and went up to an area on the hill behind her neighbourhood.

The neighbourhood up the steep hill was full of luxury homes and views of mountains and water. Lou stopped and took a rest from the tiring ride up, looking around and thinking, "I could live here with this view for the rest of my life."

While she was lost in thought, an older woman came by

walking an Afghan Hound. Lou had seen this kind of dog before, but never one trimmed and styled so fancy. Laughing at herself, she thought, "That dog has better hair than I do."

The dog walker said hi as she passed by, so Lou decided to ask if she could pat the dog. The lady pulled on the dog's leash, tugging her further away from Lou, replying, "Sorry, sweetie. Anastasia doesn't like strangers."

Lou knew dogs could sometimes be that way, so she didn't take offense. "She's very pretty though," she called out. The lady nodded as she strutted off.

When she was back on her bike, Lou rode away laughing, "Rocky would be that dog's worst nightmare."

Lou biked around the hilly neighbourhood and gawked at the luxurious homes. It seemed a little weird though. There weren't any people outside except for the woman and her aloof dog. Nobody was in their yards or out on the street. She thought it was sad that people had these great yards and an amazing hilltop view, and nobody seemed to be enjoying it. She was thinking about who she would want to live with in one of these homes as she slowly cruised down the steep hills.

Having explored another area, she pedaled the rest of the way home. Lou packed a lunch and was right on time when she pulled up to Sam's store on her bike.

Sam was not up on a ladder this time, leaving Lou feeling somewhat relieved. He was, however, unloading a truck. When Lou went to see what was going on, Sam greeted her, "Oh Hello, Lou. Wednesdays are delivery days." Lou wondered where on earth they would store this small truckload of awkwardly-shaped antiques.

She spent the day cleaning and organizing new items in the oddities room, and filing papers, but struggled a bit with Sam's system. As far as she could tell, it used to be by date when he sold or bought an item. But sometimes it was alphabetical. Lou decided she would bring up a new idea to Sam.

When they were having their afternoon snack together, Lou pitched her idea. "Sam, I was wondering, do you have a computer? I mean, you have these cameras connected to something, don't you?"

Sam looked confused at first, but then brightened up when he remembered. "Oh yes, I have had one for years!"

Lou was encouraged as Sam started digging under the front counter to find it. After a moment, he said, "Ah, here it is!"

Lou puzzled over the scene, not sure what she was seeing. When he held up a dusty box that said Commodore 64, she had to work hard not to laugh out loud. He had a computer all right, but he had never taken it out of the box.

Sam said proudly, "I've had this thing since 1984, just never got around to firing it up. Will it do for your idea?"

Lou couldn't help herself, breaking out into laughter. "We might as well put a price tag on it and display it as an antique."

Sam realized what he had said and joined her in laughing. "Let's see what we can get for it!"

Once they settled back down, Lou made the case for getting a new computer. If he had one, she could help him set up an inventory system and receipt filing. Sam was listening politely, but she could tell he didn't get why that would be better. They talked about it for a bit before they got back to work. At closing time, Lou noticed he was thinking hard about something and she hoped it would be her idea. The more she thought about it, the more she realized there was a lot to be done to make it easier for Sam to do things, and that he needed more help than just her.

Lost in thought, she rode the five kilometers to her neighbourhood. She stopped her bike in front of what used to be the little blue house, now a pile of rubble in a hole in the ground. It was surrounded with plastic construction fencing, and the driveway was broken up in chunks of concrete. Lou was shocked at how fast it had been destroyed.

Surveying the site, she spotted something in the rubble. Her curiosity piqued, she put her bike down and went to peer through the fence, trying to figure out what the object glinting in the sun was. She wondered if maybe there might be a clue to this mysterious little house and what was going on inside it. Something sketchy no doubt, but then again, she reminded herself, she was always quick to label things as conspiracies or crimes.

Pushing her bike, she went to the side of the yard and stashed it in some bushes. She continued on towards the back of the lot, looking for a way under or through the fence. The previous owners must have left something behind that could be useful or could be a clue. Eventually, she found a loose panel of fence and crawled under it, making her way around the perimeter of the foundation. It turned out there were many items left behind that might be of interest. She could hardly contain her excitement.

Then she saw it. The metal she had seen reflecting the sunlight was a big clasp on a trunk, the rest of it buried under drywall and bricks.

Lou double checked that her boots were tied and carefully picked her way through the broken tile and old wooden beams. She planned her route carefully, but she didn't take into account the loose slippery tiles and lost her balance. When she started to fall, she did her best to try to land on a crumpled ball of fabric curtains. Unknown to Lou, however, hiding away beneath them was a wooden beam with a large rusty nail sticking out of it. When she landed on it, the nail pierced the skin between her thumb and index finger, going right through her left hand.

Lou shrieked, starting to shake when she saw how badly her hand was hurt. She immediately pulled her hand off the nail, which hurt as badly as it had when it went in. Needing to get out of there safely, she took off her hoodie and wrapped it around her bleeding hand. She stood up with extreme caution. Dizzy and nauseous, she knew she still had to get back to the side of the lot and under the fence. Slowly turning around, she carefully picked her way back. The trunk completely forgotten; she was now focused only on getting home. Finally, she rolled under the fence and stopped to rest for a minute.

When her head cleared, she got up carefully, grabbing on to the fence for support. Her hand was bleeding badly, so she took a moment to wrap it more tightly. She was grateful she had been a Scout and knew how to handle first aid. She also knew that she had to stop the bleeding and get somewhere she would be seen, in case she passed out. With her hand wrapped in fabric, she put her arm in the air to try to slow the bleeding and walked unsteadily to her bike.

She couldn't get on it and ride with her hand wrapped and bleeding. With her helmet hanging off the handlebars, she steered her bike towards the front of the yard. Her makeshift bandage loosened, and with her arm above her head, blood started running down her arm. She stopped, losing her grip on her bike, and it fell over.

Frustrated and in pain, she wrapped her hand again and made a knot in the fabric, tightening it with her teeth. As she picked up her bike, tears welled up in her eyes. She was mad at herself for making such a dumb decision to walk over a bunch of dangerous rubble. Muttering under her breath, she chastised herself for being irresponsible. Then she heard skateboard wheels approaching.

She froze like a rabbit. She knew who it would be and was mortified for him to see her crying and bleeding. More so, she didn't want to tell him what she had done. But it was too late. She heard, "Lou! What happened?"

Tyler leapt off his skateboard and ran onto the grass to help her. He pulled the handlebars out of her grip and put the bike down, gently settling her onto the grass. Kneeling in front of her, he unravelled the hoodie.

Lou tried to wipe her eyes to hide her tears, but all she managed to do was wipe mud on her face. She cried harder as

Tyler tried to find where the blood was coming from. Eventually, Lou calmed herself and was able to tell him what happened. He listened intently while holding pressure on the puncture.

When she finished, Tyler commented, "Good thing I passed by when I did. I was actually on my way to your house. We found a pair of earbuds at my house and I thought they might be yours from when you babysat." He held them up, and she chuckled.

"I was wondering where those went."

He put them in her backpack, slipped it on his shoulder and helped her get up. Lou held her hand close to her body and kept it wrapped, while Tyler walked her bike and held his skateboard.

They approached her house, hearing loud music coming from inside it. They looked at each other and looked back at the house, confusion on their faces. It wasn't until they came up the front stairs that Lou realized what was going on.

Every so often her parents blasted their 80's music at full volume and, much to Lou's horror, had a dance party all by themselves. When Lou opened the door, she and Tyler's ears were blasted with "Should I Stay, or Should I Go?"

Excited, Tyler turned to Lou, yelling to be heard over the music, "That's The Clash! My favourite band!"

Lou's parents were dancing and laughing until they saw Lou gaping and Tyler smiling. They froze for a second before rushing over to turn off the music. They were a little embarrassed, but they hadn't seen Lou's injury yet. Blushing, they greeted the two of them, coming over to be introduced to Tyler. When they saw the now-bloody hoodie wrapped around Lou's hand, their smiles turned to concern.

"What happened, Bunny?" asked her father while tenderly unwrapping her hand.

Before she could answer, Lou's mother wrapped an arm around her shoulder, pulling her further into the house. "Come in the kitchen, let me see it."

Lou's father went to get the first aid kit while her mother started wiping her down with wet paper towels.

Rocky had been out on the deck and when he saw Lou at the kitchen table, he knew there was a problem. He started pawing at the door at his full height and howling. Mr. Dalrymple let him in, and he sprinted to see what was wrong with Lou.

When he saw that she already had all the help she needed, he just laid at her feet and put his head on her lap. Since Tyler was sitting beside Lou at the kitchen table, Rocky put a paw on his foot as if to say thanks.

As they were tending to her, Lou's parents found out the whole story, and got an explanation as to what Tyler was doing there. Realizing that she had never mentioned Tyler to her parents, Lou hastily introduced everyone. Lou's mom gave her fidgeting daughter a knowing look; she would be sure to ask more about Tyler later.

As her mother examined and cleaned the wound, Lou asked, "Do I have to go to the hospital?"

"No, Lou. You just had your tetanus booster last year, so you are protected, and the nail was small. It looks scary but it didn't do a lot of damage." Her mom gave her a reassuring smile. "We just have to get it disinfected and bandaged."

In the meantime, Mr. Dalrymple had gotten Lou and Tyler some juice and was preparing snacks. They were all relieved that the drama was over. Lou wasn't hungry but ate to focus on something other than Tyler being at her kitchen table. She couldn't believe that the one person she wouldn't want to see her such a wreck was him. And there he was, first on scene.

When he finished his snack, Tyler stood up to say his goodbyes. On his way out, he told Lou if she ever wanted to come out to the skate park with his friends, he had an extra skateboard to lend her. He gave Rocky a scratch and was gone.

Mrs. Dalrymple closed the door behind him. "It's a good thing your friend came by when you were hurt."

Lou was grumpy and curled up on the couch. "I'd have been fine, Mom. I was already walking home, and besides he's not my friend; we just go to the same school."

Knowing Lou had been embarrassed by the entire episode, her mom tried to bring her out of it, sitting down next to her and stroking her hair. "Well, I think he is a nice boy. Sometimes, all of us, no matter how independent we are, need help. He was your hero today and there is nothing to be ashamed of."

Lou shifted a bit, her eyes closing.

Standing back up, Lou's mother added, "Tomorrow, when you are feeling better, you can tell us what on earth you were doing on a demolition site in the first place."

Lou pretended she didn't hear, keeping her eyes firmly closed.

CHAPTER SEVENTEEN

It was a warm Friday, and Lou was at home relaxing. She had already called Sam to let him know that she hurt herself. He told her to take as long as she needed to recover. She didn't have to go to work again until the next Tuesday anyway, and felt she would be fine by then. She was grateful not to have to lift boxes for a few days though.

Lou cleaned her injured hand and put a new bandage on it. It had been a few days, and Lou was reassured to see her wound was healing. Her pride, however, was still bruised about Tyler being the one to find her crying. She hated when anyone saw her cry, but the more she thought about it, the more she realized that Tyler and her parents had barely even noticed her tears. They were all more worried about her injury. Their concern didn't make her feel weak, just loved.

"I wish Tyler would see me as more grown up," she thought. Lou had finally admitted to herself that she had a crush on Tyler and that it wasn't going to go anywhere. It made her a little sad, so she put it aside and cheered herself up by making plans for the day. First, she texted Oliver to see if he wanted to do something.

He answered right away. *"I'm good to go. What are we doing?"*

"I'll be at your place in a few minutes, I have a picnic spot in mind. Pack some food and I will too."

When Lou pulled up on her bike, Oliver was already on his. He looked around, confusion on his face. "Where's Rocky?"

Lou smiled, happy that her best friend liked Rocky. "My dad took him out for a hike. He likes to clear his head with long walks, and Rocky doesn't talk, so it works out for both of them."

Oliver accepted her explanation before looking down and noticing the bandage on her hand. "What did you do to your paw, Lou?"

"I was being nosy, and it bit me in the butt," Lou said. "I'll fill you in on the way."

Oliver laughed at her response, knowing she'd tell him when she was ready. He double-checked that his bag and chair were secured before turning his bike towards the drive. "Where are we off to?"

Lou smiled as she answered. "We're headed to the big fishing boat dock. I met a cool fisher dude who should still be there. I want to introduce you."

Oliver scrunched his eyebrows together, once again trying to make sense of Lou's explanations. When he realized where she meant, his face brightened, "Oh, where the whale-watching and fishing boats are? I've been there before, but not for a long time. How did you get yourself a friend there already?"

Lou stepped on her pedal, calling over her shoulder, "I'll tell you that story on the way, too." With that, they set off for the day's adventure.

On their way down to the water, Oliver spotted a girl walking along the sidewalk. He called out to Lou, "Hold up, I want to say hi to my friend."

They both pulled on their brakes, nearly skidding to a halt as Oliver waved and called across the street, "Hey Sandy!"

The girl waved back, motioning for Lou and Oliver to wait while she crossed to join them. As she jogged across the road, Lou noticed she looked around their age and wore a suede jacket with tassels and small beads at the end of them. Lou couldn't stop staring at the girl's hair; it was raven black and reached all the way down her back.

The girl was smiling as she dodged traffic. As soon as she made it across, Oliver said, "How was school? We missed you!" Then he pulled her into a hug. Watching Oliver be so friendly with her, Lou couldn't help but think, "This guy knows everybody around here."

Oliver and the girl were so caught up saying hello, they forgot Lou was even standing there. Lou wasn't worried, she knew Oliver would remember in a second. He would never make a social misstep like that. Lou waited patiently, smiling when they finally turned their attention to her.

"Oh, sorry!" Oliver exclaimed, looking at Lou. "Sandy, this is my friend Lou. She recently moved here from Halifax."

Sandy waved at Lou and said, "Hi, nice to meet you!"

Oliver continued, "Lou, this is Sandy. She's been away at a fancy art school in Vancouver since December. That's why you didn't meet her at school."

Lou was fascinated with the idea of a fancy art school and at the same time, desperately wanted to touch the fabric of Sandy's jacket. She jumped at the chance to ask questions. "So cool to go to an art school! What kind of art did you study? Are you going to be a professional painter, or do you carve?" Lou realized she was at risk of not even giving Sandy the chance to answer her questions, so she stopped herself before she began to pepper her with too many questions.

Sandy wasn't bothered by the barrage of questions. She was always happy to share her stories. They headed to a local café and found a picnic table outside. They ordered ice cream cones and settled in to chat. Sandy was so charming and beautiful, Lou wondered what her relationship was with Oliver. Now that she thought about it, she remembered he had mentioned her a few times, but not a lot.

She decided it was up to her to ask enough to fill in the blanks. "Sandy, what grade will you be in next semester?"

"I'll be going into grade 12. I was at a school in Vancouver that specializes in art and music for all of last semester," Sandy answered.

Oliver added, "She's an awesome painter and carver."

Sandy blushed a little. "I can't imagine doing anything else," she admitted.

Lou asked more questions about Sandy's classes, curious to know what kind of homework one would even get at an art school. When they were done with their ice creams and started getting looks from the manager, they decided they had best let somebody else use the picnic table.

Moving over to the sidewalk, Sandy asked, "Now that Lou's done her questions, I have one for you two. Did you guys have a counsellor named Cecie working at your school in the spring?"

Lou tilted her head to the side, wondering how Sandy knew that. "Yeah, we did. We really liked her. Do you know her?"

Sandy smiled and nodded. "She's my cousin."

Oliver was so surprised, he forgot to keep his hands on his bike pedals. "I did *not* put that one together," he said.

Sandy shrugged. "It's okay, there are a lot of kids in our family. I can barely keep up with all of us. So, where are you guys off to next?"

Lou pointed down the road. "We are going down to the fishing dock. Want to come?"

Sandy checked her phone and groaned. "Ugh, I wish I could but I'm late. My mom is expecting me. Hey, are you coming to the party at the Spit tomorrow? We're doing a beach bonfire."

Oliver looked thoughtful. "Depends. Who is going?"

Sandy shook her head at him, chuckling. "Oliver, you are such a social climber. If I don't give you the names of cool people, are you really going to turn me down?"

"Nah. The three of us are the cool people." Oliver smiled his cheekiest grin. "So as long as we're there, it will be a great party. Lou, can you come?"

She played it cool but she was vibrating. "Yeah, I'm in."

They worked out the details of the party, and when all was agreed, Sandy went on her way.

Lou and Oliver chatted as they resumed their cycle to the dock. "She seems really nice, Oliver." Lou said with a wink.

Oliver rolled his eyes. "I know what you're thinking Lou, it's not like that. She's going into grade twelve, and we're going into eleven. I don't think I would be in her dating pool."

Lou got the reaction she wanted, so she teased a little more, "What exactly is it like then?"

Catching onto her game, Oliver decided to turn the tables. "Is that jealousy I hear in your voice, Lou?"

She huffed, sounding a little insulted. "It's not jealousy. I was just wondering what you two are all about." Then, seeing the smile on Oliver's face, she cracked up. He had gotten her back, for sure.

When they stopped laughing, Oliver explained the real story. "I've known Sandy for my whole life. Her older sister is a massage therapist and she used to come to my house to massage my legs. Sandy would come along to keep me company and to distract me from the boredom and pain of it."

Lou nodded, trying to imagine what that must have been like for Oliver. Before she could ask, he interrupted her train of thought. "Sandy looks a lot like Cecie."

Lou agreed. "I've never met Sandy before, but I should have figured it out. They both have the same hair and smile. They look more like sisters." They carried on to the dock.

❖

Oliver and Lou pulled up to the dock and strolled down the ramp. There were a lot more boats than the last time Lou had been here. Oliver pedaled slowly, and Lou walked her bike. They laughed at some names on the boats and agreed that *The CodFather* was the best one. They continued chattering, and when they got near the end of the dock, Tank's head popped out of the door of the boat and called out, "Hey Lou! Where's your dog?"

Lou replied, "Hi Tank!" She put her bike down and took her helmet off. "He got a better offer and is hiking with my dad."

Remembering her manners, she introduced Oliver and Tank to each other. After they said hello, Tank looked Oliver and his bike over, and said with a wink, "At least you won't get tangled in a net, which is better than the last buddy Lou brought along." He chuckled at his own joke and then invited Lou and Oliver to relax. "I have a batch of iced tea brewed. You interested?"

Lou and Oliver both nodded enthusiastically and said, "Yes, please."

It was clear that Tank was happy to visit with guests rather than work on his boat. They chatted about everything from salmon stocks to the newly returned herring that had been gone for years. Lou had no idea what could cause the herring to disappear, so she started asking questions.

Tank explained, "There was a mine around here that dumped chemicals into the water for ages. When they were finally shut down, the herring eggs started returning, which brought seals and orcas back into the area."

Oliver added, "And the eagles too; when they can't eat salmon, they eat herring instead."

Lou found this whole topic interesting, finally understanding why there were fewer salmon fishing boats and more whale watching companies running tour boats.

After a while, Oliver and Lou pulled out their lunches and offered to share with Tank.

"No thanks. You two are growing, so you need the food more than I do." Tank patted his big belly and laughed.

As Lou and Oliver began eating, Tank looked up and squinted, trying to see something in the distance. His face hardened as he mumbled to himself, "What are they up to now?"

Lou and Oliver spun around, trying to follow his sight line to see what he was looking at.

At first it was hard to see, but within minutes the image became clear. They watched a boat come in towards the dock and pull into a slip a few slips away from the Fishtank. Lou couldn't tell much about it, but it had the same sort of rigging as Tank's boat did. However, it had no nets that she could see, instead displaying a hand-drawn sign that said *Sure View Whale Watching Tours*.

Lou looked back at Tank and asked, "So, what's the deal with that boat?"

Tank was still watching the newly arrived boat. "It just seems there is something not right about it. I get that people are converting their boats to whale watching tour boats because of the salmon closure, but if that is what they have done, it is a pretty poor version of a tour boat."

Oliver spoke up. "Are they new to Squamish?"

Tank nodded. Then he chewed thoughtfully on his cigar, still watching the boat. A man jumped off the boat onto the dock so he could tie it up. After several failed attempts, Tank muttered under his breath, "That guy doesn't look like he has ever held a rope before. What's he even doing owning a boat like that?"

An older woman came up on deck, her arms waving furiously. They couldn't hear her words, but from the way the man flinched, they could tell she must have been angry.

Once the boat was securely fastened to the dock, the man and the woman went back inside the boat and closed the curtains.

Tank made a *humf* noise and sat down on the bench again. Lou and Oliver restarted their discussion of Squamish marina life, but Tank's attention kept drifting back to the suspicious boat.

"That crew is suspicious. I can't figure out what they're doing, but they aren't fishing for anything as far as I can tell. And until they get fully equipped, they won't get a license for passengers, so they aren't taking people out to find orcas or anything." He rubbed his chin, peering at the boat. "They must have gotten the nav system recently, because it wasn't there when I saw it last week."

Fascinated, Lou asked, "What does the nav system do? How can you tell they have one?"

Tank explained, "You see that big white thing that looks like a giant Storm Trooper helmet and the two tall antennae?"

Lou and Oliver both nodded.

Tank continued, "That's the navigation system that lets them find the whales under the water, so they know where to take people."

Lou ran her eyes over the rest of the boat, but nothing more was happening with the people on board.

Tank frowned, worry obvious on his face. "You know, I've been fishing here for half my life; I know everybody who runs boats off this marina. Most of us are like family. But I don't know who they are or where they came from. They just showed up one day last month."

Lou asked, "Have you tried to talk to them?"

Tank huffed. "I tried, but they aren't exactly the friendly types. Barely stopped to say hi when I went over to introduce myself. As far as I know, no one else around here has had any better luck. Those people just stick to themselves."

Oliver seemed surprised, "You'd think they'd want to make friends with others since they didn't seem to be getting along with each other when we saw them."

Tank nodded his agreement. "Every single time I see them, they're arguing about something."

Lou was quiet. She was half following along with the conversation, but most of her attention was already focused on the mystery boat. Ideas about what could be going on were spinning through her head. This was definitely going in her notebook.

As subtly as possible, Lou pulled out her phone and took a picture of the back of the mystery boat. She was at an odd angle, but when she magnified the picture, she could almost make out the name of the boat. The paint was scratched and almost illegible, but she pieced it together.

"*Unsinkable*," Lou exclaimed. "Tank, do you recognize the name of the boat?" She handed over her phone to Tank, letting him take a closer look. Squinting at the phone, he made another disapproving *humf*.

"I can't believe it. *Unsinkable* was Harrison's old boat, but he died last year. I had wondered what happened to it." Tank gave the boat in question another hard look. "I wonder how a boat like that ended up in the hands of these characters."

Before they knew it, the entire afternoon passed while they chatted and speculated about the new fishers... or whatever they were. Oliver and Lou were surprised at how fast the time had passed. They packed up their backpacks and thanked Tank for the iced tea and the nice afternoon.

As they made their way back towards the land, Tank called after them, "Say hi to your dog, Lou. Tell him I secured the net and it won't trap him again!"

Laughing, Lou gave him a thumbs up. When the two kids disappeared from sight, Tank climbed on to his boat still chuckling at himself over the memory of Rocky dangling from his old fishing net.

❖

In no particular rush to get home, Lou and Oliver took the

opportunity to talk about everything they had been up to lately. Now that they both had jobs, they had less time to spend together and lots to catch up about. Lou wanted to hear more about Sandy, so she asked Oliver, "You talked about Sandy before, but I didn't clue in that you knew her so well."

Oliver answered, "She is the year ahead of us, so most of the rest of our friends don't know her as well as I do. Plus, she was away at school in Vancouver. It was a great opportunity for her; she's wicked talented."

Lou had a few female friends – really just acquaintances at this point – but she liked Sandy. She hoped they could get to know each other better. Lou decided that she would talk to her more at the party tomorrow.

As she was thinking about the party, a thought hit her. "Oliver, how are you going to get down to the party tomorrow? Your mom can't drive you and your wheelchair to the beach, she can't take a car past a certain point on the Spit, right?"

Oliver smiled, looking unconcerned. He pointed to the back of his bike. "See that metal bar behind my seat? I clip a rack to it when I need to bring my wheelchair along. I can fold up my travel wheelchair, take the wheels off, and the whole thing clips on to the rack. Easy peasy. I'll just ride my bike and set up my chair when I get there."

Lou was very impressed. Oliver explained, "My uncle custom-built it for me. I can put a snowboard on it too, and a golf bag."

Lou was astonished. "That is so cool, Oliver. You must have a very talented uncle."

Oliver was glowing with pride. "He travels a lot and lives in New Brunswick, just a few hours from where you used to live, actually, but he always comes to see me. We do fun things together and he would do anything for me." Lou pretended not to notice that Oliver's eyes welled up a little. She enjoyed getting to know Oliver better.

They reached the spot in their neighborhood where the little blue house used to be and stopped to see what had been done on the demolition site. It hadn't changed at all since they first tore it down. It was still a big pile of junk that used to be somebody's home.

Lou eyed the sight with interest. "I know going into that pile of garbage was a dumb idea, but I couldn't help myself. I am still curious about what went on in that place before it was destroyed."

Oliver smacked himself on the head. "Oh, I can't believe I forgot to tell you. I asked my mom about it and she knew the people who lived there from way back."

Lou looked at Oliver, annoyed. "You forgot? Jeez, Oliver, I've been desperate to know what happened to this house, and why it was torn down!"

Oliver held his hands up. "I know Lou, sorry about that." Lou, trying to be patient, made a hand signal to say, get on with it.

Oliver took a deep breath and began the story. "A big family lived in that little house, but all the kids grew up and left years ago. The parents were getting old, but they were determined to stay in their house as long as they could. They kept their garden and went out to stores and the local pub."

"Then how did the place end up looking like such a disaster?" Lou asked.

"The wife died about ten years ago. The husband never touched the garden again, and the house kind of started falling apart. He started throwing stuff in the yard and never cleaned it up. He would call for delivery of groceries and kept all the curtains closed."

Lou was shocked. "That sounds so sad!" She blinked her eyes and asked, "So it was the old man that I saw in the crack of the curtains?"

Oliver nodded. "He never got over losing his wife. The neighbours called the police to check on him a few months ago, and the rumour is that he couldn't speak or even move around.

He's in an institution now, and his relatives are handling his estate."

Lou felt terrible. "That is awful! That poor man all by himself."

Oliver agreed. "Yeah, I know. My mom said the relatives didn't even come to the house. They live in Florida and just hired a company to knock it down."

Lou looked again at the pile of rubble. "That is why all the stuff was still in it. They didn't even care enough to come and search for pictures or mementos. That is just awful." Lou mumbled, "Sometimes mysteries should stay that way. I feel terrible, and I think I would have been better off not knowing."

Deep in thought, the pair slowly departed. As they pedaled away from the place where the little house had stood, they rode in silence.

When they arrived at Oliver's house and got off their bikes Oliver braced himself on the frame of his bike and transferred himself over to his chair. He said, "I wouldn't do that to my parents, ever."

Lou couldn't help but think about Sam. She was still glum. "I won't let that happen to Sam either."

CHAPTER EIGHTEEN

L ou woke up with a start on Saturday morning, but not because Rocky was snoring. She woke up because he wasn't. She looked at the floor, confused when she didn't see him in his normal position on his back, giant paws in the air.

Sitting up, she spotted the open door. There was drool all over the handle, still dripping on the floor. "Ah," she thought, "he let himself out."

She grabbed a tissue and wiped off the drool before going downstairs to the kitchen. Both her parents were having breakfast and greeted her with smiles.

Her mother asked, "Did you have a good sleep, sweetie?"

Lou nodded and went over to hug each of her parents. This was out of the ordinary, but she was still feeling terrible about the old man in the little blue house. Yesterday had made her realize that some people weren't as lucky as her and her family.

Lou put some bread in the toaster and sat down with a glass of orange juice to wait. They chatted about her day yesterday and discussed what Lou and Oliver had learned about fishing in Squamish. She mentioned the mystery boat and justified it by saying, "I wasn't the one who was watching them. Tank told us about it."

Her dad looked pensive. "That's the man who has the boat down at the dock and saved Rocky from the net, right?"

Lou nodded as she chewed her toast, going on to talk about the nav system she saw and detailed how they find whales. Her parents seemed interested, asking questions about the different boats that operate from that dock. Lou shared what she knew. She also considered talking about the little blue house, but then changed her mind.

Thinking back on the day before reminded her to ask permission to go to the party. As usual, her parents ran through the twenty questions for parties they always asked and then gave her the curfew. It helped that Oliver was going too.

She finished up breakfast and went outside to find Rocky, spotting him at the back of the yard, asleep under a big tree. When she got closer, she saw a pair of squirrels in the tree chittering angrily at Rocky. Lou figured out that Rocky probably chased them up the tree and then got bored and laid down right on their stash of nuts. Lou called him. "Rocky get up, you lazy bum."

When he heard her voice, he scrambled up and ran toward her. The squirrels scuttled down the tree and kept squeaking and chattering even as they collected their walnuts off the ground.

Lou had brought her notebook with her, and she and Rocky sat in the gazebo. Lou flipped through her many pages of notes and thought, "I am so glad I keep up with my journal. I wouldn't remember half of this stuff." She wrote her notes from yesterday and made sure she included as many details as she could. Something was afoot, and she would have to remember what she saw.

Her list so far was:

- maybe illegal salmon fishing
- drug smuggling?

Lou wasn't quite sure where one might get enough drugs to fill a boat, but she left it on her list anyway. She was still thinking about what they could possibly be doing when her father strolled out with a mug in hand.

He waved the mug in the air. "You want a coffee?"

Lou rolled her eyes. "Daaad, don't you ever get tired of offering me coffee to be funny because I don't drink it?"

He sat down across from her in a big chair with a grin on his face. "It never gets old, Bunny."

Lou chuckled despite herself and shook her head.

Her dad leaned forward. "You know, I've been thinking about what you told me about Sam's filing system and the paper all over the place."

Lou closed her notebook and looked at her father to listen. He brightened as he began telling her his thoughts. "I have an old laptop with some accounting software on it. I think we could help Sam by getting a real system set up for him and get all the paper stuff into the software. I could help you learn to use it and all we would have to do is get him set up with a router."

Lou thought about it for a minute, considering his suggestion. "I think he'll say yes because he knows he needs help. I'll ask him on Tuesday." They chatted a bit more about all the things they could do to automate the heavy work he wouldn't need to do. Lou looked affectionately at her dad and asked, "Why do you want to help Sam?"

Mr. Dalrymple paused for a second, then explained, "I'm not working right now, so I want to keep my brain functional and because it's the right thing to do."

"And you are a big softy and always help anybody who needs it," Lou quipped. Her dad smiled and lifted his coffee in a toast. They sat for a while in comfortable silence.

❖

Lou had an early dinner with her parents and then started getting ready for the party. She had decided to leave Rocky at home, but when he saw she was going somewhere, he got excited and sat at the front door with his leash in his mouth. Lou's mother walked into the living room and she spotted Rocky at the door. She called out, "Come on boy, you can stay home with me tonight. We can watch a movie and I've made popcorn."

He looked undecided until his nose caught a whiff of the popcorn smell. He dropped his drool covered leash and headed off to beg for some.

Lou needed to bring some outdoor party essentials with her, but it was far more than would fit in her backpack, so she decided to quickly rig together something to solve the problem. She turned on the light in the shed and hoped for inspiration. There it was, the perfect thing. The bike trailer she had used to deliver papers in Halifax came with them on the move, and it was still in good shape. She clipped the trailer onto her bike and filled it with blankets, a folding chair, snacks, and a bottle of pop. Happy with her setup and ready to go, she ran up the stairs and opened the door. "Bye, parents!" she yelled, and closed the door before they could ask any more questions.

Lou loved to hang out on the Spit with friends, and her dad would take Rocky for walks there every chance he got. It was a long thin point of land surrounded by ocean and had little beaches along the way. The Spit was a gathering place for people all year, but the parking lot by the trail leading to it was most jam-packed in the summer. Lou was thinking about who might be at the party as she pedaled. From a distance she saw the evening was already well underway. There was a bonfire going, and she could see a number of people in chairs. Then she heard music. She smiled and peddled faster.

"This is the first legit party I have ever been invited to," she whispered to herself. "Now remember to be cool, and don't blurt out random facts, it's lame!"

Lou pulled up to a pile of bikes, seeing Oliver had just arrived as well. He took his wheelchair off the rack that was built over the back wheel and unfolded it. Next came the wheels from the rack and he snapped them onto his chair. He checked that everything was solid and transferred himself from his bike and settled in.

Lou was still absorbing what an incredible feat Oliver had accomplished in designing a rack to carry his wheelchair on his bike. She would have liked to meet Oliver's uncle who had built it; he sounded like her kind of person.

She watched Oliver adjust his clothes and check his hair. He noticed Lou staring and proclaimed, "Thou art late, you leaden-footed mushrump."

Lou snickered. "You and your Shakespearean expressions! Have you memorized the book?" Then, carrying on with the bit, she made a sweeping gesture at her trailer and said in a terrible British accent, "Good eve, my good man, please forgive my tardiness, I bring snacks for thee, Sir Oliver." They chatted excitedly and then joined the group around the fire.

Everybody was sitting around the bonfire, and Lou let Oliver pick where they would sit. He knew more people than Lou, so she trusted him to handle the important seating strategy. All the kids greeted them and started shuffling their chairs to make the circle bigger for Lou and Oliver. He ended up seated next to a very pretty girl he had been talking to all last semester. Lou smiled because it was definitely a strategic move to sit next to her. He smiled awkwardly when it was clear the girl knew exactly what was going on. Lou smiled and watched them interact. She knew all about Oliver's charm, but seeing how well it worked on somebody to make them notice him was pure magic.

She looked over to see who was sitting on her other side. To her delight, it was Sandy. She had also been watching Oliver at work and chuckled. "Hi Lou!" Sandy greeted her. Then she nodded at Oliver and added, "He is such a charmer, isn't he?"

Lou looked over at her friend and saw he had gotten a bit taller since she met him and noticed he had fussed with his hair today. He was growing up, and one of the things she loved most about him was that he never let his disability stop him from doing what he wanted. He always found a way, and on top of that, he was such a loyal friend. With a lump in her throat, she turned to Sandy. All she could muster was a nod.

Sandy knew everybody there and was very outgoing. She was particularly good at making people feel welcome – she hugged almost every person arriving. After she had greeted new arrivals, she sat back down next to Lou and opened a pop. Turning to Lou, she said, "So tell me all about yourself. I asked my cousin Cecie about you today and she had lots of nice things to say. But one thing she said was, 'Lou might be willing to share her big story, and it's not my place to tell it.'"

Lou grinned and Sandy nudged her. "Come on, spill it."

Lou started the story of the oddities theft from Sam's store, and told it in great detail. Sandy was leaning forward to catch every word. Oliver looked over at Lou and Sandy and immediately figured out what they were talking about. He smiled because Lou loved telling the story, and Sandy seemed fascinated by it.

Sandy asked, "How did you figure out what they were doing was criminal and not just odd?"

Lou replied, "They didn't seem like the kind of people who would go for a quick fishing trip after work. Also, they were scrapping the whole time. It was very weird."

Sandy's eyes were wide with wonder. "So cool, Lou! You're so smart and observant."

Lou blushed. "My parents call it 'nosy,' but I like your idea better."

The girls were laughing as they noticed kids gathering closer to the fire. It had gotten dark, so they were loading more logs onto the fire. Others were sharpening sticks for marshmallows.

Lou decided to help search for sticks since she always had her jack knife with her and could sharpen them with it.

She came back from her expedition for the perfect sticks to find Tyler sitting in her chair. The girl he took out the night Lou babysat was sitting in his lap. It was too late for Lou to melt back into the darkness; he had already seen her.

"Oh, hey Lou, am I in your chair?" he said as he and the girl moved to get up.

Lou said, "No worries, you can stay." She was surprised at the fact that she didn't even sound weird.

Tyler shook his head and stood up. "No, it's your chair, we need to grab some sticks too. We were just catching up with Sandy." They left in search of sticks, and Lou handed the ones she had sharpened to Sandy. She gave one to Oliver so he could share with his crush.

The party went late, and when it became clear that Lou wouldn't be home in time for her curfew, she stepped away to call her parents. She begged for an extra hour and promised to bike home with a group. Her parents reluctantly agreed. Lou was happy and made a mental note to bring them coffee in bed in the morning.

Lou returned to the circle of chairs and kept talking to Sandy. They shared stories from school, about nights with their friends, about their dreams after high school. Lou added that she wanted to be an engineer. Sandy was impressed and told Lou so. Lou felt like Sandy understood her, and she felt like she got Sandy too. Though she loved being friends with Oliver and their clever banter, there are just some things only another girl could get. Her mother had always said, "Your girlfriends can last a lifetime and you should treasure them."

Sandy suddenly stopped talking and looked at something over Lou's shoulder. Lou turned to look and saw a group of people walking down the Spit towards the fire. She was a little worried because they were adults and they seemed to be focused on finding something or someone at the party. She couldn't see their faces, but they were for sure coming over to her group.

Sandy jumped up, shrieked, and started running toward the group. She leapt right up on the tallest man and clung to him. He steadied himself, laughing, and said, "Welcome home, Sandy Cat!"

The people he came with also greeted Sandy warmly. As they chattered happily, Sandy guided them to the circle of chairs, and everybody moved over and offered seats to the newcomers. Sandy introduced Lou to them and explained, "These folks are my cousins."

Lou smiled, raising an eyebrow. "All of them?"

Sandy laughed and named each of them in turn. They were older, as Lou had thought, but they blended in with the crowd and seemed to know everybody. That was one of the nice things about a smaller community, thought Lou, everybody knows each other.

The night continued with laughter, s'mores, and even some amazing fire stick juggling. Lou was having one of the best nights of her life and felt like she was settling into her new home.

Lou opened and sipped a pop, deep in thought until Sandy came over to where she was sitting and said, "Lou, I want you to meet my brother." She was dragging a very tall young man by the sleeve. "Carter, this is Lou. She's the girl Cecie was telling us about, the one who caught the guys who stole Old Sam's stuff."

Lou stood up and shook Carter's hand, "Nice to meet ya."

She saw that he was easily in his twenties and wore a cool jacket like Sandy's. He had jet black hair that was cut short and was clean shaven. His eyes were exactly like Cecie's, warm chocolate brown with long black eyelashes. Lou blurted, "How many cousins do you all have?"

Carter smiled and looked at Sandy. "Jeez, I don't even know for sure; everybody seems be related in some way in Squamish or on the reserve."

Sandy laughed and said, "You asked me the other day Lou, so I checked. There are twenty-two first cousins, forty-seven second cousins and a couple of random third cousins once removed, or something like that anyway."

Carter and Lou laughed at how sure Sandy was as she declared the family count. "She probably has that right," Carter agreed, looking at Lou. "Really it feels like we know everybody around here. It's a really tight community."

As proof, Tyler walked up to them and smacked Carter on the back and said, "Hey loser, long time no see!" Carter laughed and punched Tyler in the shoulder. They sat down and joined Sandy and Lou. They all chatted for a while, with Lou listening intently. She tried to seem cool, but she couldn't stop smiling.

Sandy leaned into Lou and said, "My family is pretty big, and it is a bit of a circus when we get together but they are great. I've missed them so much. It's just good to be back."

Lou nodded. "It was probably hard, but I bet you had to be pretty talented to get into that school. I would love to see some of your art."

Sandy smiled wide. "Be careful what you wish for, I have a lot of paintings and carvings." They both laughed and kept on talking.

Oliver came over, checking his phone. "I don't know about you, Lou, but I am going to be in some serious crap if I don't beat it home in the next five minutes."

Lou looked at her phone, shocked. She couldn't believe how fast that hour had passed. Gathering her stuff, she turned to her new friend. "Sandy, I had a really great time. Thank you so much for inviting me. Hopefully I can see those paintings soon." They hugged and Sandy went to join Carter and the rest of the gang around the fire.

When Lou turned around to fold up her chair, suddenly she heard what sounded like a horse galloping toward her, but she couldn't see it in the dark. Then she realized what it was as it careened into the circle of chairs, her dad's voice shouting from behind. "Rocky, STOP!"

Rocky pretended not to hear Mr. Dalrymple calling. He greeted Oliver and Lou and sat waiting for a treat. Lou didn't want anybody to see her dad coming to get her, so she finished packing her bike trailer and tried her best to slip away into the dark and catch her father before he barged into the party. Oliver had his chair folded up and latched onto the bike, he was ready to go. They both pedaled toward Mr. Dalrymple's voice, and Rocky followed.

Lou wasn't happy when she reached her father. "Dad, what are you doing here? I was coming home on time!"

Mr. Dalrymple's smile faded. He hadn't expected Lou to get upset. "Rocky was barking at the door, so I thought I would take him for a walk. I figured we would find you on the way home."

"Dad, I'm the only person that is getting picked up by a parent! That's so embarrassing!" Rocky leaned on Lou to calm her, but she wasn't having any of it. Her face burned, and she didn't know what to say next.

Her father tried to explain that he hadn't meant to crash the party. Rocky had seen her on the Spit, and he had taken off. Oliver reassured her, "It's cool, Lou, nobody even noticed your dad."

Lou started to calm down a little. "You're probably right, Oliver. Thanks."

By the time they had reached the path by the top of the Spit, they were talking about the container terminal they could see across the water. It was lit up, but no boats were moving. Oliver contributed his usual local knowledge. "The water is really deep in that area, so super big barges load and offload all the time. I think they carry cars and stuff, but I'm not sure."

They discussed what could possibly be transported in the containers all the way until they dropped off Oliver and headed home. Lou's dad broke the silence. "You know, Bunny, I wasn't checking up on you; your mother and I trust you completely."

Lou stopped, wondering how to make her father understand. "I know you do, dad, but I have enough trouble being seen as younger. I didn't want to be teased about having my father show up at a party."

"I'm sorry, Bunny. I wasn't thinking about it that way. Next time you go to a party, maybe take Rocky so he isn't howling all evening." He smiled and kissed her forehead.

All was well as they went into the house.

CHAPTER NINETEEN

L ou strolled out onto the patio on a bright Sunday morning. She grabbed an apple on her way and sat in a her favourite chair. She had decided to relax by writing in her notebook. When she finished updating her notes, she moved on to reading the book she had been given by Mr. Patrick.

Occasionally, she glanced up from her book to watch Rocky claiming his yard from the squirrels. Or trying to, anyway. She snickered because the squirrels taunted him mercilessly. They would throw pinecones at Rocky and he would spin around barking, but his attackers were always chattering at him from a high tree branch. Lou thought, "At least he's getting some exercise."

Later in the afternoon, she got a text from Sandy inviting her over. Lou was happy to be invited to spend some time with her. Getting out of the house was a bonus. She looked up the address as she waved over her head at her mother and was out the door.

When Lou pulled up on her bike, Sandy was already in the front yard with an easel and stool set up. Lou took off her helmet as Sandy said, "Hey, I'm glad you could come over! I'm just finishing this last bit and then we can go inside. I'm dying to show you my artwork."

Lou laughed, "I'm dying to see it!" She was gaping at Sandy's nearly-finished painting and looking up at the tree in the next yard. "So, you just look at the tree and paint it perfectly free hand?"

Sandy's cheeks got red, but she smiled. "I paint what I see. I zone out a bit and it just seems to come out of my brush."

Lou sat crossed legged on the grass and watched in fascination as Sandy's perfectly ordinary brush painted delicate green leaves and solid branches. It seemed like magic to Lou. She murmured, "Sandy, I had no idea how good you are."

The girls talked for a while as Sandy made the tree even nicer than it was in real life. Every few minutes they were interrupted by people going by on bikes or in cars, walking dogs and of course, skateboards. Some called out welcome back or some other happy greeting for Sandy. Lou realized what they had said at the party was true. Everybody did know each other.

Lou smiled at Sandy after another person passed by and waved. "It must be nice to be welcomed home like that."

Sandy stopped painting and looked thoughtful. "It is nice, I missed everybody a lot. I'd never been away for that long." She gestured at the road in front of the house. "Most of those people are members of my family. This is the main road through the rez." Lou nodded with understanding.

When Sandy started to pack up her paints, Lou jumped in to help. They went into the house carrying a big wooden box of paints, the painting, and her easel. They climbed two flights of stairs up through the house, huffing and puffing from the steep stairs. The girls walked into a room full of bright canvases. Lou gazed around the room taking in all the artwork. There were sculptures and half-finished canvases and completed paintings on every wall. The room smelled pleasantly of oil paint and turpentine.

Sandy welcomed Lou into her space, "My dad and Carter

turned this attic into a studio for me. They even put in skylights and shelves for supplies."

As Sandy was returning her paints to the shelves, Lou walked around totally immersed in Sandy's beautiful art. She turned to Sandy in awe and said, "You're an amazing artist. Your paintings make my heart happy." Sandy blushed and hugged Lou.

The girls spent the afternoon in the two huge chairs that were just old enough to be comfortable. As they ate snacks that Sandy had scrounged from the kitchen and Lou asked questions about the different landscapes Sandy had painted. Lou's favourite item was the sculpture of a small bear. She said, "It looks as if you carved each individual hair on this grizzly."

As they chatted, Sandy inquired, "when you told me about the crime you saw and solved, did you really make all that spy gear yourself?"

Lou shrugged. "It might seem a bit weird, but my hobby is designing and building whatever interests me. Usually it's surveillance stuff because I like to uncover secrets. You would be surprised what you can see when you really pay attention."

Sandy understood. "Weren't you freaked out when you were filming the guys on the boat? They could've seen you!"

Lou shook her head. "Honestly, I didn't think about it until after the whole thing was over, that's when I realized I should've been more afraid, or at least careful." She snickered awkwardly, "Usually my curiosity gets going, I lose all sense of fear, and my common sense along with it." Lou laughed at herself, and Sandy chuckled along with her.

Sandy sat up straight, her tone excited. "Hey, do you want to come to a community dinner tonight?"

Lou wasn't exactly sure what that was, but she didn't hesitate to say yes.

❖

They walked over to a huge community hall where food was already being served. There were tables of food loaded up with steaming food. There had to be a hundred people eating and chatting. Lou had never seen anything quite so festive.

Between bites, Sandy asked, "So what do you think of our Longhouse?"

Lou answered, "It's gorgeous. When you said a dinner, I didn't expect so much food, and so many people. It's awesome!"

Sandy took Lou around to be introduced to many cousins, aunties, and uncles. She hoped she wouldn't be expected to remember all their names. Carter was there, and Lou recognized some of the people from the party at the Spit.

Some of Sandy's older relatives came to introduce themselves to Lou. As most people did, they remarked on her bright red hair, "So red and curly!" Lou took it in good spirit because they were admiring rather than teasing.

Sandy leaned near her ear and whispered, "The elders are well-meaning and sweet; they just think your hair is cool." Lou laughed, and they grabbed more lemonade and chatted.

Suddenly Lou had her eyes covered with a set of hands. She startled a little and then caught on, "Who's this?" she smiled.

She heard a mischievous giggle and a fake deep voice, "it's me, the Wendigo, and I am here to drag you into my cave." The mystery hands came off her eyes, and Lou wheeled around to see a laughing Cecie.

They hugged each other. "How are you here? I thought you went back to school?" Lou asked.

Cecie held both Lou's hands and smiled widely. She said, "I live closer to Vancouver now, but I always come back for these dinners. I am a starving student, remember?"

Lou and Cecie had a quick catch up before they were inundated with aunties and cousins. Cecie was being dragged away by a little kid who wanted to show her his new toy, so they hugged again and Cecie disappeared into the crowd.

Lou decided she should go home soon, so she thanked Sandy, "This was so great; I don't think I've ever been so stuffed." They promised to get together with Oliver in the next week and have ice cream.

Even though it was a bit past sunset, it was still hot and there wasn't much breeze off the water. Lou decided once she got home, she and Rocky would make camp in the gazebo and sleep outside.

❖

The next day, Lou and Oliver decided to go to the dock and see what was going on with Tank and the suspicious boat. It was a Monday, so they figured the dock would be empty of people because the whale tours mostly operated on the weekends for tourists. When Lou and Oliver arrived, they biked all the way to the end of the dock and didn't see anybody. Before they reached Tank's boat, they slowly rode by the suspicious boat to see what they could observe.

As they passed the boat, they saw that it had been out in the water recently because it looked like the equipment had been used and just tossed everywhere. There was also a net in the water, attached to a hook. The boat was dirty, and the deck covered in muddy footprints.

Lou and Oliver looked at each other and said nothing – they didn't dare risk commenting on it and being heard by someone below deck. Continuing on, they ended up at Tank's boat. Lou hopped off her bike to see if he was around, calling out to him as she climbed onto the boat. Oliver pulled his bike around the side of the bench and transferred himself onto a seat, then he moved his bike out of the way and checked his phone while he waited.

Lou came back off the boat and plunked herself down beside Oliver. As always, she was carrying snacks in her backpack. They munched on cereal bars and chatted about nothing much. It was a beautiful day, and as far as they were concerned, this was a great way to smell the salty breeze off the ocean and sit in the sun.

Lou suddenly sat straight up and spotted movement on the *Unsinkable*. Although she could see the three figures, she couldn't tell what they were up to, so she pulled her binoculars from her backpack.

Oliver asked, "What do you see, Lou?"

Lou focused the lenses. "It's the same people we saw the first time. Two men and the older woman."

Oliver nudged her arm and chuckled. "When you're in spy mode, your voice changes to sound like an official police report."

Lou punched him in the arm and went back to her observation. While she was trying to see what the people on the boat were doing, she observed Tank stepping from the parking lot onto the dock with bags in his hands.

Lou updated Oliver, "Tank's there now. He's stopped to talk to one of the people on the boat. It doesn't look very friendly." Lou kept watching and grew increasingly alarmed. The two men stepped up onto the dock and the woman on the boat was angrily pointing at Tank. Lou couldn't make out what she was saying. She made a mental note to start learning how to lip read.

Sensing this situation might escalate, Lou grabbed an old pallet and put it right in front of Oliver and said, "Hide behind this and film what's going on through a gap. Oliver grabbed the pallet, ducked down and started recording.

Lou put down her binoculars and started to make her way closer to see if she could hear anything. She ducked behind a garbage can, and when she couldn't get a proper view, she crept along the dock to get closer. She scooted closer and tucked behind a barrel, straining to listen.

Tank was clearly holding his own against the three hostile people when he said, "Look, lady, I've been fishing off this dock for over twenty years and I've always helped everyone around here. All I was doing was offering to help you tighten up your nets! You won't catch anything with your nets set up like that."

The woman shouted, "You weren't trying to help us, you were nosing around and getting in our business!"

The two men started to take aggressive postures like they were expecting Tank to do something. Then he did. He put down what he had been carrying as a warning that he wasn't afraid of them.

Lou was having trouble keeping still, and hoped Oliver was still videoing.

The woman continued, "If you think you can take on my sons in a fight, you have another thing coming!"

The two sons were scrawny, and their filthy clothes hung off them. The angry woman had stomped across the deck to get closer Tank. She adjusted her ratty sweatshirt over her sizeable belly and pushed her sleeves up to try to intimidate him.

Tank rolled his eyes. "Lady, if I wanted to, I could toss all three of you off this dock before you had a chance to lay a hand on me. I suggest you drop it."

They knew that they didn't have a chance against Tank if he wanted to send them for a swim. He loomed over them to make his point.

The two men looked at their mother to see what they should do now. She barked, "You just mind your own business. I know which boat is yours and wouldn't want to see anything bad happen to it."

Lou heard this and covered her mouth in shock. She leaned out just a little further to get a better look and lost her balance. She tried to recover, but she just made it worse by trying to grab the barrel. The cracked barrel tipped over and Lou fell flat onto the dock.

The arguing group turned around to see what was happening. Tank picked up his stuff as Lou was scrambling to her feet. He began walking to where Lou was and then turned around to speak calmly to the three stunned people. "I would advise you to never let me find you anywhere near my boat or you'll be fish food. Got it?" He didn't wait for an answer and kept walking to check on Lou. The two men and their mother returned to grumbling among themselves as they retreated to their boat.

When Tank got to where Lou was, he said, "Missy, what exactly were you doing just now?"

Lou confessed, "Um, falling on my face."

"Not funny," said Tank, "And when we get to my boat, you had better have an explanation or I will have you scraping barnacles for the rest of the summer."

They walked toward Tank's boat and said nothing. As they approached, Oliver moved the pallet and started checking his phone. Tank looked between him and then Lou, exclaiming, "What on earth have you two been up to?"

Lou explained that they had just come to visit Tank, and when they discovered he wasn't there, they had sat down to have a snack. Lou took a sip of water and continued, "When we saw you arguing with those people, I gave Oliver a place to record from that he wouldn't be seen. We couldn't hear anything, so I went over to listen and stayed out of sight."

Tank listened to their story and shook his head. "So, it didn't occur to the two of you to just stay here and mind your own business until I showed up?"

Oliver and Lou looked at each other and at the same time said, "No sir, it didn't."

❖

Tank forgave them pretty quickly, and he poured them some iced tea. They visited until Tank needed to fix something in the engine room. Before he sent them on their way, he said, "I should put the two of you to work for your stunt, but I'll save it for another time." He winked and started pulling tools from a wooden box, muttering to himself.

As Lou and Oliver made their way off the dock, they decided that it would be a good time for an ice cream. They had apologized many times to Tank, and when he didn't want to watch the video, Oliver sheepishly put his phone in his pocket. Lou felt like she was the worst spy ever for blowing their cover.

Lou and Oliver ate their ice creams, going over all the details of what they saw and what was possibly going on with those people and that boat. Lou was going to have a lot of notes to write.

Oliver asked, "So, what are we going to do now?"

Lou popped the last of her cone in her mouth and wiped her hands on a napkin. She answered Oliver, looking him directly in the eyes, "We need to find out everything about them, and to do that, we need to come back with my surveillance gear. What else do you think we would do?"

Oliver put his head in his hand and groaned. "That's what I was afraid you were going to say."

CHAPTER TWENTY

L ou woke up on Tuesday morning to the sound of rain
tapping against her window. She listened to it for a while,
comfortable under her covers. Rocky opened one eye, but he had
no intention of getting upright, never mind wet. When Lou
tugged on his tail to see if he was awake, he rolled over on his
back and snored.

The house was quiet and Lou didn't have to go to work until
noon, so she decided to update her notes from yesterday. She
flipped to a new page and wrote, "Sketchy Fishing Boat People."
Then she began her description of what happened and what she
and Oliver witnessed. She checked back in her earlier rough notes
she had made about them before. She wrote everything out in
more detail and adding a list of possible crimes. Then, as she was
planning her next trip to the dock and which of her spy devices
she was going to need, her father knocked on her door.

"Morning, Lou. I heard you moving around, so I figured you
were awake," he said as he poked his head into the room. "I'm
going out for groceries and then to get an oil change. I'll see you
when you get home from work, okay?"

"Okay, Dad, see you later," Lou said with more dismissal than
she had meant to. She was building a plan and a diagram that was

fully engaging her brain. The more she thought about the incident on the dock yesterday, the more she believed those people were hiding something. Her next day off was Friday, so she made a note to get her gear ready and head out early that day.

Lou dug around in the fridge, finding bacon and eggs, and decided she would cook herself a big breakfast to prepare for a heavy day at the store. She was going to attempt some sort of inventory; it would be an exhausting day. As she was cooking the bacon, she was not surprised that Rocky followed the smell into the kitchen.

She opened the door to let him outside and said, "So, it takes a snoot full of bacon smell to get you up and going, huh?"

He reluctantly went out in the rain to pee but was back in under a minute. Lou let him back in and laughed. "You always pee super-fast when the weather's bad."

Rocky shook himself and then sat down in a straight back and alert position awaiting his bacon. Lou held his muzzle and placed a slice of greasy bacon on his snout. He knew the drill; he could only eat it when Lou said okay.

Lou held out her finger and said, "Wait."

Rocky was vibrating right down to his tail. He was focusing so hard on the bacon his eyes were crossed, and yet he waited.

Lou took a deep breath and said, "Okay!"

He flipped his snout up, sending the bacon strip in the air. Quick as a snap, he caught it and swallowed it whole before Lou even saw it land in his mouth. Lou laughed and scratched his head. "If you weren't a dog, you could be a juggler. Did you even taste that?"

Rocky tilted his head to the side as if questioning if she had more treats. When she wasn't putting anything else on his nose, he went to the stove and licked any grease droplets he found that tasted like bacon.

❖

Lou arrived at work ten minutes early and parked her bike. She took off her helmet and walked into the store, calling out, "Sam, I'm here!"

Sam came out of the Oddities room with a clipboard and was writing something on the paper. He looked like he was concentrating hard.

He seemed confused when he first saw Lou but quickly snapped out of it. "Oh, yes, of course you are here, it's Tuesday." He put down his clipboard, tucked his pencil behind his ear and continued, "You are always on time, girl. I think that's just grand."

Lou smiled and put her backpack behind the counter. "I like to be prompt, Sam. You don't pay me to be late." Lou liked to be on time to everything, but for sure she didn't want to let Sam down. She knew she had a big list of things to do before school started again. Hopefully, Sam might let her work the occasional weekend through the winter if the store stayed open.

It was about halfway through the afternoon when they decided to take a break. Sam and Lou had been trying to count and track what he had stored in all the nooks and cupboards, and there were many. To Lou, it seemed like an impossible task, but Sam hardly cared a bit about how long it would take, so they carried on. As they sat having a lemonade, they went over the list of items they had identified and written down. Lou kept thinking that this was a new idea for him. She hadn't found any papers that had lists of the stuff he was selling.

Lou's dad walked into the store and stared at the shelves loaded with antiques and dusty parts collected off boats from as far back as the 1800s. When he spotted the Lou and Sam sitting on their stools at the counter, he smiled and said, "Are you two goofing off, or is this what you do all day?"

Lou put her lemonade down, surprised to see their visitor. "What are you doing here, Dad?" She was smiling because her dad was visiting her at work, and she felt very grown up.

Mr. Dalrymple leaned against a bookcase and answered, "I

223

needed to go to the hardware store up the road, so I decided to come and poke around this nifty place."

Sam smiled, pleased with his response. "You are more than welcome to dig around to look at anything you want. Oh, and as a family member of a staff person, you get fifty percent off anything in the store."

Lou looked at her dad and raised her eyebrows. He looked at Sam. "That is very generous, Sam, it must put a dent in your profits to offer such a deal to your employees."

Sam chuckled and shook his head. "Well, I don't rightly know if it will, I've never had an employee before."

The three of them had a good laugh and chatted for a while longer. When her dad asked Lou what they were working on she answered, "Inventory, and I'm pretty sure it will take all summer. We write down the category of items and count them, then we enter the numbers on a log. It's pretty manual."

Lou's dad thought this was a good opportunity to remind her of his idea. "You know, it would be really simple to do this in a program that tracks inventory and price, and loads it all into a bookkeeping software. That way Sam could get a handle on what is in the store, and how much profit he makes every year."

Lou was busy pulling a box off a shelf and her dad offered to help her take it down. When he looked at the items inside, he put it down quickly and looked excited. He picked up an item and dusted it off with his sleeve. "Lou, do you know what this is?"

Lou shook her head, "No, Sam hasn't taught me the names of this boat stuff yet. What is it?"

Mr. Dalrymple pulled out another item and explained, "These are sextants. They're a relic from way back in the old times when sailors used them to navigate the seas. This is how they figured out where they were headed long before we had radar and satellite to tell boats how to reach places." He pulled out two more and exclaimed, "There has to be twenty of these in this box!"

Sam came around the corner. "Oh, you found those gadgets.

I've had them for ages. I suppose we should count them and dust them off. They're pretty old, I would say."

Lou suggested they should be on display so they could get more attention from customers. Sam agreed. "Good idea, dear, maybe put them in the glass case in the Oddities room?"

Lou and her dad took the box to the back room and polished them up.

Once the sextants were nicely displayed in the case, Lou's father spent some time looking at every item in the room. He knew what everything was. Lou was curious. "Dad, I know you're kind of an antique nerd, but these are pretty obscure old things. How do you know what they all are?"

He held up and examined something that looked like a Halloween mask with electric wires sticking out of it as he answered Lou. "When you've been fascinated with old weird things your whole life, you learn a thing or two. I have to admit that I have no clue what this is." Then he put it on his face and barked, "BOO!"

A few customers came in over the course of the day, and Sam chatted with every one of them. Some people bought items and others just browsed. The store was never very busy, but when people were antique hunters and found that special treasure they wanted, they would pay almost any price.

Sam, Lou, and her dad worked together for the afternoon. When they were leaving Sam said, "Thanks for your help today, Mervin! Good job to you too, Lou! Here's your pay." She put the envelope of money in her back pocket and they waved on the way out the door.

Her bike loaded into the van, they drove away, waving to Sam. Lou looked at her dad. "Now do you get why I said he needed help? It's too much for him to manage without somebody to be there and keeping an eye on the orders and helping customers. He is a whiz at acquiring cool things, he seems to know everybody, and the phone rings all day. But I am worried he is going to lose track of stuff."

Mr. Dalrymple nodded, deep in thought. He muttered, "I know just the thing." Before Lou could ask him what his idea was, they were parked in their driveway and Rocky had stuck his head in Lou's open window, licking the whole side of her head.

Lou jumped with shock, "Rocky! How do you get out of the back yard?" She wiped the drool of her face and said to her Dad, "Mom isn't home, so maybe he let himself out of the back gate."

After giving Rocky a firm warning about getting out of the yard, they stepped out on the back deck and had a bowl of chips and pops. Lou's dad texted her mom to grab supper on her way home.

Lou asked, "What was your idea for Sam's store?"

Her dad perked up. "In my job before, I had customers who had problems tracking all the things they sold and other issues just like Sam has. I remembered a system we sold to them. I can get a free version of that software for Sam, but not with all the bells and whistles but it would work."

Lou thought about it for a second, "Wouldn't he need a computer and somebody to set everything up for him? I don't think he would want to learn a how to use software. He likes his paper system."

"I know, Lou, it's hard to get somebody to change a lifelong habit. He could actually keep his paper system, and the computer-based one can be used at the same time. It will take you both all summer to do the inventory anyway. As long as I don't have a job, I would be willing to help load things on the computer. All I need is the paper records as you do them each week. I have an old laptop that would do just fine."

"You would help Sam get all his stuff organized?" she asked, stunned.

Mr. Dalrymple smiled. "I can volunteer until I get a full-time job. I have to keep my skills sharp while I'm waiting." He took a sip of soda and continued, "All you would need to do is bring home all the papers on Thursday nights, and I'll send you back with them entered into the system on Tuesday."

Lou considered this but was still a little worried. "Do you think Sam would want this? He might be happy with the system he has."

Her dad hadn't considered that Sam might not accept the help. "He might not want it," her dad shrugged as he looked at Lou, "But we can offer and see where it goes."

Rocky was bored with all the talking, so he dropped a soccer ball onto Lou's lap. She rolled her eyes but stood up. "Okay, big lad, let's go for a walk to the dog park and you can bug the other dogs with your ball."

As they were getting ready to leave, Lou turned to her dad and said, "It was nice to have your help today, and it's really cool that you would volunteer to help Sam."

Her dad reached out to ruffle her hair. "I just want to be kind; it isn't a big deal."

But Lou knew it was.

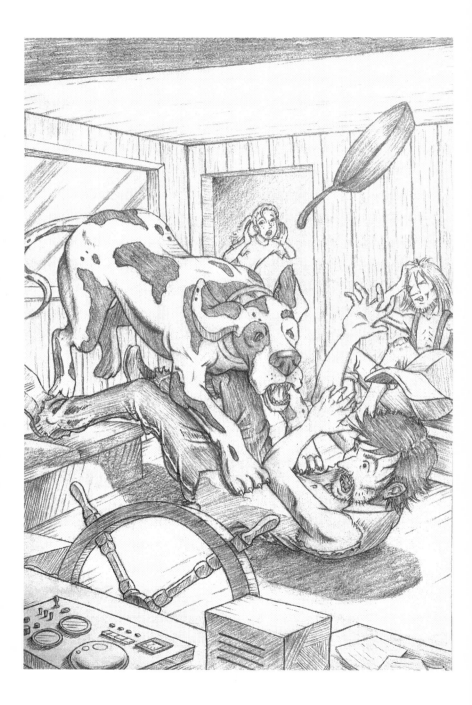

CHAPTER TWENTY-ONE

Lou texted Oliver first thing in the morning. It was Friday, and they both had the day off. Lou felt she had been working for ages without a break — but it wasn't ages, she was just tired from three long days of hard, dusty work.

They had made progress sorting boxes at the store. Sam was more than happy to have his bookkeeping put on a computer as long as he could also keep his old paper system. Lou smiled to herself, remembering how Sam reacted to getting a computer and her dad showing him what it could do for his store. His eyes had danced with excitement. He had also been pretty happy to have the extra company.

It took Oliver a bit to respond to her text, but Lou wasn't worried; she knew he was a late riser if given the chance to sleep in. She used the time to select her gear for the day. For sure, she needed the periscope, the cup camera, and—just in case—her lock picking set. When she was all set, she decided it was time for Oliver to get up. She texted him again before she and Rocky set out for his house. *"Get up, lazy bum! We have stuff to do today."*

Oliver responded, *"Ya, Ya, I'm up. You coming over?"*

Lou quickly wrote back *"On my way"* and pulled her bike out of the garage. Rocky was doing his impatient dance in the yard, anxious to head out to wherever they were going.

When Lou and Rocky got to Oliver's house, his mom was working in the garden. Lou greeted her. "Hi Mrs. Bamberg! Your garden looks great. Is Oliver ready yet?"

Oliver's mom had been crouched down as she struggled with a particularly stubborn weed. Rocky saw her pulling on it when they arrived. When Oliver's mom turned to speak to Lou, Rocky grabbed the weed in his mouth and yanked it straight out of the ground. He showered Mrs. Bamberg and himself with dirt as he shook it like he was trying to shake the stuffing out of a pillow.

Lou dropped her bike, shouting, "Rocky, drop it!"

Rocky automatically opened his mouth, and the weed dropped out and fell to the ground. He had a snout covered in dirt and looked quite proud of himself. He had made a huge mess, and Lou was frantic. "I'm so sorry! He just wanted to help." Rocky laid down and grumbled a little.

But Mrs. Bamberg was laughing as she brushed the dirt out of her hair and stood up to dust herself off. As she finished getting the last bits of dirt off her face, she smiled at Lou. "That dog is so funny! Oliver says he's practically human." Then she turned to Rocky and said, "Thank you for the help with that weed, Rocky. I didn't know gardening was among your talents!"

Lou shook her head. "Sometimes I wonder about that dog." They were both smiling when the garage door opened, and Oliver rode out on his bike.

He grinned and waved hello. "Hey, Lou! What are we up to today?"

Oliver's hair was still wet from his shower. Lou noticed when he popped his helmet on. "You're going to have a serious case of helmet hair by the time we get to the dock," she teased. He shrugged and put on his biking gloves.

Oliver and Lou spent a few more minutes chatting with his

mom and cleaning off Rocky's face. When they were ready to go, Mrs. Bamberg said, "Have a good day you two." Lou and Oliver waved and were off with the big dog loping along behind them.

Oliver asked, "What's the plan, Lou?" He was pretty sure he knew what the plan might be, considering that Lou had said they were going to look further into what was going on with those people who were nasty to Tank.

Lou answered, "I think we can figure more about those people on the dock if we get ourselves in position early enough. We should be able to watch what they're doing." Oliver rolled his eyes, but really, he loved Lou's adventurous plans and was excited to spy on the bad guys.

They pulled up to the top of the dock and were surprised that there were so many people there. It looked like everybody had decided to clean or do maintenance on their boats that day. Lou and Oliver immediately spotted the three people they were there to watch. They were busy repairing a net on the dock.

Lou looked at Oliver. "I have to get close enough to hear what they are saying to each other." She thought for a minute and mulling over ideas of how to get closer to them.

Oliver tapped her arm. "I have an idea. You can get as far as that boat over there, nobody is on it." He pointed at the boat berthed two away from the *Unsinkable*. "And how about Rocky and I tuck into the bushes up here and watch through the binoculars? If something goes down, I'll start a video on my phone."

Lou looked at her path and decided that the people on the dock would provide enough cover for her to make it to the empty boat. She agreed. "Okay, that should work."

Rocky and Oliver hid behind the shrubs, and Lou handed Oliver her binoculars. She told Rocky to lie down, which was an order he followed enthusiastically.

Lou put on her backpack and set out for the suspicious boat.

She kept an eye on her suspects and kept behind people walking on the dock to stay out of their line of vision. She crouched down behind a big water barrel and peeked around it.

A lady carrying a big cooler walked by Lou and gave her an odd look. Lou smiled and said, "I'm playing hide and seek." Seemingly convinced, the woman carried on down the dock, and Lou slipped out and used the lady as cover by following closely behind until she was able to duck onto the empty boat. As she hopped aboard, she noticed a tarp that she could crawl underneath and sit under comfortably and unseen.

Lou took off her backpack and set it down. The tarp was attached to the side of the boat with snaps. As she undid one of them to make a space for her to stick her head out, it dawned on her that she might get in trouble for trespassing. She shoved that thought out of her mind and decided she would take the risk anyway.

Popping her head out, Lou quickly realized the camera cup wasn't going to work, it would get stuck under the tarp. She dug around and found her periscope, satisfied that it would do the trick for watching what was going on.

Lou had been thrilled with how well her periscope turned out. It was a former plastic wrap box that she'd taken the cardboard roll out of and cut square holes in the sides at the top and bottom. Mirrors had been taped into it at perfect angles to see around corners and over walls, or in this case, over the side of a boat.

She pulled her phone out of her pocket and got ready to deploy "Operation Unsinkable."

Lou hit record on her phone and positioned her periscope at just the right angle. She raised them both up just above the tarp. Lou noticed that if the people on the *Unsinkable* looked carefully, they would see a plastic wrap box and half a cell phone peeking out of the edge of the tarp. She tried not to worry about it too much and kept her mind on the task at hand.

The three suspects were working on nets and one of the men seemed to be talking on some sort of old-fashioned looking radio. Lou had never seen anything like it, the thing was huge, especially compared to the little walkie talkies she had.

She could tell they were agitated and nervous by how they were rushing around and griping at each other. The older woman was keeping her voice low as she gave orders to the guy on the radio. Lou could hear a bit of it. "Tell them we'll be ready tonight."

Then the woman looked over at the other man and pointed an angry finger at him. "I swear, if you mess up one more thing, I will cut you out of the deal, Joey!"

Joey looked up at her and said, "Don't worry Ma, I won't make the same mistake as last time, you can count on me."

Lou was hoping the microphone was picking all of this up. The more she watched, the more she was convinced that they were up to something pretty serious. It looked like whatever they were planning was a big deal and they didn't want to make any mistakes.

The guy that was on the radio switched it off and turned to the two others. "They are ready and will have the crane calibrated to lift the maximum of its capacity in case we get a male."

Joey made a strained face and said, "Shelton, what does calibrated mean?"

Shelton threw a pen at him. "It means that the crane will do the job, moron. Now write down this list so you can go get some supplies. Let me and Ma do the thinking around here!"

Lou figured she would be pushing her luck by staying any longer. The last thing she wanted was to get caught spying. She packed up her gear and crept out of her hiding spot. She could see Oliver had the binoculars focused on her, so she gave him a thumbs up.

Nobody noticed her getting out from under the tarp or jumping off the unoccupied boat onto the dock. She walked normally so she wouldn't draw attention to herself, but really, she wanted to run to tell Oliver what she heard and saw.

As she approached Oliver, she bumped into Tank.

"Well hello, Lou!" He noticed her looking around, and followed her gaze to see Oliver and Rocky, who was slowly waking up from his nap. Tank smiled. "The whole gang is here! You want some iced tea? I just made a fresh batch."

Lou and Oliver looked at each other and were about to decline politely, but Rocky seemed to clue in that Tank was offering something that he understood as 'cookie.' Rocky was on his feet in a second, sprinting down the dock towards Tank's boat. Oliver and Lou chuckled and accepted Tank's offer.

They settled in and were grateful for the iced tea. Somehow Rocky had a dog chew in his mouth and laid down to munch on it. Lou suspected Tank had supplied his pocket with dog treats and was slipping them to Rocky. She smiled winked at Tank.

Knowing he was busted feeding Rocky, he quickly asked, "Have you had any more problems with the three Musketeers over there?" Lou asked as she pointed behind herself.

Tank took a big swig of his drink and shook his head. "Nothing at all. They're keeping to themselves, but they sure keep odd hours. This week I slept on my boat and heard them leaving after eleven at night. They didn't get back 'till sunrise."

Lou considered this. "Is there any type of fishing you would do in the middle of the night?"

"Not any that I can think of," Tank answered. "For sure, nothing the Fisheries agents would approve of anyway."

There was a moment of silence. All of them contemplating the strange comings and goings of the boat and its crew. Then Oliver piped up. "What if they're hunting seals? Do people still do that?"

Tank frowned. "Unlikely. If that's what they're doing, that would be real illegal. Seal hunts in Canada have only been allowed in very special cases, and not much around here."

They chatted a bit about the local area and the different types of fishing and hunting. Lou thought of a question she had forgotten to ask earlier. "What goes on in that big building, the one across the water from the Spit?"

Tank settled in, gearing up for a big lesson. He gestured with his unlit cigar and leaned back on the bench. "That's actually a group of companies and they run a container terminal." Lou gave him a questioning look. He continued, "That dock is where huge barges come and go with cargo. They load big metal containers full of stuff coming into Canada or going out to other countries on the barges. Trains and trucks deliver the containers by land, to ship them out, or pick them up from the terminal and bring them to stores and really anywhere. The ships are loaded and unloaded by the cranes you would have seen."

"So that's what we saw from across the water on the Spit? Cranes and barges?" asked Lou, thinking about something that she wasn't saying.

Tank nodded and Oliver answered, "It can be hard to see details of the terminal from the Spit. We did get to go to the terminal on a class trip in grade five. It was super cool, and so huge!"

Lou made a note to herself to research how that terminal works. She was fascinated.

The morning turned to afternoon and the trio were still chatting wildly thanks to Lou's insistent and detailed questions. When it was finally time to go, they thanked Tank for the drinks and headed off the dock and back to solid land. As they passed the suspicious boat, they noticed it was all closed up, but based on the mumbling voices they could hear, the suspects were definitely on it.

When they got off the dock and were out of earshot of anybody, Lou started excitedly chattering about what she had observed when she spied on the *Unsinkable*. She hadn't had a chance to update Oliver before, and she was desperate to tell him.

They stopped at the park so Lou could play back the recording. She hoped the phone had caught what she heard, but it wasn't great. At least it was clearer when their voices were raised.

"Ma, we haven't got one in all these nights, are we gonna do this all summer?"

"I brought you two dummies along to do the liftin' not the thinkin'.

"Do we have the stronger sedative I sent ya fer?"

As they listened, Oliver became wide eyed. "How do you even find these people, Lou? I mean, clearly they are up to something, and again you nailed it!"

"I think I just have a nose for mysteries and conspiracies. So, did you notice the bizarre phone or radio or whatever it was?"

"I did," Oliver answered. "It looked like a phone my Uncle had in the early 90s! It must have weighed five pounds at least. But I don't think it was a phone though, the guy used it more like a radio."

Lou screwed up her face, thinking hard. "Who would use such old tech? I mean, who even has that stuff anymore? Even weirder, who was he talking to?"

"Good question, Lou. I can't imagine," mused Oliver.

They continued home, still floating theories about what could be going on down at the dock. When they got to Oliver's house, he asked Lou, "I have to go to Vancouver for a doctor's appointment on Monday, do you want to come? My mom said we could go do something fun afterward."

Lou accepted right away. "For sure! I haven't spent much time in Vancouver yet, I'd love to see any of it. I'm in!"

Oliver was thrilled. "Great! I'll text you tomorrow to let you know what time we're leaving."

They said their goodbyes, and Lou headed home. When she arrived, she hugged both her parents. She was remembering how terrible the people she heard talking were to each other, and she was glad for her family.

They had a pleasant conversation over dinner, and Lou got permission to go to Vancouver with Oliver on Monday. Then she described a short version of her experience at the dock with the occupants of the *Unsinkable*, deciding to leave out the part where she hid on a random boat. Still, Lou's mother was alarmed. "Are you getting yourself into another dangerous situation?"

Lou's dad chimed in, "You can't save everybody, Lou, and you certainly aren't qualified to solve crimes. Sergeant Preston even warned you about getting caught up with bad people. They can be serious criminals!"

Lou knew that was what they were going to say. She held up her hand and said, "I promise, you guys, I won't get too involved. What I saw might be nothing. Besides, Tank keeps an eye on them too."

Lou noticed that when she left the kitchen, her parents were having an animated conversation. She knew it was about her.

Saturday morning, Lou decided to swing by the dock before work. Rocky was by her side, as always. Lou told herself she just wanted to thank Tank for the hospitality, but really, she wanted to check up on the *Unsinkable*.

She walked her bike out onto the dock toward Tank's berth and slowed down as she passed the *Unsinkable*. The tarps were off it, and it looked like it had recently been out to sea. Wet nets were piled on the deck and there were food wrappers and empty beer cans scattered everywhere. They didn't seem to be there. Lou didn't know what to think as she carried on to Tank's boat.

She set down her bike and took off her helmet next to the bollard that his boat was tied to. She noticed that his boat was moving and bobbing more than any of the other boats that were tied to the dock. Then Rocky grumbled deep in his throat. Lou put her hand on his neck to settle him, and she peeked in a window.

There they were — Joey, Shelton, and their mother — rummaging through Tank's stuff. They seemed to be looking for something and weren't making an effort to hide it, throwing his things everywhere.

Rocky jumped onto the boat before Lou could stop him and barked at the boat door. Lou tried to call him off. "Rocky come!"

He ignored her and kept barking and scratching at the door. Joey opened it before his mother could tell him not to, and Rocky ran inside. He knocked Joey onto the table pinning him with his paws. Before Lou could make her way in, Shelton picked up the first thing he could find, a frying pan, and lifted it above Rocky's head. Lou was standing in the doorway and saw what was about to happen.

She screamed, "Rocky, look out!" Rocky spun around just in time to lunge at Shelton and knock him over. He went flying and landed hard onto his back. The frying pan flew out of his hand and suddenly he had a massive dog standing over him growling just a few centimeters from his face. A big drop of drool fell onto his cheek, but he didn't dare wipe it.

Nobody was moving. Rocky was growling and still had two paws on Shelton's chest. Joey spoke first with a shaky voice. "Ma, what do we do?"

Just at that moment the boat bobbed in the water and Tank appeared behind Lou in the doorway. It took him a hot second to recognize these characters. He was glad to see Rocky had them terrified. Tank remained calm as he asked, "What exactly are you three fart-catchers doing on my boat?"

Rocky growled one more time and stepped off Shelton's chest as he went over to stand by Lou's side. She petted him silently and watched the drama unfolding in front of them.

Shelton stood up, as did Joey. Their mother was standing beside Tank's desk with her mouth moving, but nothing came out. She had two handfuls of papers that she quickly tucked behind her back.

She spoke up. "We was just looking to borrow a map of the waters, but you weren't here so we tried to..." Her voice trailed off because she hadn't been expecting him to come back so soon. She could see he didn't believe one word she was saying.

Tank put down the box he was carrying and faced her. "I know who you are, Eugenia Dumphries."

The woman looked shocked to hear Tank say her name.

Tank explained, "It took me a bit of digging to find out because nobody around here knew who you were, but I had to find out who was behind the fake company that bought the *Unsinkable*." He stepped closer to her, and she dropped the papers. He pointed in her face. "I don't know what you people are doing here, but it's not running whale watching tours or fishing. And I don't give a rip why you were digging through my boat. But I can tell you that if you come anywhere near my berth again, it will end with a long march off a short dock for the three of ya!"

Shelton recovered a little of his courage, puffing his chest out as he said, "You should watch your own self, mister!"

"Mister!" Tank took three big steps and they were face to face. Shelton realized that Tank was solid muscle and twice as wide as him. When Tank rolled up his sleeves, Shelton made a weak squeaking noise.

Tank sneered at him and scoffed, "Yeah, that's what I thought, you're just a scrawny chicken." He turned, looking at the rest of them, and shouted, "Get off my boat!"

The three trespassers stumbled out as fast as they could without another word, with Rocky right behind them growling. When they sprinted down the dock back to their boat, Rocky gave another bark to warn them not to come back. Then he went back inside and leaned against Lou.

As Tank looked around, Lou sat down and asked, "What the

heck was that all about? I just rode up to your boat, and I caught them in here. They scared me to death!"

Tank scratched his head. "I have no idea what they thought would be useful on board my boat, but I will try to figure it out. My guess is that they were looking for notes on where I've had luck with fish."

Lou helped Tank tidy the boat and peppered him with questions about his theories, his research, and anything else she could get out of him about the Dumphries.

Tank, not being the same kind of suspicious person that Lou was, summed his thoughts up. "I think they're just petty criminals who are too dopey to get into anything serious. It was a pretty amateur move rifling through my boat when they're only ten berths down the dock from me."

Lou worried she would be late for work, so she hurried picking up Tank's papers. As she stepped out of the cabin, she found Rocky fast asleep in the sunshine on the prow of the boat. She got him up and said goodbye to Tank as she and her dog rushed up the dock. They walked past the *Unsinkable* and saw it was closed up tight. The Dumphries weren't showing their faces.

"Good thing!" thought Lou as she set off to the store, Sam would be expecting her.

The next day, Lou couldn't wait to tell Oliver about the incident on the boat the morning before. She sent him a text, *"You won't believe what went down yesterday! You busy today?"*

Oliver answered, *"Sandy's coming over. Want to join? Come at two."*

Sandy and Oliver were in the front yard tossing a football when Lou and Rocky walked up to them. Rocky saw Oliver had the football in his hand, so he ran over and sat down in front of him, waiting for him to throw it.

Oliver laughed. "Are you a linebacker now, Rocky?"

Rocky stood up and wagged his tail.

Oliver looked him in the eye, sizing him up. "Well, you look ready for action. Go get it!" He threw the ball as hard as he could. Rocky went tearing across the yard, trying to keep his eye on the ball. When it started to come down, Rocky jumped and caught it.

Oliver and the girls cheered, "Woohoo!!"

Rocky came over to Oliver and dropped the ball in his lap to get him to throw it again. Oliver picked up the ball by its end with two fingers. It was covered in drool.

"Maybe another time, Rocky," Oliver muttered, dropping the wet ball before wiping his hand on his pants.

Sandy and Lou were laughing as Rocky grabbed the ball and proudly carried it around the yard.

Oliver finished cleaning his hand and called out, "Let's go, I'm craving a banana split."

When they were settled with their ice creams at their usual picnic table in the park, Lou filled them in on the day she had. "You guys won't believe this!" she started. As she told a detailed account of the drama on Tank's boat, she also told Sandy about what she and Oliver had seen when they had been there. Only when she was done did Lou finally take a breath and look at the two rapt listeners.

Sandy was the first to speak. "You must have been so scared, Lou!"

Lou shrugged. "Honestly, it went so fast I didn't have time to be scared, not much anyway. It was on my way home after work that it finally hit me, and I was shaking when I got to my house."

Oliver piped in wide-eyed, "Did you tell your parents all this?"

Lou looked down. "I haven't said anything yet. I know the kind of trouble I would be in, so I want to pick a good time to tell them."

Sandy shook her head. "With that story, there probably isn't a great time to tell your parents you were stuck on a boat with people who were going to smash a frying pan on Rocky's head. What if this Tank guy hadn't shown up when he did?"

They were all quiet after that, trying to think of ways that Lou could tell her parents and not get grounded for the rest of the summer. They couldn't think of a single thing.

CHAPTER TWENTY-TWO

As planned, Lou and Oliver headed to Vancouver for Oliver's doctor appointment. They sat in the back seats as Mrs. Bamberg drove.

"What do you guys want for music?" asked Mrs. Bamberg.

Oliver looked at Lou for the answer, so she said, "I'm good with pretty much anything."

Oliver's mom smiled and before Oliver could give his opinion, she said, "Eighties it is then!" Oliver sighed heavily as Lou started bopping her head to the B52s.

It was a beautiful day for a drive. Lou was gazing out the window when Oliver declared, "I'm having an awesome summer. How about you, Lou? Do you miss Halifax?"

Lou turned to look at him. "Maybe a little, but I'm pretty happy with my new life, and my new best friend." She reached over and squeezed Oliver's hand, and he blushed hard. Mrs. Bamberg watched the scene in her rearview mirror and grinned.

They parked at the clinic and went in for the appointment. The wait wasn't long before Oliver and his mother were called in. Lou wished Oliver good luck as he rolled into the doctor's exam room.

While she was sitting in the waiting room, Lou had time to

pull out her notebook. She reviewed all the details of what happened on the dock and wrote down a few questions as they came to mind.

1. 1.Why are they only taking the boat out at night?
2. 2.What is the story behind the fake company name?
3. 3.Tank's boat search, why?
4. 4.Where did they come from and why Squamish?

She tapped her pen against her lips and stared out the window at the Vancouver skyline, completely lost in thought about the mysterious boat crew. She snapped out of it and was about to make a list of theories when Oliver and his mother came out of the doctor's room. Lou put her notebook back in her bag and asked, "How did it go?"

Oliver motioned her to hurry up. "I'm starving. I'll fill you in over lunch."

Lou jumped to her feet, saying, "That works for me, I could eat roadkill right now!"

Oliver laughed. "Hey Mom, you know any place that serves flat squirrel?"

Mrs. Bamberg pretended to think for a moment before she responded, "As it happens, I do know a place near here. They call it the Bistro du Rodent, very fancy."

Lou and Oliver thought she was serious for a second, but when they figured out she was teasing them, they laughed and started making an imaginary menu.

Lou started the game. "I will order roasted squirrel on a bed of lettuce."

Oliver replied, "I could really go for boiled rat on a stick." This went on for a while until they entered a real restaurant. Oliver shook his head as he looked at the food options. "Look at the menu, Lou. Not one rodent dish to be found. Unacceptable."

This offered no end of amusement for the whole meal. When

they were done, Oliver's mom gave them a choice. "So, you two, would you like to go to the art museum, the science centre, or the space observatory?"

Both of them answered at the same time. "Science centre!"

After they pulled into the parking lot of the science centre, Oliver opened the side door of the van and Lou went to the back doors to pull out his chair and bring it around to where Oliver was waiting. Lou expected him to slide over, but instead he held onto the handle in the van, took three labored steps, and sat in his chair. Lou stared, "That's awesome, Oliver!"

Adjusting himself in the chair, he explained, "I've been able to do that for a while. The doctor reminded me I should be taking steps whenever I can, even when I'm not at physiotherapy."

Lou was full of admiration. "I think it's awesome, and now I plan to nag you about it when I see you being lazy!"

Oliver rolled his eyes. "Oh great, that'll be so much fun with you watching me like a hawk."

Oliver's mom got out of the van and handed him some money. "Treat Lou for the day. There is enough there for your entry fee and a snack later. I'm going to visit a friend who lives near here. Just text me when you're done."

Lou began to object, pulling out some bills of her own to show she could pay her own way, but Oliver said, "Don't bother. My mom's very stubborn when she wants to treat somebody."

Lou reluctantly put her money away. "Thank you, Mrs. Bamberg. That's super nice of you."

As Oliver's mom drove off waving, she thought to herself, "Those two are such great pals."

❖

Lou and Oliver spent the afternoon exploring all the displays. They ended up on the top floor and instead of turning to see the dinosaur and biology area, they wound up in a hallway

247

that led to a small section called 'The Science of Criminal Investigation.'

Lou stopped dead. "Oliver! Look at that sign!"

Oliver said sarcastically, "Yes, Lou, I can read." He thought about saying something else, but she was already gone. He took off after her.

He found her looking at a wall of jars behind glass, her nose practically jammed up against it. When Oliver pulled up to get a better look, he curled his lip in disgust. "That looks so gross, Lou, what's in that jar?"

Lou didn't look over at Oliver, she just kept staring at a jar with a bizarre looking creature floating in it. She explained, "Early scientists and criminal investigators used dead animals to study when bugs formed on the cadavers. It helped them figure out how long murdered, or I suppose any dead people really had been dead."

"That's disgusting." Oliver grimaced.

Lou quipped, "No, it's science."

Lou examined every jar, and Oliver only looked at the ones that didn't have animals floating in them. For a second, he thought he glimpsed a human finger in one of the jars, but looked away quickly.

They moved on to look at the wall displaying investigative tools. Oliver was bored, so he just went over to check out the microscopes you could use to look at samples of bacteria.

Lou was fascinated with the hidden cameras and listening bugs that had been used by detectives in the olden days. The modern devices used by detectives to catch criminal operations got her attention. When Oliver came to find her, she was writing furiously in her notebook.

When she didn't notice him, he tapped her on the arm. "Hey, detective, ready for a snack?"

Lou snapped her notebook closed. "For sure. I pretty much have notes on everything, so we can go."

248

While they were eating their snacks, Oliver asked, "So, what're you going to do with all the information you have on the dock people?"

Lou looked miserable. "I don't even know what to think, Oliver. What if I tell my parents, or even Sergeant Preston about what I think I saw, and they laugh at me, or worse get mad and ground me?"

Oliver looked serious. "They wouldn't laugh at you. They might give you an earful for getting yourself into another bonkers situation, but your parents are decent."

Lou cheered up a little. "I really can't just forget the whole thing and keep it to myself. What if it turned out something seriously sketchy was actually happening? These people are mean, and they could be up to anything. I just have a gut feeling that all this is bad."

Oliver was munching on a piece of licorice and waved it at her to make a point. "It could be that they're fishing illegally. All you would need to do is call the Fisheries people, or maybe the Coast Guard, and tell them. They would check it out for sure."

Lou considered Oliver's suggestion, wondering to herself whether she had enough information to take to the authorities. It was a good idea, but she felt she needed more proof. "What if we watched where they went at night to see if we can tell what they're doing?"

Oliver almost choked on his licorice. "Are you nuts?" he exclaimed. "Your parents would kill you for sneaking out at night, never mind spying on criminals. Besides, you'd need a boat."

Lou hadn't considered that. Then she lit up, "Tank would take us if we asked."

"What do you mean *us*, Lou?"

Lou looked surprised. "Wouldn't you want to help me?"

Oliver softened. "Lou, you know I always have your back, no matter how batty your plans are. I just know my mother would lose her mind if I snuck out. I'd be grounded for at least a month and she'd put all my gaming stuff in the basement forever."

Lou nodded her understanding, but looked resolute as she stated, "I'm going to do it. I'll ask Tank to take me out on his boat and see what they're up to. That way, an adult goes with me and sees what I see. If it's nothing, then I had a cool nighttime boat ride, but if it is something, then I can prove it."

Oliver shook his head. "You are really something, Lou. I don't know if I should be scared for you or proud of you."

Lou smiled. "Be proud of me, you won't regret it."

CHAPTER TWENTY-THREE

L ou worked at the store as usual for the next few days. She and Sam were making progress on their organizing and dusting. Lou's father came in for a bit each day to continue setting up the bookkeeping system. Lou would peek over his shoulder once in a while to see what she could figure out. Her plan was to work during the school year to make sure Sam's books stayed in order.

After work, she took a detour and rode down to the dock. She wanted to see if Tank would help her find out what the *Unsinkable* crew was up to late at night. She figured the chances were slim, but she had to try. Lou was happy to find Tank up a ladder working on his boat, and she greeted him warmly as she pulled up on her bike. "Hey, Tank, what are you up to?"

He answered, "Just shenanigans," chuckling at his own joke.

He was sweating and wiped his forehead with a rag when he came down the ladder from and sat opposite Lou. She decided he probably could use something to drink. "How about I get us some iced tea, if you have any?"

He answered, "That would hit the spot! It's in the fridge under the counter."

Lou came back with two glasses and handed one to Tank. He took a big swig and said, "Thanks, I needed that. I've been working on fixing my navigation system all day." He held up his glass to toast her. "I think you would make a fine crew member, Lou."

Lou saw this moment as the perfect chance to make her proposal. She forced herself to stop fiddling nervously with her phone. She sat up straight and blurted, "I have an idea, but I need your help, Tank."

He was leaning back relaxing with his eyes closed and had no idea something big was about to be dropped in his lap. "Idea about what?" he asked.

Lou laid it all out. "Okay, here goes. You know that those Dumphries people take the *Unsinkable* out every night, right?" Tank opened one eye and nodded. Lou had his full attention. She continued, "And you told me that there was no whale watching or fishing that is normally done in the middle of the night." He nodded again. She carried on building her case, "I told you about the crime I reported a few months ago. The criminals that were stealing from the store gave me the same feeling that I have when I see the Dumphries."

Tank was listening respectfully. "Well sure, these people are likely rats and up to something, but they could just be jerks."

Lou shook her head, "I know it could be nothing, but it sure feels like something. I'm almost positive there is something criminal or at least suspicious going on with them."

Tank leaned forward and put his elbows on his knees. "Okay, so let's say there is something going on. What do you want to do about it? How would you go about finding out?"

Lou went for it. "I was thinking maybe you could take me out on your boat so we could follow them one night. Maybe we could see what they are up to."

Tank's eyebrows shot up to his hairline. "You want me to take you out to follow these people in the middle of the night! On my boat? Are you serious?"

Lou nodded. "I know it sounds crazy, but don't you want to find out what they are doing out there? You found out who they are and said to yourself that they are suspicious. Aren't you curious?"

Tank took a sip of his drink and thought about what Lou was asking. He screwed up his face in concentration. He was focused on the *Unsinkable* docked and bobbing in the water. "They are some slimy characters though. Just this morning, I was positive I saw a seal in a cage on their boat."

Lou's eyes bugged out. "What?" she stammered. "Was it alive?"

Tank answered, "Oh, it was alive all right. I heard something crying, and it sure sounded like a seal."

Horrified, Lou exclaimed "Why would they have a live seal? Is that even legal?"

"No, it's not," he answered, "but when I came back to it, they had tucked it away someplace. The cage and the seal were gone. I was trying to figure out what they were doing with it. I had planned to report it to Fisheries officers, but then it was gone."

Lou could sense he was weakening about her proposal, so she pushed her request again. "It would only be a quick trip, just long enough to figure out where they go at night. We might even find out what they did with the seal and be back quickly, for sure."

Tank started to warm to her logic but stopped suddenly as a thought struck him. "Have you told your parents about your plan?" he asked in a disapproving tone.

Lou had hoped he wouldn't ask this question, but she wasn't surprised that he did. She wasn't one for lying, but she knew if Tank thought her parents didn't know about her nighttime escapades, he wouldn't go for it. She looked up at him with hope in her eyes. "If I promise to tell my parents about it before we go out, would you say yes?"

Tank felt he was being bamboozled, but he knew that once Lou got an idea in her head, it was impossible to stop her. He realized that if he said no, she'd likely find a way to go out on her own, which would be even more dangerous. No, his best bet was to take her himself, making sure the trip happened safely. "It would be very hard to watch them from my boat, it's too big to be sneaking up on people, but we could use a small motorboat I have in the boat shed. They wouldn't hear the engine over their own."

Lou gave a silent cheer. She bit her lip to keep from smiling, not wanting Tank to rethink his decision to take her out. "That sounds perfect, Tank. We can follow safely behind them, figure out what they are doing and come straight back without them even knowing."

Tank gave her a very stern look. "Okay, I'll take you out, but you have to tell your parents before we go." Lou nodded and gave him a thumbs up. "When do you want to go?"

Lou thought about it for a minute and said, "I had thought to do it on the weekend, but since they're keeping a seal in a cage, I'm not sure we can wait that long."

Tank nodded his agreement. "Okay, I'll need a day to get ready and make sure the engine is working; it's been in storage for a while. How about tomorrow night? You come over when it gets dark, and we will wait for them to go. We can tie up the motorboat behind mine, so they won't see us. Does that work in your grand plan, missy?"

Lou was nervous and excited that he had agreed. "It sure does, Tank! I'll be here tomorrow night. I can leave my bike at the top of the dock and I'll be careful to make sure they don't see me as I go by."

They spent some more time working out the details, and Lou could not have been more thrilled that she was finally going to figure out what the Dumphries were up to. Of course, there was still the small matter of informing her parents about the night boat outing. As she rode home, she couldn't figure out a way to let them know and be sure they would let her go.

She was deep in thought when she got home. The van wasn't in the driveway, and the house was dark. However, she could see some movement in the living room window. Rocky was pacing back and forth, waiting for her to come in. When she unlocked the door and turned the lights on, Rocky raced to the back door.

"Sorry, Rocky, how long have you been alone?" She let him out the door to the back yard and started looking in the fridge for something to eat.

Her phone lit up with a notification of a new text. It was from her mother.

"*Why aren't you answering my texts?*" Lou was puzzled by the message. She scrolled back and realized that she hadn't looked at her phone all day and had missed a bunch of messages and calls because her phone was on silent. She quickly skimmed her mother's texts. Her parents were going to be away for a few days because of a family emergency in Seattle. An aunt of her father's took a fall and broke her hip and they had to rush off to help her.

This put a wrinkle in her plans. Lou sat down with her phone, trying desperately to come up with a way to ask her parents about the late-night boat excursion without getting a hard no.

She stood up to let Rocky back inside and give him his dinner. He finished the whole bowl in a few bites.

Lou looked at his bowl. "A little hungry, I see?" Rocky sat in front of her and raised his paw. Lou leaned to shake his paw, then he burped in her face. "Argh, Rocky! Gross!"

She sat down to answer her mother with a carefully composed response. "*Sorry, Mom, I had my phone on silent at work and forgot to switch it back. I just saw your texts now.*"

Her mom had clearly been waiting for it because the three dots indicating she was typing came up immediately. The text came in fast.

"Ok, I am just glad you are ok. We are at the hospital now, and Aunt Aggie's surgery is in the morning. I am not sure how long we will be here, but when I find out, I'll let you know. It has been very sad for Dad, so I am glad I came with him. Are you going to be ok alone for a few days?"

This was Lou's chance to try to communicate what she was going to do. She decided to tell her mostly everything and hope for the best.

"Mom, I have a chance to go out on Tank's boat tomorrow night. There are people we're pretty sure are pretending to do whale watching tours, but they aren't. We just want to see what they're up to, from a distance."

She crossed her fingers and hoped that would be enough information to get her a yes from her mother. Lou paced while she waited for the response. Finally, her phone chimed.

"Lou, I am not happy about this. Are you getting yourself into a situation again?"

"Mom, I promise it'll just be a short ride and if anything looks sketchy, we'll come back to the dock right away."

Lou's mother took a few minutes to answer. Lou hoped she was considering saying yes instead of getting angry and saying no. If she was going to say no, Lou was going to have to decide how she would handle that.

Then the phone chimed, *"You have put me in a bad position, and I am NOT happy about it. We are away and can't really have a talk with you about this. I am going to choose to trust your judgement this time. Don't make me regret it, be careful, and wear a life jacket."*

Lou had to read it twice. Could it be that she just said yes to the whole scheme? Might this be her mother actually giving her more freedom, or was she just distracted enough to not ask too many questions? Either way, she would get to go.

❖

The next night, Lou sat on her back patio waiting for nightfall. She made herself a late dinner, took Rocky for a long walk, and changed into all black clothes. Her backpack was light, because other than her phone a flashlight and binoculars, she didn't think much else would be useful in the dark. There was no moon, so it would be dark on the water. She hoped Tank was still up for their investigation.

The sun set, and that was her cue to get down to the dock without being seen. She wished she could take Rocky and Oliver along, but Rocky might blow it, and Oliver wasn't going to take the chance of being grounded. She set off on her bike and made her way to the top of the dock. After parking her bike in the shrubs, she tucked her hair into a black hat and made her way carefully toward Tank's boat. There were lights on in a few boats, so she tried to stay in the shadows.

Lou was nervous as she passed in front of the *Unsinkable*, but the three Dumphries were inside the cabin with only a dim light. She startled when she heard something moving around on the deck of the boat. She slammed her hand against her mouth so she wouldn't blurt anything out.

She saw a seal in a cage, looking very agitated. "They still have the seal!" she whispered to herself. It looked starved and weak. Lou knew she had to keep moving, but now she was upset.

The lights were dim on Tank's boat, too. She could see him moving around the cabin. She opened the door quietly and whispered, "I'm here."

Tank startled, dropping the coffee cup he had been holding. "Aye, ya nearly gave me a heart attack!"

Lou apologized quietly and helped him wipe up the coffee. As they were cleaning up, Tank said, "You sure know how to sneak!"

Lou told him, "I saw the seal in the cage. They had him on the deck, and he had no food or water! I mean, what kind of people do something like that?"

"They must need him alive for something," Tank muttered. "I can't imagine if they were illegally hunting seals, they would risk being caught with one in a cage. I just can't figure it out, but hopefully we'll see tonight."

Lou spent the next while helping Tank prepare to launch the boat. She was distracted by the memory of the terrified seal trapped in a cage. She couldn't stop seeing it.

CHAPTER TWENTY-FOUR

T ank and Lou were still deep in conversation when they heard an engine fire up down the dock. "That's them!" exclaimed Tank while already grabbing his giant flashlight and a paddle. He whispered, "Come over this way, we can go down the back ladder to the motorboat. I have it tied up where they can't spot us."

Lou was relieved that she hadn't tried this on her own; Tank was just the person to have on a mission like this. They climbed into the small boat and Tank started the engine up. He had been right. It only made a chugging sound, whereas the *Unsinkable* was loud. They pulled out just a bit past the end of the dock so they could watch the bigger boat head out onto the water.

They followed the *Unsinkabl*e at a good distance, but they weren't worried about the Dumphries noticing them. Lou figured they were so focused on whatever they were doing that it wouldn't occur to them that anybody was watching. Their screens were lit up and the big radar unit was spinning on the top of their roof. Tank stared intensely at the other boat. "What are you nimrods looking for?" he muttered to himself.

Suddenly there was a flurry of activity on the *Unsinkable*. Lou and Tank both pulled out binoculars. It was hard to tell who was who, but they could see three people scrambling around. One of the dark figures ran to the back of the boat to the seal cage and dropped it in the water.

A gasp escaped Lou's mouth as she watched the caged animal drop into the water. She could see that the cage was floating, and it was attached to a long rope tied to their boat. The Dumphries were yelling at each other, but Lou couldn't make out what they were saying.

The *Unsinkable* started moving slowly through the water. The Dumphries had flashlights, and they were looking for something. Suddenly a pod of orcas appeared alongside their boat.

Lou couldn't believe what she was seeing. "They are being attacked by killer whales, Tank!"

"No, they aren't being attacked," Tank reassured her, "Although the orcas seem to be the reason these three are here." He continued to squint into his binoculars to watch every move.

Once the orcas surrounded the *Unsinkable*, the boat started to move quickly in a specific direction.

"Where are they going?" Lou wondered aloud.

"The only thing in that direction is a small cove," Tank replied. "There's nothing but rocky shore and shallow water there."

As the Dumphries were moving toward the cove, they dropped a net off the side of the boat.

"What kind of net is that?" Lou asked.

Tank reeled back in disbelief, suddenly realizing what they were doing. He lowered the binoculars and rubbed his eyes hard. Not speaking, he lifted the binoculars and peered through them again. Lou was bursting with curiosity, but she wisely decided not to flood him with questions. Finally, he pulled the binoculars from his eyes to look at Lou. "They're using the seal as bait to catch a whale."

Lou forgot to close her mouth for a second. She couldn't

believe what he was saying. "Are they trying to kill a whale? They can't do that!"

Tank looked back through the binoculars, adjusting the focus as well as he could in the dark. "Well, they might be trying to, but I don't see a harpoon or the type of gun they would need. They're big animals and don't take kindly to humans trying to kill them. I don't know that the three of them have the strength to use a harpoon, but I can't imagine what they would be doing other than that."

Tank turned off their motor and controlled their direction with a paddle. They floated as close as they could to observe what the Dumphries were attempting to do, whatever that was, for another hour, until Lou started yawning. By then, it was almost one in the morning.

Tank spotted her mid-yawn and powered the motor back up. "Let's get you home. From the looks of it, they aren't the best whale hunters. I don't think we're going to see them doing anything else tonight."

By the time they got back to Tank's boat, Lou was asleep under his big raincoat. He woke her up with a gentle nudge. "Wake up, girly. You're going to need to save catching criminals for another day."

Lou sat up and rubbed her eyes. "What are we going to do now?" she asked sleepily.

"I'm going to put your bike in the back of my truck and take you home," he replied. "It's late and I'm pretty sure your parents would be flipping out if they knew you were still out at this hour."

Lou was wide awake now, peppering Tank with questions and theories for the entire ride home. Her main thought was that they should alert the authorities about what was going on.

Unfortunately, Tank disagreed. "I am no police officer or anything, but we didn't really see them trying to hurt a whale or anything. They could just say they were figuring out how to spot whales because they're new to the business or something. Caging the seal is illegal, but they kept it hidden away."

Lou was disappointed, but she knew Tank was right. The Dumphries would lie about all of it. She was discouraged that they didn't have enough evidence to report them to the police yet. She and Tank were first-hand witnesses which is ideal in prosecuting a case. But for what crime? She mulled this over as he drove her home.

Lou waved at Tank, and she went in the door. Rocky had no interest in going outside, so she just got in her pajamas and flopped into her bed. Too tired to even brush her teeth, Lou fell asleep within seconds.

❖

Lou was still dead asleep when her phone started ringing the next morning. She answered it with a grunt. It was Oliver. "Hey, Sandy and I are at your house. Come open the door."

Lou stood up and stretched, Rocky did the same. She made her way downstairs and opened the back door. She saw Oliver had pulled his wheelchair off the rigging on his bike and assembled it. He came racing up the ramp, right behind Sandy.

Sandy paused at the door, taking in Lou and her pajamas. "Sorry for waking you up, but we couldn't wait to hear your story from last night!"

Oliver rolled through the door and added, "And we were hoping for some breakfast!"

Lou wiped the sleep from her eyes. "Okay, here's the deal. I am going to go brush my teeth and you guys can start some eggs." Lou went upstairs while Sandy and Oliver started rifling through the kitchen.

When Lou came back downstairs, she was much more awake. She saw the table set and orange juice being poured by Oliver. He smiled at her. "No offence, Lou, but you look pretty rough!"

Sandy was at the stove scrambling eggs. She turned to glare at him. "Oliver, that was mean! You never tell a girl she looks bad, even when she's been out on a boat for half the night!"

They all chuckled, and Lou started putting bread in the toaster. She caught sight of her reflection in the side of the toaster and grimaced. "I am seriously scary looking. I had wind blowing through my hair all night and I probably still smell like fish."

When they finally sat down for breakfast, it took Lou an hour to tell her story. Oliver and Sandy were shocked and upset about the caged seal and the hunting of the whales.

Oliver asked, "How did they know where to find the pod?"

"They have sonar or radar or something and they can see where they are under the water," Lou replied. "The pod we saw were mostly in shallow water so we could see their fins. The Orcas were hunting that seal in the cage."

Sandy looked at Lou with a worried expression on her face. "So, what're you going to do next?"

Lou thought for a moment. "We're just going to have to go out again and try to catch them before they hurt a whale. They came super close to one or two of them, it was scary. We need more eyes on them, though. It was just Tank and me, we didn't see everything they were up to. They might have had harpoons or some other weapon that we couldn't see from where we were sitting."

Sandy was thoughtful. "What if we had people in canoes and kayaks watching them? They would be quiet and hard to spot at night."

Oliver turned to look at Sandy. "That's a good idea, but where would we get people to come out in the middle of the night to stalk these guys?"

Sandy grinned. "I have cousins with canoes who would be very interested in catching anybody messing with the wildlife in Howe

Sound. Literally, I could have ten of them out in their canoes on short notice."

Lou smiled, already busy formulating a plan.

Lou put Rocky on the back deck for the day. She filled his water bowl and gave him a scratch. "Have a good day and don't bark at everything. It bugs the neighbours." He looked confused, but then put his head down on his paws and pouted.

Lou, Sandy, and Oliver couldn't contain their curiosity. The intrepid adventurers hopped on their bikes and went down to the dock. It wasn't too busy, so they tried to be inconspicuous and look like they were innocently visiting their friend Tank.

They went by the *Unsinkable* very slowly, pretending to look at other things. They shouldn't have worried though. Mrs. Dumphries was busy yelling at her sons and wasn't paying attention to anything happening on the dock. "You morons!" she shouted. "Weren't you supposed to keep the seal alive?"

Shelton threw his hands in the air. "We had him locked in the cage, he must've slipped out somehow this morning!"

"Slipped out, did he?" She was furious as she turned and focused on Joey. She pointed a finger at his face. "I don't suppose you know how the seal got away, do you?"

Joey's chin started shaking. "I'm sorry, Ma. I just couldn't do it anymore. He was so skinny, and he probably would've died if he didn't get some fish."

Mrs. Dumphries turned bright red and looked like her head was going to pop off in rage. She shook Joey's collar and yelled, "I should've known you would be the weak link in this plan! How am I gonna to explain why we don't have one yet when he calls? You just can't do anything right!"

She was still yelling at him when Lou, Sandy, and Oliver reached Tank's boat. Lou and Sandy put their bikes out of the way on the dock and Oliver turned around to position himself where he could still see the drama on the *Unsinkable*.

Lou knocked, calling out, "Tank, it's us!" She heard some movement in the cabin and saw the boat bob in the water. He was in there.

Suddenly the cabin door flew open, and Tank filled the doorway. He was rumpled, and his beard and hair looked more like a Yeti than a human. He was wearing an old t-shirt with paint stains on it, and shorts that were probably from the 80s. He had a cigar behind his ear and a coffee in his hand. He blinked as if to figure what time of day it was.

"Morning, Tank," Lou said from her position on the dock. "We just wanted to check in and talk to you about a plan we have. Oh, and this is Sandy, she's fully updated on the situation."

Tank shook his head, not looking surprised in the least to find the kids standing there. "Oh, I knew you would show up with a plan, I just didn't think it would be so soon! Nice to meetcha Sandy. Lemme just get another coffee. He went back into the cabin and came out dressed in his overalls, holding a cup." He walked over to the bench near his boat and sat down, grunting. "Okay you three, hit me with your scheme."

Lou started off. "Sandy, Oliver, and I figured that if we had more eyes on the *Unsinkable*, we could maybe figure out what they're trying to do. We can only fit a couple of people at a time in your boat, and even then, we can only watch them from one spot."

Tank took a sip of coffee and nodded. Lou took that as approval to continue. "We need to position more people on the water, so they can see everything that's happening. If we send people out in canoes, they can move around in shallow water and can be waiting there when the *Unsinkable* sets out."

Tank was looking for holes in the plan to see if was watertight. "How would we know where to position these people in canoes? We don't know where the *Unsinkable* will go."

Oliver spoke excitedly. "If they are trying to kill an orca, they would have to corner it. The only place anywhere near here is the cove they went to last night."

Lou added, "And they had them right where they wanted them. I'm just not sure why they didn't succeed last night. Also, they need another seal, or some other bait. They were fighting over the seal slipping away when we walked past them."

Tank chucked, "I wondered what the ruckus was. They've been at it all morning. So, where are we going to get these extra people in canoes?"

Sandy told Tank about her cousins and how quickly she could get them to help. "My cousins all live around here, and I know for a fact they don't like poachers very much."

Tank took a closer look at Sandy. "You're one of the Joe family, aren't you?"

Sandy did a ballerina bow and swept her hand. "The one and only!"

Tank chewed on his unlit cigar and smiled. "I know many of your kin. I almost married one of them when I was young."

Sandy's eyes were wide with surprise. "Which one?" she asked, her voice filled with curiosity.

Tank smiled in the cheekiest possible way. "Now that's between her and me."

Lou decided to save Tank from anymore awkward questions. She waved her arm to capture everyone's attention. "Does it sound like a plan that could work?"

Tank leaned back on the bench, giving Lou his full attention. "Run it by me, step by step."

Lou straightened up; her expression serious. "We'll have to pick a night soon before they manage to hurt any more wildlife. My plan for that night would be that you and I watch them from your boat to see when they're preparing to leave. We would have Sandy's cousins on the beach near here. If the Dumphries head out, we can text Sandy and she can signal the others. We follow them and just watch. If we see that they're actually going to kill a whale, we'll charge them in your boat and spook the whales so they can get away unharmed." Lou thought some more and asked, "Do you have any flares?"

Tank nodded yes.

Oliver spoke up. "Me and my friends can set up on the Spit in case the Dumphries change where they're hunting. We might be able to see them with binoculars."

Tank rubbed his chin, thinking it all through. "What if they have another bust of a night? How are we going to get all those people in position night after night until they reveal what they're doing?"

Oliver was the one to come through with an answer. "I don't know, but the Dumphries seem desperate, they have to keep trying. If we do all this as we planned, I think we would have enough evidence to go to the police. We'd have plenty of eyewitnesses, and more information. We could give the authorities everything we have, and they'd have to look into it."

No one disagreed with Oliver's statement. One more night of observation, this time with a bigger group, would hopefully give them a chance to catch the Dumphries in the act.

CHAPTER TWENTY-FIVE

I t was Friday, Lou's day off. She got up early so she could talk to her parents before her mother went to work. She had avoided the conversation about the criminal surveillance from a few days before, but now that they were back, she knew they would have questions.

She came downstairs to find her parents in the kitchen. Her mother exclaimed, "You're up early! I thought this was your day off."

Lou hugged her dad on the way to steal a piece of bacon that her mother was cooking. "It is, but I need to talk to you guys about something important."

Her mother was nearly finished cooking. She quickly plated the food and then they all sat down at the table with their breakfast plates, ready to listen.

Lou exhaled, "Oliver and I have been spending time over on the fishing dock. With Tank, mostly."

Her parents exchanged looks and nodded.

She continued, "There's been drama with some strangers who showed up this summer. They seemed sketchy pretty much as soon as I saw them. Tank did some research to check them out and he thinks they are running a fake company and they don't really run whale watching tours."

Lou's dad put his coffee down and fixed his eyes on Lou, his gaze stern. "Tell me you aren't investigating another dodgy criminal?"

She shrugged. "Sort of, three of them actually."

Both parents shook their heads, but before they could say anything, Lou continued, "I didn't mean to, but it was all right there. And I told you about the fact that Tank is sure that they aren't legit operators licensed to take out whale watchers. He also told me they only take their boat out at night. On top of all that, they broke into Tank's boat and were looking for who knows what."

She could see her parents opening their mouths to comment, so she took a quick breath and told the rest of it. "Me and Tank followed them out one night to see what they were up to. We saw them throw a seal in a cage off the boat. We think they were using the caged seal as bait. Then a pod of orcas surrounded their boat."

Lou's mother was horrified. "You saw them do all this? Is that what you were doing the other night when you said you were going out on a boat? You neglected to mention that you were out in the middle of the night watching dangerous criminals!"

Mr. Dalrymple looked alarmed. "Lou, you could have been hurt! I can't believe you were so reckless!"

Lou's mother got up and started pacing around the kitchen. "Lou, you lied to me when you sent that text. Not being honest and clear about what you were doing is the same as lying!"

Her dad was the first to take a gentler tone; he always was the first one to calm down. "Lou sweetie, that was incredibly dangerous to do what you did. We weren't even home to be there if something went wrong."

Lou argued, "But we were never close enough to even be noticed. Tank made sure of it."

Her dad frowned. "I know Tank is a great fellow. Everybody in town speaks highly of him, but can you see where we're coming from?"

Lou started to justify her actions again, but she thought better of it. She nodded and said, "I know I pushed the boundaries, and I am sorry I scared you guys. But I would do it again in a minute. Sometimes I feel old enough to decide what I care about, and we need to talk about the things I feel are important too."

Lou's mother sat down and looked at her. "You scare us when you do things like this, honey, and that is why we're so upset. And you're right, you aren't a little girl anymore. We need to start trusting that you are making good decisions about bad situations. However, following criminals in the dead of night was not one of them. Are we agreed?"

Lou nodded again as her dad took her hand and kissed it, saying, "You're our whole world, Lou."

Having made peace with one another, they returned to eating their meals, each lost in their own thoughts. Unaware of the earlier discussion, Rocky stuck his nose against the window, letting everyone know that he wanted to come in. Lou got up and let him inside. He immediately lumbered into the living room and all they could hear was him rustling around. He came back into the kitchen proudly holding a blanket between his teeth and dragging it along behind him. As they watched, he placed the blanket beside the table and used his paw to make a nest out of it. When Rocky was happy with his accomplishment, he flopped down on the blanket and grumbled in satisfaction.

Lou and her parents shook their heads and snickered.

Seeing that her parents' mood had lifted, Lou figured there was no time like the present to finish her conversation.

"So... there is another thing I need to talk to you about."

Lou's father rolled his eyes. "Have you done something else that will get you grounded?"

275

She smiled, trying to look innocent. "No, Dad. It is more a case that what I am planning to do *might* get me in trouble again."

That got their attention.

She straightened up in her seat, wanting to show her parents that she was serious. "Tank and I have seen enough to know that we can't just walk away and ignore whatever is happening. The people on the boat we were watching still haven't gotten what they are looking for, which we think might be to try to kill a whale." She looked both of her parents in the eye before she continued. "But, we don't have enough proof to send to the police."

Her father raised an eyebrow, wondering where Lou was going with this discussion. "This is our only chance to figure out what they're doing. The Dumphries don't know they're being watched; so they aren't being careful. If the police come around asking questions, they'll move somewhere else and keep trying to do whatever it is they are doing. So, it just makes sense that we have to watch them at a distance."

Mrs. Dalrymple scowled. "Who is the 'we' you are talking about?"

Lou answered, "Tank, Sandy, Oliver, me and some others. I'm not going alone... we have a whole plan. Sandy's cousins are coming to help. They will be in canoes hiding in crags and between rocks, observing everything. Oliver and his friends will be on the Spit with binoculars in case they go that way this time."

Her father was surprised by the level of detail in her plan. "And when did you intend to do this?"

Lou swallowed. "Tonight."

The next hour was pretty intense but Lou had all her arguments ready, having planned for her parents' objections. She promised that Tank would radio call the Coast Guard if there was trouble and leave it to them.

Later that morning, Lou told Oliver all about her conversation with her parents. Lou had gone to his house when her mother finally left for work.

Eyes wide with disbelief, he said, "That sounds brutal!" He offered her a chocolate bar and opened his own.

"It *was* brutal," she admitted in between bites. "I think they honestly believe I have no sense. But..." Lou paused for effect, "the good news is, they're letting me do it!"

Oliver gaped.

Lou explained, "In the end, they appreciated that I was honest with them. It took me a while, but when they realized adults would be there to help, they agreed, but they sure weren't happy about it. I guess I finally convinced them that we will have enough people to make sure we can keep each other safe. It was a reluctant permission, but still, it worked."

Oliver said, "That's surprising, but great!"

Lou looked over at Oliver and nudged him with her elbow. "Are you coming or what?"

Oliver squirmed a little. "Yeah, I told my mom about it and she said yes, but she is coming to the Spit with me and my friends."

Lou beamed with excitement over Oliver's news. "That's actually pretty cool, if you think about it."

Oliver and Lou spent the day lining up everybody who was in on what Lou was calling: 'The Sting.'

Sandy sent a text saying, "*We're good to go, I have five cousins in canoes lining up at dusk. They'll get on the water out of sight of the dock.*"

Lou replied, "*Oliver and his buddies will be on the Spit and Tank and I will be in the motorboat. I'll text you when the Unsinkable heads out.*"

Sandy wrote back, "*Aye aye, captain.*"

Lou was a bag of nerves at supper. Her parents had said

nothing more, but Lou could tell that they were nervous too. When it was time for Lou to leave, her mother repeated the advice she had given Lou her whole life. "Stay safe, Lou, and please don't be reckless."

The sun was just about to set when Lou set out on her bike. She wished Rocky was coming, but she knew there was a good chance he could wreck the whole thing. She sent a quick text to Oliver. *"Are you good to go?"*

He answered right away. *"Everybody's heading to the Spit around ten."*

Lou sent him a thumbs up emoji and got on her bike. She took a deep breath and set off towards the dock.

CHAPTER TWENTY-SIX

When Lou arrived on the dock, the *Unsinkable* was dark and she couldn't tell if anybody was in the cabin. Along with her many other worries, it hadn't occurred to her that the Dumphries might not be doing anything tonight. How awful it would be if the very evening she had brought all these people to witness something, and it wasn't even going to happen!

Tank's boat also looked dark and uninhabited. She put her bike on the deck of his boat, out of sight. As she started toward the cabin, he popped up at the back of the boat, startling her.

Lou screeched. "OH! Jeez, you scared me to death!"

Tank apologized, "Sorry, Lou, I didn't mean to. I was just loading up essentials and I heard you climb aboard."

"It's okay, I'm just a little nervous about this." She waved her hand around. "I'm worried about everyone that's coming out tonight, and I'm hoping it all goes to plan."

Tank smiled gently, "At first, I thought your idea was a little harebrained. Now I know you have a good nose for sniffing out bad guys and are an excellent planner to boot. I'm sure this will work out. I know a lot of the people that are coming, and they all care about the wildlife around here. You have a good team."

Lou blushed and picked up a life jacket. "I hope I don't need one of these tonight." She hesitated for a moment and said, "It's so great that you have believed in me enough to do this crazy spying. I'm super grateful."

Tank looked bashful but smirked at Lou. "Let's see what those boneheads down the dock are up to."

Tank and Lou hopped off the boat onto the dock and immediately stepped back into the shadows. The Dumphries were just arriving back on the dock and were headed to their boat. Joey and Shelton were carrying a huge cooler between them. Lou looked up at Tank and he shrugged as he whispered, "I have no idea what they are up to."

They watched the comings and goings on the dock for an hour until it was fully dark. Tank nudged Lou and whispered, "We might as well wait inside, they don't usually leave for another hour or so."

Suddenly, they heard the old engine of the *Unsinkable* fire up. Mrs. Dumphries was on the dock untying the rope and swearing at her sons. Lou couldn't hear them before, but she heard that part.

Lou glances at Tank, her eyes wide. "Tank, they're leaving! We have to go now!"

Tank scrambled into the little motorboat and started untying it. Lou grabbed her life jacket and rushed into the boat.

He started the engine and began backing the motorboat away from the dock. "They're headed in the same direction as last time." He focused on the water and keeping their motor from revving too loudly.

Lou had her phone in her hand and was frantically sending texts. *"They left early, get everybody in position!"*

Oliver and Sandy got the message and started moving fast. Sandy sprinted along the rocks from canoe to canoe, being careful not to shout and reveal their positions to the Dumphries. She spoke softly to each canoeist. "They're on the move, head out now!"

Sandy watched her cousins paddle away to take up their positions on the water. She admired them for helping, but even more for taking her seriously. Lou needed her and her family, and they stepped up. She hopped in her own canoe and went straight to the Spit, being careful to stay clear of the *Unsinkable*.

Oliver was moving fast. He had just gotten out of the van in the parking lot closest to the Spit and was getting on his bike. He turned back to his mother and called out, "Come on, Mom! Lou says they're on their way out to the cove! They left early, and we have to stand watch."

Mrs. Bamberg waved him on. "Go ahead, Oliver, I'll meet you there in a minute. I need to grab the spotlight."

Lou got messages back that everybody was almost in position. She couldn't see any of the canoes, but that meant neither could the Dumphries. She and Tank were following the *Unsinkable* at a distance, focused on any activity they could make out in the darkness.

As the suspect crew did the other night, they headed toward the small cove. Their sonar was spinning, and the *Unsinkable* took a couple of sharp turns and changes of direction. Tank said, "I bet they're trying to find the pod of whales that hang around there." Lou nodded and tried to get a better look with her binoculars.

The deck of the *Unsinkable* was hidden in darkness, Lou had trouble making out the moving shadows. Then a light flashed on, and she could see Shelton and Joey maneuvering the big cooler onto the end of the boat and dumping it.

Tank explained, "That looks like a pile of fish. I bet they're baiting whales!"

Lou could see everything better now that they were using a light. That's when she saw fins appearing above the waterline. She squinted her eyes, looking carefully, and finally saw three canoes in the distance. They were deep in the shadows close to shore, watching. Thankfully, the Dumphries weren't looking around; they were busy and didn't notice that they were being observed.

Lou suddenly realized that if they were actually planning to harpoon an orca, they would be doing it soon. The plan was that if they looked like they were going to injure a whale, everybody would surround them and scare off the whale pod. Tank was ready to radio the Coast Guard at any moment.

Lou's heart was pounding. She thought, "I wish I wasn't so nosy; I wouldn't be out in a boat in the dark watching this horror show." She gave her head a shake and looked through the binoculars again.

They didn't see anybody holding a harpoon – all the boat seemed to be doing was dropping their net. It had ropes on both sides of it and looked more like a hammock than anything. As they watched, Mrs. Dumphries signaled her sons to grab each end of the net as it submerged. Then they waited and slowly moved to the inner rocks of the shore.

Tank smacked the side of the boat. "They aren't trying to kill it. They are trapping it in that net!"

Lou was about to ask him a question about how that would work when she saw the *Unsinkable* start to rock and pitch in the water. Lou whispered, "Is it actually in the net? How did they catch it so fast?"

"Dunno, maybe the bait worked, or they cornered one against the rocks. For sure they have one though."

Lou was totally focused on the spectacle going on in front of her. She noticed the canoes were now spreading out a bit. Maybe they had a plan. She certainly hoped so.

That's when she saw Joey holding a pole. He stood on the deck and aimed it at the net. He seemed to change his mind and stepped back, shaking his head. Shelton marched over to Joey and grabbed the pole out of his hand and plunged it into the water.

Lou squeaked and slammed her hand over her mouth. "Are they killing it?"

Tank mused. "No, whatever that pole is, it is too small to be a weapon. My bet would be that it's a sedative shot to keep the animal calm." Within a minute or two the boat stopped rocking in the water. There were a few fins circling the boat, but when it fired up its engines, the fins disappeared from sight.

Tank declared, "That pod is always around here. They had one new baby this year, a male. I bet that is the one in their net."

The canoes could had a better view that the orca wasn't being hurt. Lou hoped that their plan was the same as hers and Tank's, to see where they were taking it.

The *Unsinkable* started slowly moving west. Joey was securing the net with more ropes as they went. Lou asked, "Where are they going? What's over there?"

Tank thought for a second. "The Spit and the container terminal are the only things I can think of. I know that the container terminal wouldn't be open at this time of night, but it's the only place in that direction that would make sense."

Lou suggested, "Maybe they're hiding the whale somewhere?"

Tank shrugged and kept following the *Unsinkable* wherever it was leading them. Lou was peering through the binoculars, trying to see anything that would give her a clue. She knew it wasn't good, whatever they were up to.

More frantic now, Lou was thinking about what could happen to a whale now that the *Unsinkable* caught it. "Tank, shouldn't we radio somebody now?"

Tank squinted at the scene that was unfolding. "Now that I am pretty sure they will be caught red-handed, I'll call the Coast Guard." He was about to click the radio and then hesitated.

Lou kept watching the *Unsinkable* and when she didn't hear Tank speak, she asked, "What's wrong?"

Tank muttered, "The *Unsinkable* has radios too. What if they catch my signal?"

Lou's face dropped. She hadn't considered this.

The two of them stared at each other, realizing that their whole plan could crumble They could be in serious danger if the *Unsinkable* were to hear their radio call.

Tank decided, "We're just going to have to take the chance. We can't let them get away with this." He paused for a second and announced, "They're using those old school radios that look like something out of World War II, so I'm going to have try to it and hope they won't pick up our signal."

Lou nodded, agreeing with Tank's logic. She picked up the binoculars and aimed them at the *Unsinkable*, hoping to tell if the crew aboard hears the call.

Tank took a deep breath and clicked on his radio and said, "Coast Guard, Coast Guard, this is fishing vessel Fishtank, over."

"Coast Guard, Fishtank, what is your emergency, over."

"Coast Guard this is Fishtank, we are in view of a vessel called *Unsinkable* and we think they have an orca trapped in their net."

Tank explained where they were and the direction they were heading. The response from them took a bit but then they heard, *"Fishtank, this is Coast Guard. We are on route, ETA 15 minutes."*

When *Unsinkable* showed no indication that they had heard Tank's call and the Coast Guard were safely on their way, they both breathed a sigh of relief.

Lou suddenly remembered where she had seen those radios before, "Tank! I have a spy magazine that has a bunch of pictures of vintage surveillance and communication gear. I saw them using those radios on the dock, they are old Russian technology!"

Tank scratched his head. "Where would those dopes get Russian radios?"

The *Unsinkable* sped up, making it clear they were now heading to the container terminal. It was dark, and it looked like nobody was at the terminal. All the floodlights were off. Lou couldn't figure out why they would be going there, but she called Oliver and said, "They're heading to the container terminal. They have a whale trapped in a net floating beside their boat. We have to stay out of sight a bit, so your guys need to be watching for them."

Oliver was speechless. "They stole a whale?"

Lou answered impatiently, "Just tell everybody to watch closely, and if anything happens, call me. Tank radioed the Coast Guard and whoever else can come fast. Over and out." She disconnected the call.

Oliver told everybody what was happening. They all moved as far out onto the Spit as they could go to watch the boat. Lou sent a text to Sandy that said, *"They're heading to the container terminal, we're staying back a bit, let the others know. They might be able to slip by them to get a better look."*

Just then, Oliver saw the *Unsinkable* come around the corner of the huge cement bollards that protected the container dock. He could see the boat listing to one side, but otherwise it didn't look like anything was wrong. Then he saw a couple of canoes with paddlers dressed in black slipping through spaces between the posts under the terminal dock and around the back of the *Unsinkable*.

By the time Lou and Tank silently came around the same corner, the *Unsinkable* was already positioned under a tall crane. A huge spotlight flashed on and lit up the crane and the boat.

Tank stared; worry etched in his face. "Now I know something is wrong. There is no way the loading company would let a crane be operated in the middle of the night with only one spotlight. That whole place should be lit up like a Christmas tree!"

Lou tried to make sense of it. "So now the crane is going to lift the net with the whale in it? What on earth do they think they are going to do with that whale?"

Tank was thinking hard as he looked around. "You see that barge with a container on it over there?" Lou nodded. He continued, "That crane only goes in one direction, so I bet they're putting the whale in that container is probably full of sea water."

Lou's mind was racing as fast as her heart was pounding. Who would want to trap a whale, and why? She glanced over at the canoes, who were all in a holding position. She didn't know what to do other than watch, which is what everybody else was doing, too. They seemed frozen in place.

As the crane started to move toward the net, men came out on the deck of the barge with flashlights. Lou elbowed Tank to get his attention. He looked over and saw the men signaling to the Dumphries from the top of the barge. They were speaking a language Lou couldn't understand.

Tank knew though. "What would Russians want with these three petty criminals?"

Lou said, "Looks like they kidnapped a whale for them. It seems like they are delivering it or something."

As the crane lifted the net out of the water everybody could see by the light on the crane. There was a young whale struggling weakly as he was taken out of the water and suspended in the air. Everybody gasped at the same time.

Then, in a second, everything was lit up with lights so powerful it looked like daytime. Two Coast Guard zodiac boats with spotlights came speeding toward the barge. The waves they created almost tipped Tank's boat and the canoes. They came to a stop between the *Unsinkable* and the barge and pointed their rifles at the Dumphries.

A group of police officers came running along the terminal dock. They stood facing the barge, weapons drawn and pointing rifles at the men on the barge yelling, "Lie down, put your hands on your head and don't move!"

The Dumphries frantically looked around for an escape route. They weren't going anywhere because canoes came out of the shadows, blocking any hope of speeding away. They were surrounded.

Sandy spotted the canoes from the Spit and gasped. She whispered to Oliver, "They are so close to that boat!" Oliver didn't look away from the scene that was unfolding and just held her shaking hand.

Mrs. Dumphries stood on the side of the boat by the net

yelling at the canoes to get out of the way. She was cutting the last ropes that attached the net to the boat. She was still trying to let the crane lift the whale.

One of Sandy's cousins shouted back, "You better sit down and zip your stinkin' lip."

The Dumphries were thinking about objecting, but when they looked around at the Coast Guard zodiacs and the number of canoes around them, they sat down and, for once, stayed quiet.

Lou and Tank decided that they should get out of the way. They pulled up to the Spit and beached the boat. As they watched, an officer climbed up the crane and made the operator lower the whale. When the net was back beside the boat and dipped in the water, the whale revived a bit. The Joe cousins started cutting the whale loose from the net.

Lou couldn't believe all this was happening. She looked around at the people on the Spit. Oliver, his friends and his mom were all watching the drama. Then she saw her dad standing next to Oliver's mom.

"Of course, he came," she smiled.

Then she heard a heartbreaking cry. The little whale was calling for his pod.

Tank was watching the whale slowly being cut free of the net. He observed, "The Joe family knows these waters and these animals better than anyone. If anybody can save that little guy, it'll be them."

More police cars came racing onto the terminal dock with full lights and sirens; they parked by the ramp to the barge and started boarding it. The sailors who were face-down on the deck of the barge were hauled up and put in handcuffs. The officer who had been up on the crane brought the operator down and handcuffed him too.

In the meantime, the little whale was struggling to get out of the net. He knocked one of the Joes into the water and got himself more tangled. The Coast Guard boats pulled up beside the *Unsinkable* and transferred the Dumphries off their boat and put them in handcuffs. One Coast Guard boat departed to bring the Dumphries to land and hand them over to the waiting police officers.

Lou looked out in the direction the Coast Guard boat had gone and saw something moving in the water. She picked up her binoculars and yelled, "The orca pod is here!"

Oliver turned on his spotlight to light up a large section of the water. Everybody turned their attention to where Lou was pointing. She quickly counted eight fins. "They must have heard his cries," she murmured, tears filling her eyes.

Everyone's eyes were focused on the whale and the incredible effort being made to cut the net. When the last bits of the ropes and net fell away from the whale, he smoothly slipped into the water. Lou and Oliver were about to cheer when they noticed he wasn't moving. The whale didn't swim off or dive down, it just floated. Lou started to panic.

Everybody, even the police and Coast Guard officers were now watching the pod approach the juvenile orca. Nobody wanted to move or make a sound as the whales swam around him to identify him as family. The bigger whales swam under and beside him. They gently nudged him to get him moving away from the dock. To the relief of all the people watching, the little whale revived and gently moved his tail. The pod guided him out to the open water, slowly swimming beside him so he could keep up.

When they were safely out of sight, Lou let out a "WHOOHOO!" Then the rest of the people on the Spit joined in. They were hugging and cheering and when Lou hopped out of the beached boat, she ran up to her father and hugged him hard. They were both in tears when her dad said, "I'm so proud of you, Bunny. You are incredible."

There was a lot of excited chattering going on. Sandy found Lou and clutched her in a huge hug. She spoke through her tears, "This was the coolest thing I have ever seen. I don't know if anybody would have caught these guys if you hadn't raised the alarm!"

Lou held both her hands. "We all made such a great team. I wish I knew who the people on the barge were, and what they were going to do with the whale."

Sandy agreed. "I think we all would like an explanation for that. It was so freaky."

Oliver came to join the conversation. "So, what happens now?"

As if to answer his question, the *Unsinkable*, now covered in police tape, was being tied up and towed away. The Coast Guard boats left, and they waved on the way by. Some of the police cars left with their back seats full of criminals.

One police car picked its way along the Spit, trying to avoid the potholes. It parked in front of the group and a smiling officer got out. It was Sergeant Preston.

"Oh, I should have known you would be involved in this somehow, Lou Dalrymple."

Lou smiled and shrugged. "I go where I'm needed."

Sergeant Preston said, "I am going to need some time with you and your conspirators to get this full story, aren't I?" Lou just shrugged her shoulders and smiled.

Sergeant Preston took the names of every witness and asked them to get some rest and come to the station in the morning. Then she snapped her notebook shut and said, "Are you all curious about what was going on?"

The whole group nodded and stepped closer to hear her speak. Sergeant Preston started, "We had gotten a call from Fisheries and Oceans a month ago giving all law enforcement a head's up that they had suspicions, but no direct evidence, that the Russian military was reviving their training programs for whales and dolphins."

Of course, Lou was the first to blurt out, "What do they want to train them for?"

Sergeant Preston continued, "I don't know much about how it works, but I am told they have been stealing whales and dolphins from anywhere they can and transporting them back to underwater pens. The last time they got caught doing this sort of thing, they were teaching whales and dolphins to spy on whatever country they were brought to. They wore tracking and listening devices. It never worked very well, but I guess they're trying again because I have a jail full of Russian Navy guys disguised as barge sailors."

Lou was thinking fast. "And what about the Dumphries?"

The answer she got was pretty much what she expected.

"Those three petty criminals smelled money. The payment they could earn per whale was massive. We'll take their statement when they get to the station, and then they'll have an uncomfortable sleep on a cold steel bunk."

Sergeant Preston found Lou's eyes in the group. "And you, Miss Lou, are once again at the centre of all this."

Lou's dad came and stood by her side, then so did Mrs. Bamberg and Tank. They didn't say anything, but Sergeant Preston got the meaning. She shook her head with a chuckle and said, "The rest of you ought to know better."

They talked for a little while longer until the kids all started yawning. Tank stretched his back and said, "Well, that was a good night's work. I'm going back to my boat. Lou, I'll keep your bike for you for when you need it."

Lou yawned again and picked up her backpack. She thanked Tank sincerely. Sandy hopped back in her canoe to meet up on the shore with her cousins. She waved and called back, "Ice cream tomorrow?"

Lou and Oliver laughed and shouted, "Yes!" at Sandy as she paddled away.

As everybody who had watched the drama unfold walked up the Spit to the parking lot, they congratulated Lou and Oliver for being heroes. All Lou could come up with was a wave, she was so tired. Her dad took her backpack off and carried it for her.

Oliver was his usual excited self. As they got to the parking lot, he said, "This is going to be the best story ever for when we get back to school!"

Lou rolled her eyes; she didn't even have the energy to tease him.

CHAPTER TWENTY-SEVEN

Lou slowly opened her eyes and looked around. She was in her room, but it didn't feel real yet. She was still halfway in a dream about whales and seals trapped in underwater pens.

She didn't notice Rocky approaching her until he put his head on her stomach. "Oof! Rocky, you scared me! Your head is so heavy!"

Still, she massaged his big floppy ears until he started getting even heavier. Lou pushed him off her, saying, "Don't go back to sleep on top of me!"

When Lou and Rocky went downstairs, her parents were already making breakfast. Her mother came over and gave her a long hug. As she was stroking Lou's hair, she said, "That was quite the adventure you were on last night. Your father told me about it when you two got home."

Lou flopped down on a chair at the kitchen table. She was exhausted but knew they would need to discuss what went on last night. "I really didn't expect any of what happened Mom, I swear. I'm not going to pretend I had it all figured out from the start, but I knew it was something. I had no idea it would be so big!"

Her mother answered, "You know what, Lou? I never know

what you're going to get up to next, but I have to say this adventure was astounding and dangerous."

Mr. Dalrymple had been standing there listening, but now sat down to join them. "I agree with your mother. You were in over your head, Bunny."

Lou's dad turned to her mother. "Roberta, you should have seen our girl though. She was on the motorboat that was tracking the whale, then the Coast Guard speedboats came in to save the whale. There were police everywhere on the dock arresting the criminals."

As he spoke, Lou's dad realized he should probably calm his excitement and say something fatherly. "But you know, Lou, these situations don't always go well, and you put yourself in danger."

"I know, Dad. I just appreciate that you guys let me go and do what I needed to. It was important." She looked at her father. "I knew when I saw you on the Spit that you had my back. It was the best surprise."

Mrs. Dalrymple was not quite over the whole thing yet and chastised Lou, "You can count on the fact that we will be asking more questions the next time you try to pull a stunt like this."

Lou picked at her food and felt tired and moody. She mumbled, "Sorry, Mom."

Once they had finished breakfast and were cleaning up the dishes, there was a knock at the door. Rocky was the first one at the door to greet their guest.

Lou opened the door and was taken aback when she saw who it was.

"Sam, what are you doing here?" She smiled and opened the door wide.

Sam stepped in. "Hello, Lou. I'm actually here to see your parents. Are they home?"

As if on cue, Lou's parents stepped out of the kitchen and greeted Sam warmly. Mrs. Dalrymple said, "Come on in, Sam. We were just putting on a fresh pot of coffee!"

Sam took off his shoes. "Don't mind if I do. Thank you, Mrs. Dalrymple." He picked up his dented old briefcase and walked into the kitchen. Rocky came along with him and nudged his hand for a pet. Sam chuckled. "Rocky, my boy, you are some character."

They chatted comfortably as they sat around the kitchen table, then Sam got to the point of his visit. He put the briefcase up on the table and opened it, rifling around while muttering under his breath. He seemed to finally locate what he was looking for and said, "Aha, there it is," and closed the rickety briefcase. He held a crinkled piece of paper in his hand.

Sam seemed to be preparing himself to say something important. "Well, it's like this; I'm not getting any younger, you know. It was pretty darned clear how far behind I've gotten when you were helping me with the new technology for my store."

He took a sip of coffee and continued, "I'll just come out with it. I want to retire."

Lou realized that this meant she would probably be out of a job. She wanted to try to convince him to stay and just get more help, but she decided not to interrupt.

Sam continued, "So, I got to thinking, how can I retire before I sell all the stuff I have in the store? I looked at the reports you did for me that added up what my junk was worth. I figured out it would take me ten years to sell it all. Then I got to thinking, maybe I should just sell the store to somebody with all the stock in it." He looked over at Lou's dad and said, "I was hoping you might buy it."

Mr. Dalrymple's eyebrows shot into his hairline and he stammered, "Me? What do I know about running an antique store?"

Sam was prepared for this. "You have the bookkeeping smarts and are good with computers, all you need is some help with buying the right things that the customers want. That's where I would come in, I would stay as a volunteer assistant and show you

297

the ropes. I can work fewer hours, and you would have a tidy profit."

Sam pushed the piece of paper over to Mr. Dalrymple's side of the table. "I put some numbers of my own together. That is the price of the building and everything in it."

Lou's dad started reading it and made sure her mom could see as well. Mrs. Dalrymple looked up from the scrap of paper and asked Sam, "Are you sure you want to do this? Retire, I mean?"

Sam nodded, a little sadly. Lou was busting to see what the paper said but knew better than to be nosy about stuff like that. When the Dalrymples finished reading it, Mervin said, "I would have never thought of this idea in a million years, but I have to admit you've intrigued me! Obviously, I'll have to discuss it with Roberta and get back to you."

Sam stood up and said, "Well, then, I'll leave you to it." He said his goodbyes and was out the door.

The Dalrymples had a lot to talk about. Lou waded into their conversation, pointing out, "Dad, you love the cool stuff and antiques, and you know what everything is. You've already done a lot of work on Sam's business and you need a job. It seems like a no-brainer to me."

Lou's parents both laughed a little, but it was clear that it wasn't quite that simple. Her father said, "I will crunch some numbers to see if owning this store is better than a normal job in the long run." He looked over at his wife. "It would be a big change for us, and it's a decision we need to make together."

Lou's mother started clearing the table, looking over her shoulder as she picked up a plate. "Mervin, I haven't seen you this happy in a long time. Lou is right. If the numbers work, it's a great solution as far as I am concerned."

❖

That afternoon, the Dalrymple family showed up at the police station as requested. They weren't prepared for what they saw when they came through the doors. Every desk had an officer and a witness being interviewed. Lou spotted Oliver and his mom, Tank, and Sandy first. Then she saw another row of desks with three of the Joe cousins making their statements too.

Lou saw Cecie's uncle at the front desk. He spotted her and waved hello. "Hey Lou! Nice work with the whale. My nephews told me all about it this morning." He looked at his watch. "Oh, we have prisoners coming through, can you all just have a seat over there?" He pointed at chairs in a small waiting area.

Lou's family did as they were asked and sat. Within a minute, officers started walking out of a back hall toward the front door. Each one of them was escorting a person in handcuffs out the door. Lou realized these must be the sailors from the barge. They looked foul and angry, and they smelled of fish. Lou asked her dad, "Where are they taking them?"

Mr. Dalrymple shrugged and quipped, "I don't know, but it won't be a fancy hotel, that's for sure."

Then three more officers came out with the Dumphries. Joey and Shelton had their heads down and looked miserable and defeated. Their mother was scowling and tugging at her handcuffs, then she saw Lou and yelled, "YOU! You should've minded your own business and left us alone."

Lou looked away and said nothing. Her mother put her arm around Lou's shoulders. "Don't pay any attention to that garbage."

Constable Joe called out to the officers walking the criminals out, "I hope you guys brought the big truck!" He chuckled a bit and saw Lou looking curious. He explained, "Those are the sheriffs. They take the people we arrest to their cells in the courthouses to see a judge.

Lou asked, "Are they taking them out of Squamish?"

Constable Joe nodded. "Don't worry, they're never coming back here. They'll stand trial in Vancouver first and likely sit in jail for many years."

Finally, Sergeant Preston came out and escorted the Dalrymple family to her office. As she closed the door and they were sitting down, she said, "Thank you for coming in today. We really need your testimony, Lou. These people are facing some very serious charges, and your facts are important."

Lou asked if she would need to testify in a court or anything like that. Sergeant Preston assured her, "Probably not, they've been caught red-handed and will hopefully confess to their crime. They'll likely be sent back to Russia to serve their jail time." Lou was a little disappointed she wouldn't get to testify but was satisfied that there was no way they'd get away with it.

Because Lou and her dad were witnesses, they spent the next two hours making sure they gave every detail and all the events were in the right order. They described boats, and people, and locations, anything they could think of that might be useful to the case.

When they were done, Sergeant Preston tidied up her notes. "Well that ought to do it. You must be exhausted Lou; it was a big night for you. Oh, and speaking of last night, I was pretty sure I told you to keep out of the sleuthing business."

Lou shrugged and blushed a little. "I know, but it was a whale, I couldn't help myself."

When they were done in the office and walked out, all the officers were interviewing another load of witnesses, mostly her and Oliver's friends who had been on the Spit watching.

Lou wanted to see Sandy and Oliver but decided it would have to be another day. She just wanted a nap after all this. Her mom put her arm around Lou, and they left the building.

Sandy knocked on Lou's door the next morning. Rocky had now improved his door opening skills and grabbed the handle in his mouth and let Sandy in. Lou was in the kitchen and hadn't gotten to the door before Rocky decided that opening the door was his new job.

Sandy stepped into the house and scratched Rocky's ear. "Cool trick, dude. Good thing I'm not a robber or something."

Lou was shaking her head. "Honestly, I think he would let anybody in just because he's so excited about his new talent. We're going to need to keep that door locked now. He hasn't figured out how to unlock it yet. Come on in, you want some orange juice?" Sandy accepted and the two girls sat at the table.

Sandy lifted her glass. "Well, here's to saving whales!"

Lou picked up her own glass and clinked it against Sandy's. She marveled, "That was nutso, huh?"

Sandy answered, "It was scary, amazing, and maybe another forty words to describe that whole adventure."

Lou agreed and added, "Your cousins were so brave! Those criminals didn't have a chance."

Sandy smiled and finished her juice. When she drank the last drop, she proposed, "I was thinking we should get Oliver out of bed and go to the park. We could have a picnic and spend a bit of time together without criminals and scary boat rides to deal with."

Lou answered, "That's a good idea, but I also want to check on Tank to make sure he's okay."

Sandy agreed and with Rocky running alongside them, they set off on their bikes to see if Oliver was out of bed yet.

Lou knocked on Oliver's front door, and to her amazement, he was up and dressed. "Oh, hey, you guys! I was just going to text you to see what you wanted to do today." Then he noticed they were on their bikes. "Hey, wasn't your bike on Tank's boat last night?"

Lou answered, "I think my Dad must have gone to get it early this morning."

The three of them decided the first thing they would do was

to check on Tank. They got on their bikes and headed towards the dock.

As they were making their way down the dock, they saw the *Unsinkable* was no longer there, and another boat was tied up in its place. It was called *The Kraken* and it made the three of them laugh.

They saw Tank working on his boat. Oliver to catch his attention. "You never take a rest, do you?"

Tank looked up from his task and waved a screwdriver at Oliver. "There is no rest when your boat is as old as this one is. You should see the holes I patch every summer, but she stays afloat. That's all that matters! What brings you lot here today?"

Lou answered, "We just wanted to check on you to see how you are. We also wanted to know if you had heard anything about what went on the other night. Have any of the other fishers said anything?"

Tank chuckled. "There are no secrets on the docks; the whale and the Russians are all anybody is talking about right now. There are some crazy rumours out there, but I try to squash them when I can."

"The people or the rumours?" Oliver asked, smiling cheekily.

Tank rolled his eyes. "I was just about to take a break, anybody want lemonade?" Rocky perked up as if Tank had offered him a treat, so when Tank tossed him a cookie, Rocky inhaled it and sat to wait for another.

When their glasses were filled, everybody settled in and got comfortable for a visit. Lou had been wanting to ask, so she just dove straight into it. "So, is it just me or has this been the coolest thing ever?"

Oliver's eye grew wide as he remembered the scene. "I couldn't believe the coast guard boats! They were moving so fast! And did you see one of the officers climbing up the crane?"

Sandy jumped in, her voice excited. "When all those police cars came screaming in, it was so cool! Those guys on the barge were running around like chickens and had nowhere to go. It was almost funny!"

Oliver smiled at the memory. "And Sandy, your cousins were unreal! They were so careful freeing that whale! They were on that boat before anybody even saw them. How did they keep the Dumphries from attacking them?"

Sandy shrugged, "We wouldn't have heard it, but I imagine Carter made it clear they would regret trying to stop the rescue. He is one tough dude."

Tank looked at the trio of teens sitting around him, still unable to believe what they had done. "You kids sure are brave and smart. That plan was pretty darned good."

They spent the rest of the morning talking about everything that happened on the water, in the police station, and what the Dumphries might be thinking right about now. Oliver snickered at the thought of the three of them sitting behind bars. "They sure aren't having a good time in a jail cell."

When they had finally discussed every detail, it was time to go. Lou, Rocky, and Oliver started up the dock. Sandy lingered behind, explaining, "I'll catch up in just a minute." She waved them off and turned to talk to Tank, who listened intently and nodded in response to whatever she was saying.

When Sandy caught up to the others, she didn't offer any explanations as to what she had been talking to Tank about. Lou was curious, she didn't ask about it though. By the time they got to the ice cream shop, they were talking about other things and Lou forgot to ask.

CHAPTER TWENTY-EIGHT

I t had been a week since Lou and her friends had prevented the whale from being stolen. Every morning at breakfast, Lou sat down to read the local newspapers. The story was in the headlines all week: "Russians Attempt Theft of Local Orca — Youths Save the Day" or "International Whale Trade Stopped by Local Citizens." She cut out all the articles and printed the online pieces. They were all carefully pasted into her scrapbook.

At first, Lou read all the articles and was excited when she eventually found her name. They didn't even mention Tank at all. Lou decided that newspapers don't worry about details, just headlines, and she eventually stopped reading them. She knew what really happened, and that was enough.

Later that day, Lou got a text from Sandy that said, "*Hey Lou! Can you come to a community gathering on Friday? Same place, one o'clock, dress up and bring your parents too!*"

Lou texted her back, "*Okay!*"

Before she could write her next text full of her usual questions, Sandy sent another message. "*Before you ask me twenty questions, don't. Just show up and wear something nice* ☻."

❖

Friday came, and the Dalrymples got themselves ready. After some discussion about how dressed up they should be, they settled on their outfits. Lou wore a bright pink skirt that sat just above her knees, and a white flowy blouse. In typical Lou style, she wore bright white tennis shoes with shiny metal tips. Her hair was up in a bun, but no matter what she tried, bits of unruly hair came loose and curled around her face. She thought about wearing her backpack but decided against it. She had a feeling it wouldn't be a backpack kind of event, so she filled a small purse and went out the door.

When Lou and her parents walked into the main hall of the longhouse, the smell of food made Lou's stomach growl. There were already a crowd of people there, but Sandy spotted them right away from across the room and waved hello.

Mr. Dalrymple looked around, clearly impressed. "This place is amazing, and boy does the food smell good."

Lou gaped at the beauty of this longhouse. She had been in the building before, but not in this large main room. It was built with huge logs and one of the walls was all windows. There were paintings and carvings everywhere, just like at her school.

She couldn't believe how crowded the room was. "Look at how many people are here, it's like the whole community showed up." Her parents nodded in agreement, all of them feeling a bit overwhelmed.

Mrs. Dalrymple looked surprised as she was suddenly whisked away by a tiny little old lady. Lou watched as her mother moved through the crowd as she was being escorted to the buffet.

Sandy stood beside Lou and nodded toward the lady. "That's my Auntie Pauline, she's mostly deaf but pretends she can hear you, it's hilarious. She's totally sweet and adorable, but she probably thinks your mother needs a meal."

Lou watched her mother at the buffet and appreciated that she had worn a floral summer dress. She looked really lovely, but she could see why an elderly lady might think she needed a snack. Lou smiled at the thought of it.

Then she saw that her father was mingling. He was wearing a beige golf shirt a size too big and his pants were rumpled. Her heart went soft just to see him chatting comfortably with Carter and some of the younger men in the community smiling. Her mind wandered, thinking back to when he showed up at the Spit on the night they stopped the whale from being stolen. "Even though I told him he didn't need to come, I was so glad he was there. I guess I'll always need him." She concluded to herself.

Sandy and Lou were still chatting when they saw Oliver and his mother come in, followed by Tank. Lou was surprised to see him there, and even more by how Tank looked when he wasn't on his boat. He was wearing slacks and a blazer with a dress shirt and his hair was neatly combed. He had even trimmed his beard. Before Lou could make a remark to Sandy, she noticed the room had suddenly gone silent.

People started shuffling into different positions, and a few ladies were digging through boxes on the floor at the side of the hall. Someone else was setting up a microphone at the front of the hall. Sandy disappeared from Lou's side and was replaced by Lou's mother. It felt as though everyone was following a set of instructions that Lou didn't know about.

Sandy reappeared at a doorway at the side of the hall, sending Lou a text. "*Grab Oliver and Tank and come over here.*"

Lou figured Sandy had something planned, so she gathered the others and they went where they were told.

As Lou, Oliver, and Tank worked their way through the crowd, Lou saw a group of little kids in formal aboriginal regalia. They wore brightly coloured tunics with intricate designs and beaded headbands. Their soft leather boots were covered in beaded stitching in incredible patterns. A man carrying a huge drum painted with beautiful artwork stood with them. He was wearing a beaded leather vest and his jet-black hair was tied with leather straps and feathers. He gathered the children and they made their way through a doorway. It led to a hallway and he arranged them in a lineup.

Lou, Tank, and Oliver met Sandy at the entrance to the hallway where she directed them toward the end of a line. They greeted the Joe cousins as they went by, as Sandy arranged them all in a row. Lou whispered to Oliver, "What do you think is going on?"

"Not a clue." Oliver shrugged.

A group of women made their way toward Lou, Oliver and Tank carrying piles of colourful fabrics. When they began to unfold them, Lou saw that they were beautiful ornate blankets. She had never seen anything like it.

One by one, the women put them over their shoulders. When it was Lou's turn to receive a blanket, she saw it was Sandy's Auntie Pauline. She held up the blanket and Lou crouched down a little so the tiny woman could reach up and place the blanket over her shoulders. Auntie Pauline smiled broadly and rubbed the top of Lou's arm affectionately.

Lou clasped the blanket around herself and watched as Tank and Oliver received their blankets too.

The next minute the kids and the drummers started moving and Lou's line followed them out the door into the main room. The floor at the front of the room was now covered in cedar branches, creating a gorgeous, fragrant carpet. The kids began dancing to the drummer's beat as the group stepped forward out into the hall. The little dancer's tunics and vests had small carved paddles dangling from them. The paddles were made of carved oak and made a bright, tinkling sound as they moved.

Everyone in the room was smiling at the breathtaking talent of the dancers. As Lou and the others followed behind the drummer, they clutched the blankets around their shoulders. Lou realized they were going to be led around the people gathered in the room. She felt a little stunned but couldn't stop smiling. The dancers had everybody's attention and the more people smiled, the more enthusiastic the children were.

When the group had made a full circle around the room, they made their way up the centre aisle to the front of the hall.

The ladies who had presented the blankets were at the front, standing alongside a woman waiting behind a microphone. She watched the dancers and acknowledged the line of people going by with a nod. Lou sucked her breath in, almost forgetting to keep walking. She had never seen someone so stunning and elaborately dressed before. The woman wore a big hat that looked like a woven basket. Her colourful dress and long-embroidered jacket swept behind her as she stepped forward to speak. When the woman turned, Lou saw the full pattern that was embroidered on the back of the coat. She swallowed hard and whispered, "It's an orca."

The drummer moved off to the side by the door where they had come in and the dancers sat down in front of him. The dancers were trying to hold still, but you could see an excited buzz in their faces. Some of them fiddled with the feathers on their boots.

Lou had goosebumps the whole time. When the lineup was positioned at the front of the room facing the crowd, Lou glanced at Oliver and Tank. They both smiled nervously, and Oliver gave a subtle thumbs up.

The woman stood looking more dignified than anybody Lou had ever seen. She then put up both her hands with her palms facing her and made a gentle circular motion that looked very much like she was gathering the people in the room. She started speaking in a language that Lou didn't understand, but she loved listening to the tone and rhythm of it. The speaker then switched to English. She introduced herself as a band Elder, saying, "Welcome, my sisters and brothers, and honoured guests." She turned slowly and seemed to look everybody in the eye. Lou was transfixed.

Oliver nudged Lou's arm. She bent over, leaning down until their heads were close together. He whispered in her ear, "This feels super special." Lou nodded, keeping her eyes locked on the speaker.

When the songs and dancing ended, the Elder announced, "Today is a memorable celebration." Her eyes held the room in silence with a powerful warmth. She put up her hand and gestured. "Can I have Carter, Wally, Martin, Eugene, Sandy, and Simon Joe step forward?"

They all shuffled forward. She waited for them to get in to position and began speaking. "We all know what happened in our waters recently. Serious crimes were being committed under our noses. You should know that these young people from our family, our band, and our hearts protected the orca that would have been taken and harmed. The criminals wanted that whale for purposes of war, but they have been stopped. Today, we show the Joe family our thanks and respect. They have fulfilled their responsibility as guardians of our traditional lands and waters."

The room erupted in hoots and clapping. The little kids got up from where they were politely sitting and hugged their heroes. There was much chatter as the Joe cousins returned to the crowd.

The Elder wasn't done yet. "Oliver, Tank, and Lou, would you kindly come forward?" The three of them looked at each other in surprise and took a step forward to stand beside the microphone.

"I would also like to speak about our honoured guests. Tank, Oliver, and Lou, we acknowledge and honour you as protectors of the animals we all treasure." She scanned the crowd in silence, then continued, "You put yourselves at great risk to rescue an orca. You showed great bravery."

Lou was beaming. She had never had such a special honour before and felt very proud. She was proud of her friends, proud of her own courage, and proud of this amazing community she could now call home. She looked around and spotted Cecie and Sandy standing together. Lou gave Cecie a little wave.

The Elder then thanked everybody for attending. She made special mention of the young people learning by the example set by the people who went out into the night to save a dignified and important creature. When she finished, everybody smiled and applauded.

She continued. "These teachings were handed down from my grandmother Maggie. Please accept our gratitude and respect and we hope you will cherish these blankets as we cherish you.

Then she smiled widely and said, "Now, everybody, please eat and enjoy yourselves."

Everyone began moving around and chattering, most headed to the buffet. Lou, Oliver, and Tank took off their blankets to admire them. Tank had a tear in his eye. "I have never been so honoured, I don't even know how to thank them." Lou put her hand on Tank's arm and patted it.

Lou and Oliver marveled at each other's blankets. After careful thought, Lou said, "I'm hanging this up in my room, it's gorgeous."

Before Oliver could answer, they were overwhelmed by a crowd of people. The Dalrymples, Cecie, Sandy, and Mrs. Bamberg descended on them all at once to examine their blankets. Oliver and his mother hugged for a long time. Everybody was so excited about the meaningful ceremony and the exquisite blankets.

As the afternoon wore on, everyone stuck around, mingling and telling stories. It wasn't until dinnertime rolled around that the crowd began to thin.

Lou said goodbye to her friends and walked out with her parents. Her mother was carrying the blanket, admiring it as she walked. Lou and her dad strolled along in a comfortable silence. Then Lou remembered what she had wanted to ask all day. "Dad, are you still thinking of buying buy Sam's store?"

Her dad had a thoughtful look on his face. "I am still getting my head around the idea. Sam kind of sprung the idea on us. I honestly had never considered running my own business before."

Lou's mother put her arm around her husband's waist. "Mervin, you have been nerding out with those antiques all summer. You have been busy, but you've also been happy. I think it would be perfect. I would support any decision you make, but my vote is for the store."

Lou added, "Mom's right, and she didn't even see you at work like I did. You put your whole brain into a job you weren't even being paid for. If school made me as happy as the store makes you, I would have gone to summer classes!"

Mr. Dalrymple laughed. "Okay, you two, I know better than to go against the advice of the two smartest women I know! When we get home, I will crunch the numbers and see if it'll work for our family."

Lou and her mother gave each other a high five and got in the van. It had been a very good day.

Lou pulled up to the store on her bike in time for her shift the following Tuesday. It was a beautiful August afternoon and her thoughts were turning to plans with Oliver and Sandy on the weekend. She was pretty sure a drive-in movie was on the agenda. She parked her bike and noticed her dad's van was already there.

As she walked into the store, she saw her dad and Sam sitting at the counter going over documents. They looked up and greeted her with big smiles, her dad saying, "Oh hi, Lou!"

Lou eyed the pair, wondering what they were doing together so early. "I wondered where your van was when I didn't see it in the driveway."

Mr. Dalrymple explained, "I came in early to work out the deal with Sam." He looked happy and smiled broadly.

Sam jumped in. "It seems you have a new boss, Lou," grinning at his own clever remark.

Lou's chin dropped. She looked at her father. "Actually? You bought the store? What happens to Sam? Do I still have a job?"

Her dad laughed, holding up his hands to stop her questions. "Whoa, slow down, Bunny. Yes, you still have a job, and yes, I bought the store. We're just signing the deal and making it official. Sam still plans to live above the store and work when he wants to. He promised to teach me how he finds the stuff that he sells in the store and to introduce me to his customers."

Lou's brain leapt into action, already thinking about a plan for the next steps. "We're going to need a website."

The next day, Oliver knocked on the back door around breakfast time before letting himself in.

"Oh hey, Oliver," Lou called out. "Come on in. I was just making breakfast. Are you hungry?"

Oliver gave her a look. "Lou, you are perfectly aware that I don't need to be hungry to eat."

She started cooking bacon, the smell quickly spread throughout the house. Upstairs, Rocky woke up and came flying down the stairs towards the kitchen. He knew if he was a good boy, he would get a strip of bacon. He startled a little when he spotted Oliver but then went over to greet him with a lick on the side of his head.

Lou rushed to the rescue, passing Oliver a paper towel. "Rocky, I know you like Oliver, but did you really need to give him a bath?" Oliver laughed and wiped his face.

As she put two plates of eggs and toast on the table, Lou noticed that Oliver's wheelchair had some damage. "What happened to your chair?"

Oliver surveyed the damage, explaining, "Well, that's sort of why I came over. I have to tell you what happened. It was epic, Lou, you should've seen it. I was riding my bike yesterday, and I had this chair in its carrier on the back of my bike because I needed to go into a store. I was going down that hill on Broad street, you know the one?"

Lou nodded, so he continued. "I ended up bombing down the hill and caught a pothole. I was worried a tire blew and then I heard a crash behind me. I had to go back and get my chair, hoping that it wasn't trashed. I had no tools, and nowhere to brace myself."

Lou listened to his story, rolling her eyes. "And as usual, you didn't think to ask for help."

Oliver glared back at her. "Ha ha ha, Lou, very funny." Then he continued with this tale. "Anyway, the freaky thing was that I rode back to get the chair and just slowly moved off my bike and stood up. It wasn't pretty, but I have taken more steps in physio, so I decided to try it."

Lou stared, wondering whether she had heard him correctly.

"Lou, I took at least six steps and got my wheelchair attached to my bike standing up." Lou's eyes were wide. Oliver took a deep breath before confessing, "That's the most steps I've taken since I've been in this chair. I can't wait to tell my doctor. He told me to keep pushing, and even though I was tired after, I still did it."

Lou had tears in her eyes. "I wish I could have seen you! I'm so happy for you, Oliver!" She got up and hugged him hard.

When she started to pull back, Oliver held onto her shoulders, looked her directly in the eyes and said, "I will walk again, Lou. Just watch me."

CHAPTER TWENTY-NINE

The last days of August were sunny and hot, so Lou and her friends spent their afternoons hanging out on the Spit enjoying the cool ocean. None of them were thinking too much about school starting up again. They focused more on just being relaxed and happy. Rocky spent all day with them, occasionally going for a dip in the ocean to cool off.

Lou and Rocky made their way home before dark. Lou had a long day, and Rocky looked exhausted too. She showered and watched TV with her parents for a bit. When she was nodding off in her chair, she decided it was time for bed. Rocky was already passed out on the floor of her room.

As Lou was drifting off to sleep she realized she was running out of days to get organized for school. She muttered to herself, "I'm gonna need a list." That was the last thing she remembered before she drifted off to sleep.

❖

The next morning, she woke up and immediately got to work making a list of school supplies in her notebook. When her checklist was complete, she snapped her book closed and went downstairs. She found her mother in the kitchen and went over to give her a hug. "Where's Dad?"

"Take a guess," her mother chuckled. "He's been at the store since six this morning. I got up to have coffee with him, then he was gone. The man is pretty focused on that store."

Lou peeled a banana and let Rocky inside. "Well, I know there's gonna be a whole list of things I have to do when I get to work. He likes lists."

Her mother looked at her pointedly. "That's for sure, and he's not the only one." Her gaze softened as she placed her finger under Lou's chin and said, "I couldn't be prouder of you two. I'm pretty lucky." She kissed Lou's forehead.

Rocky decided he wanted in on the moment, pushing his way in between them. Lou reached down to scratch his back. "Don't worry Rocky, we still love you too."

As she ate breakfast, Lou's mother hummed a tune while she tidied before heading to work. Lou's mother had been much less stressed and grumpy since they came to Squamish. Lou and her dad were pretty thrilled with that.

When it was time to go, Lou pedaled to work on her bike. It was raining hard, and she regretted not replacing her raincoat. It no longer fit, and she just hadn't gotten around to getting a new one.

She walked into the store, spotting her dad up on a ladder. "Hi, Dad. Where's Sam?"

Mr. Dalrymple strained as he carried a heavy box down the ladder. When he was safely on the ground, he wiped his forehead and explained, "Sam isn't going to be working every day anymore, but he'll be in this weekend."

Lou nodded. "That makes sense considering we have the grand reopening on Saturday." She took the box from her father. "Mom's idea to have an open house to celebrate the new management was great!"

Lou answered, "I think it will be great for business."

Her dad agreed, "I happen to know that Sam intends to wear a new cardigan for the occasion."

Lou chuckled as she put the box on the counter. She froze where she stood when she saw who came out of the stockroom.

"Oh hey, Lou! I was hoping to see you here."

It was Tyler. Lou was too surprised to speak; she had almost forgotten how nervous he always made her. Oblivious to her awkwardness, Tyler explained, "Your dad posted an ad for a store helper and I got the job!"

This news stunned Lou and helped her find her voice again. "That's great! But I thought you were going away to school."

Tyler answered, "I decided not to go away, and instead I'll go to a local college in January when my program starts. I figured I had better earn a few bucks while I waited, so when I saw the ad, I thought this job would be cool."

Lou knew her dad needed more help than a part time fifteen-year-old, and once school started, she wouldn't be able to work as much. She was relieved he'd found someone, especially someone as nice as Tyler. "I guess we'll be working together this week."

Sweeping his bangs off his forehead, Tyler smiled at her. "It'll be cool. You can show me the ropes."

Lou almost blurted out, "Do you still have that girlfriend?" But she didn't. Instead, she turned red and picked up a random box. As she walked away, she gave herself a stern talking to. "I seriously have to get over this guy before I embarrass myself." Chuckling a little, she got back to work on her dad's list.

It was a sunny Saturday morning when Lou's family got up early and headed to the store. They had a lot to set up as they were expecting a crowd to help them celebrate the store's grand reopening.

They put up tents, loaded coolers full of pop and hot dogs,

and wrangled giant bags of ice. As always, Lou's dad insisted on using charcoal for the barbeque, so she dragged a huge bag of it out of the van. As she finished emptying the charcoal into the barbeque, Sam and Tyler turned up with coffee and donuts. Then everybody got to work setting up tables and chairs under a giant tent.

Rocky, ever the life of the party, was greeting people when they began to arrive and generally getting in everybody's way. Lou had put a bright red kerchief around his neck and when somebody would admire how handsome he looked, he would sit and put his paw up. Lou saw him bugging Tyler and was about to go over and rescue him, but she realized Rocky was being pretty charming and Tyler didn't seem to mind.

Sandy arrived with her makeup box and found Lou inside. "Hey girl, I'm ready to paint faces!"

Lou was happy to see her. "Can you do me and my mom before we start? She wants balloons on both cheeks."

Sandy smiled in agreement. "For sure. I'll do hers first. Am I setting up at one of the tables outside?"

"Yeah, that first one is fine," Lou answered. "I'll be out in a minute. I'm going to get Tyler to have his face done too. I think he would rock a dinosaur on his cheek to entertain the kids."

The girls both giggled and rushed off to get ready since it was almost time for people to arrive.

Once people started showing up, the Dalrymples served hotdogs and pop to everybody. Sandy had a steady lineup of little kids excited to get their faces painted. Sam kept busy doing tours of the store, telling people about the history of every object.

Tyler had put on some fun music. As soon as a child got their faces painted, they moved into a group and started dancing. They wanted the "dinosaur guy" to dance with them, so he did. Lou couldn't stop laughing at Tyler's new fan club.

Lou was walking around cleaning up the tables and serving lemonade when she noticed a group of people walking into the

320

parking lot. She put down the plates she had collected before running towards them, yelling, "Cecie!"

As Cecie and Lou hugged each other, Cecie said, "It's good to see you, Lou. Quite the party you have here!"

Lou was brimming with excitement. "I'm so happy you came, and with so many members of your family!" She recognized many of the Joe family members, and even Cecie's Uncle Bobby – the police officer was already at the food table, loading his plate with hot dogs. Her auntie was over at the barbeque chatting with Lou's mother. There was a new flock of kids circling around Sandy as they waited to get their faces painted.

Tyler was sent out to get more hot dogs and buns. They hadn't expected such a great turn out.

Cecie and Lou sat down for a chat while the party carried on. Oliver kept trying to come sit with them, but he always had kids scrambling all over him asking for rides on his lap.

Cecie laughed, shaking her head. "What an exciting summer you've had, Lou."

"For sure. It was a little crazy though," Lou answered thoughtfully. "I never thought my fun hobby would lead to me solving real crimes, particularly ones as big as I stumbled into this summer!"

Cecie patted Lou on the back. "You've certainly made a name for yourself around here, everybody knows you now. Not only that, I think my aunties might want to adopt you."

Lou laughed, not at all upset by the idea. "They can borrow me anytime!"

"Speaking of the aunties, I promised I'd drive mine home. I'll see you again soon." Cecie gave Lou a final hug and went to find her wandering relative.

The crowd thinned out by late afternoon. When Lou's dad served his last customers, he shut down the barbecue and packed everything up. Tyler folded up the tables and took down the tents. Lou took care of garbage and offered to help Sandy pack up her stuff. As they were chatting, Oliver came over and joined them. "Thanks for inviting me, Lou. This was fun."

Lou took one look at Oliver and burst out laughing. "Your clothes are covered in face paint stains and potato chip crumbs."

Oliver looked down, noticing the mess for the first time. He began frantically wiping his clothes off, but only made the stains spread. Grimacing, he explained, "I think I gave every kid here a ride today."

Sandy took pity on Oliver, deciding they could all use a treat. "Do you guys want to go for ice cream?"

Lou didn't need to think twice. "That sounds perfect. Let me check if my parents need me to do anything else. I'll be back in a second."

Oliver turned to Sandy with a concerned look on his face. "I don't have my bike, do you?"

Sandy answered, "No, Cecie dropped me off this morning with my stuff. The ice cream shop isn't too far away. We can all walk. I better ask Lou's dad if I can put my stuff in his van, so I don't have to carry two suitcases of face paint and brushes around."

At that moment, Lou and Rocky came running back. "We are good to go, everything is packed up! Sandy, my dad wants to know if he should take your suitcases home if we are going for ice cream."

Sandy chuckled. "I think he read my mind!" She rushed off to put her suitcases in the van and let Lou's dad know her address.

When she returned, the group strolled off toward the ice cream shop at a slow saunter. Even Rocky was low on energy. They all had a long day.

❖

"I'm going to try something new. Pistachio please, two scoops," Lou said. Sandy and Oliver ordered their usual choices – chocolate banana for Sandy and black cherry for Oliver.

They settled onto their usual picnic table and enjoyed the ice cream, the sunshine, and their friendship.

Rocky knew it must be a special day because he got a vanilla soft cone of his own. He practically inhaled it and spent a good deal of time licking his lips. At one point he started shaking his head. Lou said, "What's wrong, dude? Brain freeze?"

When he didn't stop, Lou stood up and went over to see if something was wrong. When she got closer, she noticed a lump on the side of Rocky's face. She lifted his lip and looked under it. She burst into laughter as she removed what was stuck under it. He had been trying to shake out half a cone that was lodged under his lip.

Lou held up the half cone for Sandy and Oliver, "this is Rocky's medical emergency." They all cracked up and Lou gave it back to him to eat.

Rocky looked embarrassed and laid down against Oliver's wheelchair, sniffing at it. When nobody was looking, he tried to lick the side of Oliver's seat as subtly as he could. He was trying not to get caught, but Lou saw him. "Gross, Rocky! What are you licking?"

Oliver looked down, chuckling. "It's okay. The kids at the party dropped everything they were eating on my chair. He's doing me a favor by cleaning it." Lou rolled her eyes and gave up.

Sandy stretched her legs out to catch the last rays of sun. "I'm pretty happy to be back at school with you guys this year. My time away was good, but I want to do my final year at Eagle Wind."

Oliver nudged her. "You know you'll have Mr. Patrick, right? We will too. He even gave us books to read over the summer! Just Lou and me."

Sandy's eyes widened. "I've heard that he does that, but only for his best students. I never got one, so you two should be honoured."

Lou and Oliver shared a secret smile. In truth, their

assignment hadn't felt like homework. They had both read and reread their books, always finding something new in them to love.

Sandy sighed. "It feels like summer has gone so fast. We go back to school next week!" Her phone rang, interrupting whatever else she was planning to say. She listened for a moment and then said, "Okay," before ending the call. "Sorry guys, I have to jet. My mom needs me to come and help her with some canning. I swear she spends half her life canning fruits and vegetables!"

Lou and Oliver said their goodbyes, not yet ready to make their way home. They watched Sandy walking away, and she turned to wave. Rocky jumped to his feet and followed her. Sandy thought he would tail her all the way home, but at the park gate he nudged her hand, turned around and ran back to Lou. Sandy shook her head. "That dog is smarter than he looks."

Rocky ran back to Lou, sticking his head on her lap so she could reward him with an ear scratch. "Well, aren't you the gentleman? Did you escort Sandy to the gate?" Satisfied, Rocky flopped down at Lou's feet and reached one of his front paws and placed it on Oliver's foot. He closed his eyes, confident that neither of his people could move without him knowing about it.

Oliver looked down at the sleeping giant dog and felt loved. He daydreamed for a bit, thinking back on all of their summer adventures. "This summer has been great, Lou. I'm glad we're friends."

Lou nodded. "Me too, Oliver. You were my first friend when I came here, and now you are the best friend I've ever had."

Oliver had a lump in his throat but smiled warmly when he heard Lou's confession. He realized he felt exactly the same way about her. "Lou... I haven't told you, but I have never brought anybody else to my doctor's appointment. I was always worried about getting bad news and then ending up crying and stuff. You're the first person I trusted to come along."

Lou put her hand on his and patted it gently. "You never have to worry about that with me. Have you not noticed that I'm a total nerd, uber clumsy, and get myself into all kinds of trouble? I know you still care about me anyway, so we're even."

They watched the sun go down, lost in their own thoughts. Lou's voice broke the silence, her tone full of wonder. "We solved two crimes this summer. Two! Do you know how cool that is?"

Oliver replied, "Well, it was more you, Lounado, but it sure was exciting."

Lou shook her head, still amazed by all that had happened. "If you had told me when we left Halifax what a crazy summer I would have, and how many good friends I'd make, I wouldn't have believed you."

Oliver leaned forward, looking Lou in the eyes. "You belong here, Lou." When she smiled in agreement, he leaned back and turned his gaze back towards the horizon.

They sat quietly and watched the ocean. The calm waters reflected the deep yellow and orange colors of the sunset. In the distance, they could see a few canoes slipping slowly through the water. Lou took in the scenery, hardly able to believe that this was now the place she called home.

When the sun went down behind the mountain range on the west side of Howe Sound, they decided it was time to make their way home.

Lou pulled herself to her feet as Oliver began pushing his chair wheels. Together, they slowly left the park. Rocky lagged behind until Lou called to him to catch up. "Come on, big dog. It's time to go home."

And in that moment, Lou, Oliver, and Rocky were as happy as anyone could be.

EPILOGUE

As life got back to normal in Squamish, the big orca rescue story wasn't front page news anymore. People started going about their usual business, but everybody kept a closer eye on the waters of Howe Sound from then on.

After Sergeant Preston arrested the container terminal manager who had made the deal with the Russians, she hired two more officers who would keep a better eye on the container terminal.

Tyler continued to work at the store and broke up with his girlfriend.

Sandy and Cecie went on a camping trip and decided that they picked the rainiest weekend ever. Their moms and aunties greeted them at home with hot food and towels.

Tank repainted the name on his boat and added beautiful design of an orca.

Amy got engaged to a nice musician and their wedding was planned for Christmas.

Sam and Mr. Dalrymple started selling their antiques and oddities online. Sam didn't quite know how the internet worked, but he was happy to pack shipping boxes. Mrs. Dalrymple got a promotion at her job and now she calls herself the top banana.

Lou and Oliver kept exploring but took a break from looking for crimes for a change.

Rocky made the mistake of trying to eat a porcupine. It did not go well.

ABOUT SQUAMISH

As Lou's family got ready for their move clear across the country, she did hours of research to find out everything she could about her new home. What she discovered made her more excited than ever to get to the West Coast.

Squamish, where they would live, is nestled between the ocean and the mountains north of Vancouver, in British Columbia, Canada. It sits at the northern tip of Howe Sound, which further south flows into the Pacific ocean.

The winding highway that passes through Squamish overlooks the water of the Sound, and at times allows a glimpse of the incredible wildlife that lives there. The humpback whales splash with delight during their migration season in the fall. There are groups of sea lions mischievously playing together on the rocks that line the waters. Orcas swim in family pods snacking on fat salmon. When they breach the water their skin gleams and reflects the sun in their dazzling performance.

The Stawamus Chief looms over the gentle town – a watchful, huge granite monolith. The Chief is a playground for rock climbers, hikers, paragliders and base jumpers. Endless bike trails criss-cross the rain forest. Peeping through the cloud forest as it rises to the heavens, the Sea to Sky Gondola looks down on the hurried waters of Shannon Falls. Bright colours dance in the bay when kiteboarders challenge the breeze on a windy day.

The First Nations population of the region are the Squamish Nation, descendants of the Coast Salish aboriginal people who governed the region before recorded history. As stewards of the land, their traditional territory protects countless natural resources and spectacular wildlife.

Lou fell in love with Squamish the first time she saw it. She knew she could be happy there.

- Tammy McIntyre (Squamish resident)

ACKNOWLEDGMENTS

I can't count the number of people over the course of my life who have told me I should write a book. I disregarded them because only authors can write books, not suburban working moms like me.

One day almost ten years ago I treated myself to a costly ticket for a writer's conference. It was a dream come true and I was hooked.

Jump forward a few years and I started writing a blog and working with others online. It was my happiness to get my stories out, so that they would read by other people. As I dove deeper into my new virtual squad, I met authors who collaborated with each other and wrote actual books. These have been my pod people ever since.

It took me two years of building up my courage and jotting down ideas before I could start the first line. It wasn't until a dear friend asked me to help with her book series that I was pushed to write my own.

Lynn Morrison, my writing partner and author of a series of cozy mysteries set in Oxford, England, has been my mentor, inspiration, and relentless cheerleader. She has been the one who taught me not just how, but that I could. I am forever grateful for her friendship and support.

I also learned that writing a book is a team effort. The people who stepped up and leant me their talents are the ones I would like to acknowledge.

Lynn's daughters were my first reviewers. Avid readers both, I am forever grateful to Adele and Georgia. I appreciate them for liking Rocky better than their mother's wyvern.

As I wrote, there were scenes in the book I wanted to get just right and needed very specific advice. I never thought I would get such incredible support, but when I asked, two very special people responded.

Xelémilh Doris Paul, a Squamish Nation Elder, ensured that I honoured and showed the respect of the beautiful culture I wove into my story. Her advice on important sensitivities and ceremonies was invaluable.

Fernando Romero leant a hand for Oliver's portrayal as a wheelchair user. He made sure Oliver's portrayal was realistic and respectful.

The readers of my draft manuscript spanned a number of age groups. The adults were great, but it was the kids who gave me the most insight. They warmed my heart with their excitement about the story. I am so grateful for Greyson, Katie, Pacifique, Claude, Jack and Sam. What an amazing crew of readers!

The setting of this book is Squamish, British Columbia. It is a beautiful and diverse area that goes from ocean to mountain in breathtaking vistas. I wanted to explore it in person for this book. My guide was Tammy McIntyre, who is local to Squamish and has great passion for the area. She was the perfect person to guide us to the best-kept secrets the tourists don't know about. Her advice was incredibly helpful.

No authors are perfect, so their editorial team is critical. It is no small feat to edit a book, no matter the age level it is written for. I have had the challenge of receiving large sections of chapters with big red strike throughs and gentle suggestions. Lynn Morrison, Anne Radcliffe and Erika Gow (who doubles as my daughter), are every kind of sharp and fussy. Grammar and content had to be perfect. For all the revisions and consistency corrections, I am eternally grateful that they had the same goal as I did, to make the book great. The grandparent reviewers have been gems, so helpful!

This brings me to this book's illustrator, Trevor Watson. He worked tirelessly for months to bring the characters from my imagination to life in the pages of this book. There is a certain satisfaction that happens when, after endless iterations, a character or scene jumps out at you and all you can say is: "That's it! That is what I pictured!" If there is any magic in this book, it's the characters drawn by the hand of an artist of exceptional talent.

Along the way, there were cheerleaders lined up to make sure I didn't close my laptop on this book. Hopefully they know how vital their roles have been in getting me through it. A kind word of encouragement goes a long way, I have been so grateful.

If I learned anything in this journey, it was that it's never too late to start a new thing. If you are dreaming about it, take the first step, write the first line, paint the first stroke.

Why you? Why not you?

To all my loved ones, helpers, and cheerleaders, thank you.

ABOUT THE AUTHOR

Inga Kruse is a proud Montrealer, transplanted to British Columbia twenty years ago. She has enjoyed a career spanning over thirty years. Now in retirement, she has made a lifelong dream come true, writing her first book.

She travels at every opportunity, and sometimes even takes her teenagers and husband along. Europe draws her back more than any other place in the world.

Inga has worked on blogs helping develop writers under a pen name for a number of years. This is where she met the people who love word babies as much as she does. Her writing journey has been epic and wonderful.

Inga can be reached by email at: ingakruse00@gmail.com.

Manufactured by Amazon.ca
Bolton, ON